For all the mothers.

PROLOGUE

The young woman stands in the doorway of the house, her hand on the heavy wood of the doorframe. *Will this be strong enough to contain him?* she wonders, feeling the heft of the oak on her palm. *Will this house keep him safe, and keep the village safe from him?*

It is an old house already, then. Even when they were children, there were rumours about it. That it belonged to a ruthless sea captain, that a corrupt judge had lived there, a pirate, a mad monk. Isobel does not believe any of that, but the house, nonetheless, has a certain *feel.* Maybe all old houses feel this way: creaky, sad, as if it has contained too many sobbing arguments, too many dissatisfactions and reminders of what could have been.

There is one story that is true and it is connected to this house, now. A tragedy that will keep her brother pacing the halls, tortured by the memory. He, like her, often wakes in the night, but he does not wake crying. Instead, he wakes, convinced that he is drowning.

Isobel cannot count the nights she has stayed awake in the wee hours, whispering to him, stroking his sweat-matted hair, crooning old lullabies to calm him. Yet, he is not by any means a child.

She is so tired. She has been all he has for a long time now, and it has taken a toll on her heart. She feels frayed. Dim, like a flickering light at the edge of darkness. She has to get out.

Maybe all old houses are sad, she thinks. Isobel is sad. She feels life slipping away from her. She is still young; she still has a future ahead of her. Yet, being confined to this house with him stills her heart.

I cannot stay here and lock myself away from the world, even if that is what he wishes for himself, she thinks. Isobel imagines being locked inside the house, the heavy front door closing slowly. She imagines the vision of nature outside – blooming, full of life – slowly disappearing as the heavy oak door swings shut.

She knows that doors and walls are not what he needs. Yet, it is all she can give him: all he will accept from her.

A sanctuary

That is how he sees it. So, that is what she has found for him, at the edge of the village they have lived in all of their life.

A prison.

That is what she thinks it is. Despite the fact that he will be perfectly free to come and go as he pleases. But, this is what he wants. He wants to hide away here, and pretend that he was never alive.

Isobel signed the papers in the solicitor's office earlier that day and, now, she stands in the doorway of his new home – hers, though she will never live there – with trepidation in her heart.

Am I doing the right thing? she asks herself, as she has asked herself repeatedly over the past weeks. She still has no definite answer. She loves him, but she is afraid of him, too.

She hopes that the house will hold him, care for him, heal him.

She cannot stay: if she does, she will lose herself completely.

She has offered to take him with her, but he refuses to leave, and so there is the house. The house will keep him safe.

The house will be the love she cannot give him in any other way. He will not allow himself to be loved. Not now. Not after what happened.

That is the way she thinks of it as she closes the door behind her and walks up the gravel path, her heart breaking. If the door is to close, then she must be on the side of light and life. She cannot – will not – wall herself up inside a mausoleum.

Behind the door, she hears him sobbing again.

1

Dear Catriona,

I hope that this letter finds you well.

I am writing to you because, as you may or may not know, your great-aunt, Isobel Annabel McGovern, passed away a month ago. I know that Isobel was estranged from her family, and indeed, she informed me that she had not seen or spoken to you since your childhood, so this letter may come as a surprise.

Our client, the late Miss Isobel McGovern, has instructed our firm to be the executors of her estate. I am pleased to inform you that you are the recipient of an inheritance.

The following is the text from the will that regards your inheritance. This is an unusual inheritance in terms of its conditions, as you will see below. However, your great-aunt wished me to tell you that she regretted her absence from you and your sister's life, and hoped that you might one day understand more of her story and her life.

To my two nieces, Catriona McGovern and Bridget McGovern, I leave my house: Castle View, in Loch Cameron.

Ownership will lie with both sisters equally, and depend on them both living in the house – with their respective families, if necessary – for at least one calendar year.

During this time, Castle View's gardens and interiors must be maintained to a good standard. I have employed the services of a gardener and housekeeper for many years, and have left instructions with Mr Matthews that the gardener be retained as staff and paid from my estate in perpetuity, or until Castle View is sold.

If it is mutually decided after one calendar year of full-time mutual cohabitation that both sisters wish to sell the house, they may notify John Matthews of Matthews and Douglas, Solicitors, of their intentions in writing, put the house for sale on the property market with a good, reputable estate agent, and divide the profits equally.

If, after one calendar year, Catriona and Bridget mutually agree that one of them would like to live in the house alone or with their family, they may do so if they notify John Matthews of Matthews and Douglas, Solicitors, of their intentions in writing.

If either one or both sisters opt not to live in the house for the minimum required time, the house will be sold by Matthews and Douglas, Solicitors, and the profits donated to the Barnardo's children's charity.

However, it is my hope that Catriona and Bridget will choose to live in the house together for a great many years, and keep Castle View in the McGovern family for as long as possible.

I enclose the relevant paperwork for you to sign to start the process of the transfer of title deeds, if you are willing to proceed. Of course, I am also available on the phone and by email for any queries you may have, and look forward to speaking with you soon.

Yours sincerely,

John Matthews

Matthews and Douglas, Solicitors

'Look at this! Can you believe it?' Catie McGovern held up the letter she'd received from the solicitor to show her fellow librarian, Lilian Green. 'I just got this in the post before I left for work. I can't take it in, actually.'

Catie and Lilian were opening up Loch Cameron's Stella Ross Memorial Library as they did every morning: turning on the aged computer system and the book scanners, shelving stray books and making a cup of tea before they opened the library's old, ornately carved oak doors. The library had been closed for many years, but had reopened a few months ago. Catie – who had grown up in Loch Cameron, but been away for many years was still adjusting to being back.

'Ach. You know, that website's going to be the death of me. It's down again.' Lilian tutted, staring at the screen of her computer. 'How are we supposed to run a functioning library if it doesn't include a decent online service? I mean, I know we've got the oldies that love to come in person, but we're supposed to offer a full service to everyone. There's lots of people that love renting the ebooks online, listening to audiobooks... we're going to get loads of complaints, again. All because we can't get the investment we need.' She made an *agh* noise.

Lilian sat down behind the issue desk, pulling her yellow handknitted cardigan around her shoulders for warmth. 'Sorry, hen. What were you saying?'

'No, that's okay. The website is a pain,' Catie agreed. 'I'll call Colin.'

Colin was the freelance web designer that maintained the library's clunky website; Catie wasn't convinced that he was really the best person for the job, but it had fallen to her to communicate the website's many failings to him and try to get it fixed. Lilian had flatly refused to talk to him any more since they'd had a blazing row about the contact form on the website, which Lilian maintained still didn't work properly.

'Thanks, hen. You do better with him than I do.' Lilian rolled her eyes. 'What were you saying about a letter?'

'I got this in the post today,' Catie said, handing Lilian the letter this time. 'What do you think?'

'This is like something out of a film!' Lilian read the letter carefully. 'So, your great-aunt has left you a whole *house*?'

'It looks that way, yes.' Catie shook her head. 'I dimly remember my great-aunt Isobel, but the letter's right: I haven't seen her since I was maybe six or seven. My mum and dad don't hear from her, I don't think. She's sort of the black sheep of the family.'

'Very odd. Very odd *indeed*,' Lilian mused, handing the letter back to Catie. 'What does your sister say?'

'I don't know. We hardly talk.'

'You'll have to, now,' Lilian said.

'I know. I'm not looking forward to it,' Catie admitted with a sigh.

In fact, Catie and her sister Bridget had hardly spoken since Catie had moved back to Loch Cameron, a few months ago. Before she'd decided to come back – taking a job at the newly reopened library – Catie had been working at a small, independent bookshop in Aberdeen.

It had worked out fine, being far away from each other, after some of the arguments they'd had. It wasn't even just one argument, not really: they'd never got on. Not since Catie was ill as a young child: she'd had leukaemia, aged six. Her memories of that time were hazy, fortunately, but she remembered endless hospital stays, and her mother at her bedside. Bridget had often been kept away from the hospital. Catie hadn't wanted that, but she'd been too ill and too young to argue.

After that time – Catie, when she thought of it, thought of the indeterminate, grey-green hospital room: quiet, with dim light and hushed voices – Bridget had been distant. Argumentative. She had vied for their parents' attention. Played up, started fights with Catie over nothing. They had argued constantly, after Catie's recovery. It was as if Bridget just couldn't forgive her sister for being ill; couldn't forgive her for taking the attention away from her.

Yet, when Catie and Bridget's dad had recently had a stroke, Catie had felt wrong being so far away. She'd wanted to be closer to her parents, and when she'd heard about the position for librarian at the old Loch Cameron library, it had seemed like perfect timing.

However, though she'd been spending plenty of time with her parents, Catie had managed to more or less avoid Bridget altogether since she'd been back.

'Wait. Let me see that again.' Lilian held out her hand for the letter; Catie passed it to her. 'Castle View?' Her eyes widened. 'I thought that was what it said.' She got up to open the front door to the library, leaving Catie behind the wooden issue desk. 'You know that's the mystery house,' she said, over her shoulder.

'What mystery house?' Catie asked.

'There's a big detached house up on its own, overlooking the loch but down the way from Queen's Point. It's been empty for years, I'm sure of it. There's a gardener that goes in every week, and a housekeeper. So, the gardens are kept neat and, apparently, it's beautiful inside.' Lilian was caught in a blast of icy cold air when opening the door.

'No way! Why haven't I ever heard about it?' Catie asked, aghast. 'You're saying that this is my great-aunt's house? The one I've just inherited?'

'Seems like it. I'm sure it's called Castle View. When you go past, there's an old house name sign at the end of the drive. Tall gates, too. Proper mansion, it is.' Lilian nodded, confidentially. 'You maybe don't remember it because you've been away a while. But it's a bit of a local legend. No one's ever known who owned it.'

'What about the gardener and the housekeeper? They must have known,' Catie said, smiling automatically at a mum who had walked into the library, holding a toddler's hand. They gravitated straight to the picture book shelves.

'I don't think so. We were talking about the house not so long ago at my crochet group, and one of the girls was saying that she knows the housekeeper. Said she's been working there years, goes in one day a week, cleans, polishes, vacuums, but has no clue who she's doing it for. Just gets paid every month by a solicitor.'

'Wow. This is a lot to take in.' Catie frowned. 'And I have to live there with my sister. If this great-aunt Isobel knew us at all, she'd know that was impossible.'

'Why?' Lilian peered at Catie over the top of her glasses. 'She's your sister, so you must have lived together before, no?'

'We really don't get on.' Catie sighed. 'It's a really long-standing thing. We're just very different.'

'Did something happen between you?' Lilian asked, curiously. 'Or do you just rub each other up the wrong way?'

'Ah, kind of,' Catie demurred. She didn't want to get into all of it, now; the arguments, the buried resentments. It was too much, especially for a work colleague she didn't know that well. 'You know what sisters are like.'

'Well, I have brothers. So, not really, but I can guess.' Lilian gave Catie's shoulder a squeeze. 'Listen. I'm here for you, okay? If you need a chat.'

'Thanks, Lilian.' Catie looked at the letter in her hand

again. 'I mean, this is super exciting, on one hand. A whole house!'

'I know. I'd lop off a toe to be given a free house. And a big one, at that.' Lilian looked wistful. 'Even if it was a bit spooky.'

'It's quite a thought,' Catie agreed. 'I mean. I've never owned a house. And this just comes out of nowhere! I can't get over it.'

'It is very weird,' Lilian agreed. 'You can't just... take it for yourself?' She widened her eyes. 'Is that possible?'

'As much as that idea appeals, no. Look. The letter is really specific.' Catie pointed to the lines that said she and Bridget had to live in the house, together, for a whole year, for them to inherit Castle View. 'It's cohabit or lose it completely.'

'Bad luck. You really don't get on, huh. It's not like you just have a sisterly tiff now and again?'

'No. She hates my guts. I've never really known why,' Catie sighed again, feeling the excitement of the offer of being given a whole house – apparently a big one – fade. 'It's such a shame. I've always wished that we could be friends.'

'I'm sorry, hon. That sucks.' Lilian reached for her hand and squeezed it. 'What are you going to do?'

'I guess I've got an uncomfortable conversation ahead of me,' Catie said reluctantly. She really didn't want to talk to Bridget. But what choice did she have?

Catie got out her phone and opened up a message chat to her sister.

Hi. Did you get a letter from a solicitor today? We need to talk. she wrote, and pressed SEND.

She watched the screen for a minute; she could see that the message had been received, and that her sister was replying. The dots flashed on the screen repeatedly for a few minutes, and then stopped. Catie watched her phone, but Bridget didn't reply.

Well, I guess this is going to go pretty much as I expected, she thought, as a customer approached the issue desk. *Badly.*

2

'Mum. You are literally the most embarrassing person in the world.' Skye, Catie's fourteen-year-old daughter, brushed her mother's hand away from her forehead, looking around at the empty track they stood on. 'Get off.'

'Your fringe is in your eyes,' Catie said. 'And there's no one here. How can you be embarrassed?' She looked up and down the lane theatrically, holding out her hands to point in both directions.

They were standing in front of the house that Great-Aunt Isobel had left Catie and Bridget in her will. Lilian had been right: there was indeed an aged brass sign bolted onto the stone wall at the edge of the property, next to a tall, black, cast-iron gate.

CASTLE VIEW

'So, this is the place,' Catie mused, zipping up her parka. It was windier up here than it was down in the village: the house was on higher ground, and stood alone on the tussocky ground above the loch.

'Apparently so,' Skye said, disinterestedly. She tapped at her phone.

To the left, the land curved away around the loch towards Queen's Point, an outcropping of land that housed several whitewashed cottages. They could be seen in the distance, but Castle View sat alone on the other side, overlooking the Loch Cameron Castle.

Loch Cameron village stretched along the opposite side of the loch to the castle, which stood on a hill, across a small, arched iron bridge which was painted blue. The village itself consisted of a small high street with perhaps ten or twelve shops, the Loch Cameron Inn, a hairdresser's, a community centre and the village school.

The castle itself was a huge, fairy tale thing in grey stone with turrets and manicured gardens that stretched down to the glittering loch below. Catie had always admired it and, like most people in Loch Cameron, felt proud to be a part of a community with such an impressive legacy.

The castle had stood at the edge of the loch for many hundreds of years. Catie knew that there had been a structure – a fort, originally – on the banks of Loch Cameron for much longer than the present castle had been there, but the present castle had been built in the 1700s. She'd learnt about the history of the castle, the village and the Cameron clan at the tiny primary school in the village she and Bridget had attended, before they'd gone to the closest secondary school which was some villages away.

Catie had visited the castle many times; they'd gone on school trips when they were children. She knew that her parents and her sister had attended some of the May Day parties that the current laird now held at the castle for the community. The parties were intended as an annual treat for the villagers in the spirit of community cohesion, where there were mountains of free food and drink, fireworks, a bonfire and dancing until the early hours. The laird paid for all of it, and could apparently usually be found reciting traditional Scottish poetry at some point in the evening.

Nowadays, the Laird – Hal Cameron, who was younger than Catie – was engaged to a glamorous American girl that Catie had seen around the village a few times. Apparently – her mum had told her with great enthusiasm – they were getting married soon.

'Should we ring the bell?' Catie asked, wondering what would be enough to spark Skye's interest. She'd had to black-mail her daughter to leave the house at all by promising that they'd get dinner on the way home from the food truck on the high street. It only came once or twice a week, but there was always a huge queue for its fish finger sandwiches, crab mac 'n' cheese and sweet potato fries, among other things.

Not that she could afford it. The move to Loch Cameron from Aberdeen had all but wiped Catie out, financially – she hadn't had much of a buffer saved in the first place. She tried to save money every month, but it wasn't easy, as a single parent on a low salary. And moving house was expensive, even when you were renting. She'd had to come up with a deposit for the new place and, typically, the flat they'd lived in before had skimped on repaying her deposit because, they claimed, that they had needed to bring in a professional cleaning company when Catie and Skye moved out.

That had annoyed Catie. She and Skye were extremely clean and tidy, and Catie had done a thorough floor-to-ceiling deep clean when they'd moved out. Plus, she knew that she had personally improved the flat when they'd been there: she'd painted it all white, covering over the dubious brightly coloured walls when they'd moved in, repainted the skirtings and the doors and turned the whole place from a badly splodged, grubby rainbow nightmare to a much more rentable, clean and peaceful haven.

Nevertheless, her old landlord had retained most of her deposit, so she'd had to take out a small loan to find the money to move to Loch Cameron, cover the new deposit – even though it was reasonable – and the first two months' rent, which was the agreement. All so she and Skye could be close to her mum and dad, now that her dad was ill and they needed her.

She was happy to do it, but she was also, now, broke.

Catie was also annoyed that her sister Bridget hadn't wanted to come to look at the house. They had both had the letter from the solicitor – Catie had phoned Bridget that night, after she'd got it – but Bridget had refused, saying she was busy, and that she wasn't interested in the house in the first place.

You and I both know that living together would be a disaster, her sister had said. *So, why entertain the idea?*

However, Catie couldn't *not* come and at least see the house. Just out of curiosity, if nothing else.

'Mum. Can I have these?' Skye turned her phone around to show Catie a pair of expensive branded trainers.

'Why? Have you grown out of the ones you have?' Catie looked at the price on the screen and winced.

'No. They're just cool. The other girls have them.' Skye pouted.

'Skye, I'm sorry. I can't afford those right now. Maybe something cheaper?' Catie said, a little distractedly.

'But, Mum... you don't know what my life is *like*. Wearing second-hand stuff.' Skye persisted, a slight whine in her voice.

'Skye. Your trainers weren't second-hand. Don't exaggerate.' Catie sighed. 'And I thought you liked vintage clothes, anyway.'

'There's vintage and then there's charity shop,' Skye insisted. 'You don't know what the girls at my school are like. They pick up on the slightest thing.'

'You wear uniform. That's the point of it, so you all look the same.' Catie looked at her watch.

'But we don't. Coats. Shoes. Trainers. Bags. All that stuff makes a difference. They can tell we're poor.'

'Well, the uniform cost an arm and a leg, and it's the best school in the area, so why don't you make the best of it?' Skye didn't seem to understand that Catie was working so hard just to keep them both afloat, and even just affording the uniform and the travel costs to Skye's new school had been difficult.

She'd chosen that school for her daughter because it was the best state school in the area, and it would give Skye the best possible start in life. It was more than Catie had had; she and her sister had gone to the closest secondary school, and it was all right, but it wasn't stellar, either. The fact that Catie had gone to university later in life was a testament to her own determination to make a good life for herself and Skye, but she certainly hadn't been handed it on a plate.

'Ugh. You don't get it.' Skye rolled her eyes and went back to her phone. 'There's a school disco coming up and everyone's going I haven't got anything cool to wear.'

'Yes, you do. You've got some lovely things,' Catie replied, reaching out to smooth her daughter's hair with fondness.

'No, I don't. You don't understand, Mum. All the kids wear these particular brands. And if I don't wear it too, then they'll just think I'm even more of an outcast than I am.'

'Oh. Well, why don't you make yourself something to wear? You always have such lovely ideas.' Skye had loved fashion since she was a child, and in the past year, she'd started making her own clothes. Catie had got her a second-hand sewing machine, and Skye had taught herself to use it. Catie had found books on pattern cutting and fashion design at the library, and Skye had already made herself a number of dresses and skirts. Catie had admired Skye's efforts; she really had a good eye, and it was probably the first time that she had been interested in a hobby outside of school.

'*Mum.* No.' The tone of Skye's voice suggested that nothing could be more ridiculous than her wearing something she'd made to the school dance. Catie sighed, knowing that she was never going to win this particular argument.

'You do know that I've inherited that house, right?' Catie pointed at its grey stone exterior through the gate. It was a prepossessing sight. Catie thought that whoever had built it hadn't bothered to keep it in accordance with the pretty little white cottages that populated most of Loch Cameron. Not only was Castle View much bigger than a cottage – it was a tall house, looking like it had three or more floors – it had more in common with the castle itself, with its slate roof and long, lead-lined windows. Dark coloured curtains hung behind the windows, giving the house a closed up, secretive feel. Ivy had grown up one side of the front of the house and wrapped around the windowpanes; it had grown over one of the windows almost completely. Yet, the grey gravel drive was well-tended: Catie could see that weeds had been fastidiously kept at bay.

Despite the fact that the gardens were well-tended and pretty, the house gave off a sense of gloom. If it had been a person, Catie thought that the house would have resembled a woman with a manicure, smart clothes and her hair blow-dried straight, crying alone in her car. 'You might get to live in it. Are you not interested at all? Not curious to see inside?'

'You said we weren't going to live in it,' Skye said. 'I heard you on the phone last night.'

'Hm.' Catie frowned. Skye had a habit of not appearing to ever be listening to anything that was said to her by an adult – she was an attentive and vivacious conversationalist with her friends – and then repeating it word for word if she was accused of not listening.

However, it was true that Catie had said she didn't think she'd live in the house: she had phoned her best friend Simran the night before for a chat. Simran lived in Aberdeen, where Catie and Skye had lived for most of Skye's life.

'That's wild, babe.' Simran was by now well versed in the intricacies of Catie and Bridget's relationship. 'Do you really think you can live together?'

'Honestly, no,' Catie had confessed. 'She's not going to want to live with me. She can barely stand to be in the same room with me for five minutes.'

'So, what are you going to do? Sell it?' Simran had asked.

'We can't. We only get to sell it if we've lived in it together for a minimum of a year. I double checked with the solicitor and if we don't do that year, the house gets sold and the proceeds are given to charity.'

'Oh. Good news for the charity. Not so good for you.'

'Well, yes. I mean, I'd be lying if I said I didn't want the house. Skye and I have always lived somewhere rented.' Catie had sighed. 'The thought of owning somewhere for once in my life... it's quite something.'

'So, suck it up for a year, babe!' Simran tsked. 'It can't be that bad, living with your sister. Can it?'

'Hm. You don't know my sister,' Catie had replied, glumly.

Catie had left Loch Cameron aged twenty, convinced that she couldn't spend another minute in what felt like a restrictive, isolated village community. She'd wanted adventure. She'd wanted to see the world. She hadn't wanted to go to university; at the time, she'd wanted to be a florist.

Catie had got as far as Orkney, which was beautiful but remote, and there wasn't a huge demand for florists there, or in the Isle of Skye where she'd moved after – in her mind at the time, both places were rugged and rural and exciting. But she'd realised that she wanted more from where she lived than breathtaking rural beauty. She was still in her twenties: she wanted bars and restaurants and friends.

So, in her late twenties, Catie had moved to Aberdeen, which was where she'd met Skye's dad, Greg. He'd walked into the florist she was working in at the time and asked her advice about a bouquet for his sister. He later confessed that he'd been working up the confidence to walk in and talk to her for two weeks, having seen her through the shop window on his way to work every day.

When Catie was thirty, Skye was born. Two years later, Catie and Greg had split up and Catie had decided to retrain, going to university as a mature student and training in information science.

Simran and Catie had met at Catie's first library job, at a performing arts college. They'd bonded in the staff room, laughing about the drama students' complete inability to be quiet in the library, and the hilarious moments that they overheard, whether that was a teacher asking for a sunny room for animal study – her lions needed to bask – or a student with blood trickling down from his hairline who cheerily explained that his head injury had resulted from his partner's overenthusiastic performance of a period dance.

'Mum. *Mum!* Are we going in or what?' Skye broke into her thoughts. 'Ring the bell. See if anyone's in.'

'Oh. Right. Okay.' Catie pushed the button on a panel by the gate, under a keypad. The house may have looked gothic and slightly spooky, but as far as the entry was concerned, it was all mod cons, Catie thought.

'Is someone supposed to be here?' Skye asked, peering through the cast iron gate. 'Did they say anyone would be here?'

'Yes.' Catie frowned, pressing the bell again. There was no way of knowing whether it was ringing in the house, but the button lit up.

'So, how come the laird doesn't own this?' Skye followed her mum's gaze to the man who was now walking up the drive towards them. He was about thirty, tall, well-built and startlingly handsome. Catie blinked. He certainly wasn't what she'd been expecting. 'Well, Great-Aunt Isobel owned the house, which is unusual in Loch Cameron because the laird owns most

of the property and land, and acts as a landlord for most people,'
Catie explained as the man drew closer. 'Great-Aunt Isobel
bought it from the laird a long while ago. I'm not sure why.
Anyway, since she never lived in it, apparently the laird offered
to be the custodian of the house. Made sure it was looked after.'
Catie shrugged. 'I don't really understand the ins and outs.'

'Is that the laird, then?' Skye frowned. 'It doesn't look like
him. I've seen him in the village a couple of times.'

'No. That's not him. It must be an employee of his.' Catie
lowered her voice and smiled as the man approached the gate.

'Catie?' he asked, looking from her to Skye.

'Hi. Yes. That's me.' Catie stumbled over her words, feeling
embarrassed for no apparent reason. He was remarkably beautiful: high cheekbones, dark auburn hair that fell in soft waves
onto his forehead and soft blue eyes that met hers with an
amused curiosity. Up close, she estimated he was about six foot
two or three and was wide in the shoulders. He was dressed
casually in faded blue jeans and a band T-shirt of some kind
with a black hoodie over the top.

Catie was sure she'd never seen him around the village
before. Surely, she would have remembered. *Not that he's
anywhere near your age,* she thought. *Women in their mid-
forties are probably invisible to men like him.*

'Oh. This is my daughter, Skye,' Catie added. Skye looked
briefly up from her phone and nodded.

'Hi. I'm Matt. Come in.' He pressed something on his side
of the gate, and the gates swung open creakily. 'Welcome to
your new home, ladies.'

3

'We haven't actually decided what we're going to do, yet,' Catie said as she fell into step next to Matt, walking up the gravel drive. 'The will is a little... tricky.'

'Oh. I guess these things can be a bit complicated sometimes,' he said. Catie noticed that he didn't have much of a Scottish accent, but that his deep, resonant voice had a slight transatlantic emphasis.

'So, are you the person who looks after the house?' Catie asked as they approached the wide wooden front door. It was easily twice the width of any front door of any house she'd ever lived in, made of what looked like a heavy wood like oak. It featured beautiful carvings of twisting vines circling an upper glass panel, and the whole thing was varnished a luxurious glossy dark brown.

'Ah, no. The laird asked me to show you around,' he said, a little shortly. 'Come in.' He stood aside and ushered Catie and Skye into the entry hall.

Inside, Catie stepped into a wide hallway. A thick, dark red circular rug covered most of a dark wood panelled floor – Catie could see that they were the original floorboards and not modern wood – and a round reception table made of a matching dark wood stood in the middle of the rug. On the table was a tall crystal vase, and Catie was surprised to see that it contained a bouquet of white roses. She stopped for a moment to smell them: they were real.

'We thought it'd be nice to present the house to you at least relatively alive,' Matt said, watching her. 'There's been a regular housekeeping service and gardener for many years, so I'm told. Obviously, by the time you'd move in, we'd make sure it had a thorough spring clean, and there's quite a lot of furniture that comes with the house, as you'll see. Some of it has been moth-balled quite a long time, though.'

Matt led Catie and Skye across the wide entry hall and into a large, sunny kitchen through a door to the left.

'Kitchen,' he said, unnecessarily. 'Surprisingly light in here, isn't it? The house looks quite grim from the outside.'

'Oh. Wow. It's lovely,' Catie breathed. 'Yes. You'd never think it would be like this. Looking at the house from the outside, I mean. It's quite forbidding. And this is... so homely.'

The kitchen was square, with a terracotta tiled floor and light wood farmhouse style units that gave it a cosy, homely feel. There was a large white ceramic Belfast sink with brass taps under a wide window that overlooked the garden, and a collection of copper saucepans hung from one of those old-fashioned devices Catie had only seen in magazines or on TV before. It was a dark brown wooden rack, hung in the middle of the ceiling, with a rope attached so that the pans could be lowered when needed and raised out of the way when they weren't.

Under the copper pan rack, there was a central kitchen island also made of wood, featuring a large wooden chopping board and a stack of orange cast iron cookware that Catie recognised as an expensive French brand, famous for lasting a life-time. A long wooden kitchen table, surrounded with eight chairs, stood at one side of the kitchen, and an old-fashioned

French dresser stood on the other side, filled with blue and white china. It was definitely vintage, Catie thought: that type of vintage pattern featuring rural scenes.

Skye stood in the middle of the room, looking about her in amazement, then got out her phone and started taking pictures.

For once, she's interested, Catie thought wryly.

'This is insane,' Skye said. 'Look at this place! It's like, straight out of *Downton Abbey* or something.'

'Well, I don't think the house really qualifies as a stately home, darling,' Catie said. 'But it is very nice, certainly.'

'Yeah, well, it's super old fashioned.' Skye took photographs of the blue and white china. 'Would we even eat off these dishes? Does anyone actually live in houses like this?'

'Well, we never have,' Catie said, smiling shyly at Matt. 'And, I don't know if those plates are dishwasher safe. They look too old. Beautiful, though.'

'And there's a room off the kitchen,' Matt continued, opening a door in the corner of the room. 'You'd think there would be a larder or something back here, but it's been kept as a study, I'd say. Take a look.' He flicked on a light switch and stepped back to allow Catie to step past him and peer inside.

The light flickered on slowly, revealing a wooden desk, pushed up in the corner. The study seemed to be a long, narrow room off the kitchen that might have been a larder at one time, but now held the desk and a day bed covered with a plain blue throw along the opposite wall. She blinked as the light flashed.

'What's that?' she asked; the scene was imprinted on her eyes, but incompletely. She had thought that she saw a shadowy presence in the room, hovering over the bed. Her heartbeat quickened.

Yet, when the light finally came on – the bare bulb made a *pinging* noise – Catie could see that there was no strange figure on the bed. Instead, there was a kind of tapestry hanging on the wall behind the bed, and in the dark, it had looked like a figure was standing there. She swallowed uneasily.

'Strange place for a study,' Matt commented as Catie edged her way into the room to look around.

'Hmm.' She walked to the desk and inspected it cautiously. There was a stack of old notebooks on top of it, a pot of pencils, and a few pictures cut out from magazines or newspapers and taped to the wall with aged sticky tape. Catie wondered what had prompted these choices: a picture of a basset hound, an old postcard of the loch and a couple of sketched portraits. They didn't seem finished, but one showed a young man's smooth, clean-shaven face, and another a different man with a beard and heavier features, his mouth open in what could have been a scream.

The picture of the man with the screaming face gave her pause. It was disquieting. Why would anyone draw such a thing, and then put it on the wall where they would have to look at it when they sat at their desk?

To distract herself, she opened the desk drawers; they were empty, apart from a few paperclips and another blunt pencil.

Skye had followed her into the little study, picked up one of the notebooks and sat down at the edge of the bed to flick through its pages.

'Look at this. All drawings. Looks like all of the same guy.' She held the book out to Catie. 'Some of the drawings are good. It's like, life class or something. Some of the pages are really detailed.'

'Wow. This person was talented. I wonder who this man was, though. That he – or she – wanted to draw him so much.' Catie took it and looked through some of the pages. Some of them showed the young man's naked torso: either this had been a life class, or this had been an intimate relationship.

'Well. More to see,' Matt prompted them, and Catie had to admit that she wasn't sad to leave the little room. It had an air of something in it that made her uncomfortable, and it wasn't just because it was small, airless and without a window. The study was so... sad, somehow. It troubled her.

'Shall we go on?' Matt said, politely. He had a confidence about him: something in his voice, perhaps, which had a deep timbre, or his way of speaking, which was smooth and unhurried. She wasn't quite sure what it was, but there was something that suggested to Catie that Matt was used to taking charge. She found it irritating. She didn't like being taken charge of. *I'm not a stray sheep that needs herding,* she thought, crossly. But, then he smiled at her, and it was as if the sun came out on a cloudy day. She was taken aback at the sudden warmth of it; there was a twinkle in his eye that suggested a quiet devilment.

She wondered what Matt was making of her and Skye. Was it obvious that they were quite out of their depth in such a grand house?

'Yes, please,' she said, politely, a little thrown by Matt's smile, which made him seem very different – it lit up his face, and made him seem warm and approachable. Catie gestured to her daughter who had started talking to her phone, held up in front of her face. 'Skye. Are you doing a live stream thing? Please don't broadcast this to all your friends. It's private.'

'But it's a cool house,' Skye retorted. Catie smiled apologetically at Matt.

'Can you give us a moment, please?' Catie asked him, quietly. He raised his eyebrows in amusement.

'Sure. I'll be in the entryway when you're ready.'

'Thank you.' Catie waited until he'd left, and then gently took Skye's phone from her and stopped the live recording.

'Mum!' Skye made a face. 'All my friends were watching!'

'Darling. Could you please focus on what we're doing?' Catie asked, patiently. 'We've got this lovely house to look around. I thought this would be fun. Something nice we could do together.'

'It's our house. We can do what we like,' Skye muttered.

'Well, actually, this is a private residence that we don't own. Not yet. And even if this was our home, I don't want people looking around it without my permission. Homes are private places, Skye! What's stopping someone who likes the look of something in the house finding out where it is and breaking in?' Catie appealed to her daughter in the same gentle tone.

'That wouldn't happen.' Skye pouted. 'How would anyone even find out where I am?'

'It would be extremely easy to work out where this house is. Your friends and followers probably already know you live in Loch Cameron, and Loch Cameron isn't a big place. I suspect you've already posted pictures of the house from the outside.' Catie raised an eyebrow.

'Fine.' Skye rolled her eyes. 'Just because, finally, we might have something cool, but, sure, whatever. Can I have my phone back?'

'When we've got home.' Catie slipped it into her pocket. 'Come on. We've got the rest of the house to see.'

Catie led her daughter out of the airless little room and snapped off the light, sending the study back into darkness.

'Ugh. That is so unfair!' Skye muttered, but Catie just smiled and squeezed her daughter's hand.

'Everything okay?' Matt asked as they met him in the hallway.

'Fine, thanks.' Catie smiled brightly. 'Shall we?'

'Of course.' He led them through another door, this time into a large lounge with an imposing fireplace. This room featured heavy blue curtains at the windows, and there were two large olive-green velvet sofas that were covered over with sheets. Catie peeked under one of the sheets and ran her hand over the velvet pile; it was soft and luxurious.

'These look like they've hardly been used,' she remarked.

'I wouldn't know, I'm afraid. I'm just really doing a favour for the laird, showing you around,' he repeated, a little mulishly.

'Oh. Sorry. Well, we appreciate your time,' Catie said, a little archly. Matt was giving her the impression that he resented doing her or the laird a favour, and whilst that might have been true, she hadn't asked him to be there. 'I didn't actually anticipate I'd have to come and view a house I inherited out of the blue today. It's been a bit of a shock, to say the least.'

'Not sure I'd complain if I'd inherited a nice big house,' he said, airily.

'I wasn't complaining! I was just saying, perfectly reasonably, that it's been a lot to get used to,' she said, annoyed by his tone. With everything that had happened recently, Catie hardly needed some random man judging her. Even if he was startlingly attractive, and she could see from the way his jeans hugged his thighs that his quad muscles were huge.

'Right,' he said, noncommittally. There was an uncomfortable silence.

'Shall we look at the bedrooms?' Catie asked, to change the subject. It didn't really matter what this guy thought of her, anyway: she'd probably never see him again.

'Sure. This way.' He led them back out to the entry, and they started up a wide, wood carved staircase.

'What's your role, then? Working for the laird?' Catie asked, to be polite.

'I do sort of work for him, but actually I haven't been back in Loch Cameron very long. Been working abroad,' Matt explained.

'Oh. Doing what? I thought I could hear that in your voice. You've been in America, or thereabouts?' she guessed.

'Yes. California. I work in tech,' he said, shortly. 'Bit more involved than showing women around houses.'

'Oh. I see,' she said, politely.

His sudden shift in energy surprised her. He was hot, but

he had just come across as a little entitled. *You're very important and busy. We get it*, she thought.

They'd reached the top of the stairs, where there was a wide landing, then another stretch of stairs leading up. 'Three bedrooms and a bathroom on this level, and another three bedrooms and another bathroom on the next level,' he explained, flatly. 'Then, there's the attic space which is now a master bedroom and ensuite. It's pretty nice up there.'

Catie asking him about his job seemed to have put Matt into a bad mood.

'The thing is, the will says that the only way we can move into this house is if Skye and I move in with my sister. And we really don't get on,' Catie explained. She didn't really know why she had said anything; as soon as she had said it, she regretted it. This guy had no interest in whether she got on with Bridget or not.

'Oh. Okay.' Matt looked at his phone as the screen lit up. Catie couldn't help noticing the corded muscles in his neck as he looked down, and then his strong hands, holding the phone: he had wide palms and thick fingers, and, where he had temporarily pushed up the sleeve of his hoodie, she could see that his forearms and wrists were strong.

'Um. Look, I have to get this. Can you guys show yourselves around for a bit?' He looked up, distracted.

'Umm... All right.' Catie nodded, and Matt jogged back down the stairs.

Charming, the voice in her head said. It was certainly a little flaky of Matt to disappear in the middle of showing her and Skye the house.

She heard him answer the call, his voice growing muffled as he got further away. Catie exchanged glances with Skye.

'Whatever. It's better looking around on our own,' Skye said, and opened a bedroom door.

'Umm... Hi?' Matt called up the stairs, a moment later. 'Listen, I've got to rush off. I'll leave the keys on the table in the hall, so you can let yourselves out. The gate just has an open button to leave. It'll close behind you,' he shouted.

Catie went to the top of the stairs and looked down, but Matt had already left. She heard the sound of the front door slamming shut.

'Well, I guess it's just you and me, kiddo.' Catie smiled brightly.

'That guy's kinda rude.' Skye had a habit of voicing what Catie was thinking.

'Hmm. I can't help but agree,' Catie said. 'But, walk a mile in another person's shoes, and all that.'

'What does that mean?' Skye made a face.

'It means, don't judge other people. You don't know what they might be going through. What kind of day they might be having.' Catie wondered whether she would be able to work out how to lock the house up properly: she had a moment of dread, imagining her and Skye leaving the front door open, or not being able to work the gate and having to shin over the high garden walls.

'Ugh. I don't care. You sound like one of those middle-aged mumfluencers.' Skye rolled her eyes.

'Well, I am a mumfluencer. I'm your mum. And if you don't watch out, I'm going to *fluence* the hell out of you.' Catie caught Skye and gave her a hug. 'Come on. Let's go and have a nosy around.'

'You're so lame,' Skye muttered, but at least she was smiling now. Catie missed the days when Skye was her little shadow; her sweet, huggy little girl. Nowadays, she had no idea what was going on in her daughter's life, most of the time.

'Ehhh. I'll take it,' Catie said. 'I'm old. But, you know what? I just inherited a house with seven bedrooms. So, who's the real hero?'

'You and Auntie Bridget inherited it,' Skye corrected her.

'Ugh. Don't spoil it.' Catie sighed and started climbing the stairs to the third floor. How was she ever going to convince Bridget to move in here with them?

~

That night, Catie had a vivid dream. It was something she hadn't dreamt for a long time: a day she had purposefully forgotten.

In the dream, she was lying in bed in a hospital room that was once as familiar to her as her own bedroom. In her adult life, Catie couldn't have told you what colour the walls of that room had been, or what pattern the print of the blankets were – the blankets piled on top of her in an effort to keep her warm. Yet, in the dream, she knew. She remembered everything: the smell of the antiseptic, the hum of the nurses' chatter in the corridor outside.

'Shhh. Bridget, your sister needs her rest. John, can you take her down to the cafeteria or something?' Catie's mother is speaking in an exasperated tone that Catie feels in the air, though she is too weak to say anything. She can feel the panic in the room; her mother's tiredness, her father's frustration.

Bridget, her sister, younger by two years, is bored by the long hours in Catie's hospital room. She has abandoned her colouring book and has started running around in laps, counting the same things over and over again: the monitor, the chair by the bed that their parents take turns sleeping in, the end of Catie's hospital bed.

'John. Please.' Catie's mother raises her voice. 'Take her out for a while, will you?'

Catie wants to say, *please let her stay,* but she can't speak. She has a tube down her throat, her throat is sore from it, and she is very, very weak. She closes her eyes, and the room dims around her. She feels her mother's hand holding hers.

'Come on, trouble,' her father's voice says. Bridget protests. She is bored, but she wants to stay in the room.

'I want to stay with Kaybear,' she whines. Kaybear is her pet name for Catie.

'Not right now, sweetie.' Their dad picks Bridget up in his arms. 'Catriona needs quiet. She's really poorly.'

Catie wants her sister there too, but they leave, and the room quietens.

Now, all Catie can hear is the beeping of the machine she is wired up to, and her mother quietly sobbing.

She doesn't want to be the one with the problem. She doesn't want to be the reason Bridget is sent away, and she doesn't want her mother to cry. But she is unable to say any of this.

4

I really think we should talk about the house Catie sat at the library issue desk, texting her sister.

I didn't even know we had a great-aunt Isobel Bridget replied.

Dad's aunt, Catie replied, patiently, even though she suspected that Bridget knew all of this already, and was just hedging. After all, Bridget lived with their parents still; she must have heard about their great-aunt. *Moved away years ago. Dad says she was always a bit of a black sheep. They never heard from her for years.*

When Catie had received the letter from the solicitor, the first thing she'd done was call her mum and dad. Her mum had filled her in on Great-Aunt Isobel; her dad's speech still wasn't too good after the stroke, though it was improving.

Oh.

Catie was annoyed by her sister's monosyllabic response.

She moved abroad. America. So, what do you think about it? Catie prompted her.

About what?

Castle View, Catie texted, patiently.

I don't know, I'm busy, Bridget replied.

Catie resisted the urge to reply that she too was busy, but that making a decision about Castle View was important. She didn't know what to say to her sister to make her understand how important this was: if Bridge did think it was important, then she was doing a really great job of appearing as if she didn't. Catie sighed.

The sound of the library door opening made her look up from the library issue desk; it was an automatic response at the sound of someone coming through the main entrance.

Half the reason that Catie had the time to text Bridget was that she and Lilian were having their usual IT issues and, today, all the library's internal systems were down. For once, Catie was thankful that the library was as quiet as it was, because it meant that she didn't have to explain to many people that they couldn't take any books out, or use the internet. The only person currently in the library apart from her and Lilian was Mr Snellthorpe, a retired gentleman who lived in the village and came in to read the newspaper most days.

Luckily, the person entering the library was Skye, who had just arrived from school. Some days, she would do her home-work in the library while Catie was working, and then they'd go home together at six, when the library closed.

'Hello, love. How was your day?' Catie leaned over the issue desk, and Skye planted a dutiful kiss on her mother's cheek.

'All right,' Skye replied. 'Got any biscuits?'

'In the back. Just custard creams.'

'Ugh. Why don't you get any decent ones in?' Skye muttered, still heading into the little kitchenette at the back of the library and coming back with a handful of them.

Catie hovered over her daughter as she took off her jacket and got settled at one of the tables to study.

'So, school was all right?'

'Yeah.'

'You sure?'

'Mum! I've got work to do. Can you just leave me to it?' Skye raised her voice; Mr Snellthorpe, in the corner, shot them both a frown.

'Fine, fine,' Catie whispered, and walked back to the issue desk.

She was about to call the library's frustratingly ineffective IT consultant when the young guy who had shown her and Skye around Castle View walked in. She remembered him instantly. Although they'd managed to lock up the house, Catie kept worrying that she'd done something wrong, and that she had left the house alarm on or something.

'Oh. Hello.' She frowned, distracted. 'Come for a book? I'm afraid the issuing system is down, so you'll have to come back another time if you want to take anything out.'

'Err. No. Hal sent me, actually.' Matt shifted from one foot to another, looking slightly uncomfortable. 'He says he's emailed you.'

'Oh. Email has been down too, I'm afraid.' Catie stuck her tongue out playfully at her computer, 'What did Hal send you for?'

'Well, he says that you need some help with your website and your systems.'

'We do. They're terrible.' She raised an eyebrow. 'Is that you? You're the help?'

'At your service.' He gave her a wry look.

'You didn't seem to want to be *at my service* before, at Castle View,' she said, a little archly.

'Hm. I guess I didn't think you needed servicing then.' He raised an eyebrow.

'And now I do?' she shot back.

'No. Sorry. That was—' She could tell from his expression that he regretted what he'd said instantly.

'Slightly unnecessary?' she interrupted, one eyebrow raised.

'I know. Sorry. It just slipped out. Sometimes my mouth gets ahead of my brain.'

'I see.' Catie chuckled, despite herself.

'Listen, I wanted to say, I'm sorry for deserting you at Castle View the other day. I had a phone call from work, and it was something I had to attend to. I needed my laptop and I hadn't brought it with me. I'm sorry, though. I was supposed to be helping you. I shouldn't have left you there on your own. Can you forgive me?' he pleaded, his expression earnest. 'Catie. I'm sorry. I can come across as rude sometimes, but I don't mean it.'

Catie regarded him for a moment, not saying anything.

'It's all right. Skye and I licked everything in the fridge and put it back,' she replied, deadpan. Matt looked blankly at her for a moment, then realised she was joking, and let out a sudden laugh.

'Wow. I thought you were serious for a minute. Thought I'd left a lunatic inside someone's private property. And, I don't think there is anything in the fridge? Maybe an old jar of mustard. Circa 1996.'

'Delicious. Well, luckily for you, we're mostly sane. But we could have done anything. You'll never know if I wrote BUM somewhere on the wallpaper in every room.' She shrugged, grinning.

'Well, that's the thing with these baroque wallpapers,' he replied, equally as droll. 'Generally full of hidden swears from passing visitors, armed with a biro and a desire to make trouble.'

'The devil makes work for idle hands,' she quipped back. 'Was it baroque? I thought it was more chintz.'

'Full disclosure. I don't actually know what either of those words mean.' Matt shrugged with a grin, that same sudden smile she had seen before: it lit up his face.

'Well, I must say you're very timely, because nothing seems to be working today,' she admitted. 'So. Yes. Forgiven, if you can get my systems to work.'

'All part of the service.' He pointed to the old-fashioned wooden library counter which had a section that flipped up on hinges to allow staff to go behind it. 'May I?'

'Sure.' Catie stepped out of the way to allow Matt through, watching his strong hands and muscular forearms flex as he raised the divider and lowered it.

Steady, girl. She looked away.

'I thought you owned your own company. Or companies,' Catie said. 'If you felt like an errand boy showing us the house, isn't library IT support also a little below your pay grade?' She wondered what his actual job was. Jack of all trades? General handyman? She couldn't quite work it out.

'Hm. I did, yes, but... I guess you could say I'm having a break,' he said. 'At least IT support is vaguely related to my actual specialism.'

'Well, it's very kind of Hal to send you,' she said.

'He's nothing but kind, eh.' Matt grimaced. 'The saviour of Loch Cameron.'

Catie took note of Matt's sardonic tone.

'He seems okay to me,' she said, non-committal. Perhaps Matt didn't get on with his boss.

'So, how's it going at Castle View?' he asked, sitting down at the main computer and frowning at the screen. He started tapping away at the keyboard.

'Oh. Well, we haven't moved in. My sister is being... difficult.' She looked over at where Skye was studying, not wanting her to overhear her saying anything bad about Bridget, but Skye seemed to be reading a novel and not paying Catie any attention.

'Yeah. Families, huh.' He raised an eyebrow.

'Do you miss California? she asked, being polite, since he was helping her out. 'You said that was where your business was.'

'Yeah. I miss it. I mean, I like Scotland. It's home, y'know?

But I...' He trailed off. 'Well. I guess I've been away a long time.' He peered at the computer screen and frowned. 'When was this last updated?'

'Umm. Not since I've been here,' Catie replied. 'Is it bad?'

'Hmm.' Matt frowned. 'I might be a while.'

'Well, if you can get our email and issuing software up and running again, that would be a great start,' Catie admitted. 'And our website needs a total overhaul. I haven't seen anything as clunky as what we have for many a year.'

'Agreed. I looked at it yesterday.' He took off his coat and twisted around to hang it on the back of the chair. Catie's eyes were drawn to his muscular neck; he had a tan, which was noticeable for Loch Cameron, where nobody had one. Matt wore a plain white T-shirt which hinted at his muscular physique underneath, and, not for the first time, Catie found herself admiring the definition of his arms and his nicely defined jawline, which, today, was covered with a light stubble.

'Coffee? Tea?' she asked, to break her feeling of awkwardness. She couldn't just stand there, ogling him. It was... she searched for the word. *Unseemly*.

That felt like quite a Victorian word, but that was probably fitting. She was ancient compared to him.

'Tea would be great. Thanks.' He looked up and caught her eye, flashing her that warm smile. There was a playfulness in his eyes, and a boyish quality that made her smile in return.

'You're welcome.' She went into the kitchenette and switched on the kettle.

She busied herself getting two mugs down from the shelf above the little worktop, put a tea bag into each one and reached into the small fridge she and Lilian kept for milk, their lunches and Lilian's home-made vegetable smoothies, which always looked and smelled suspicious to Catie. *Each to their own and all that*, she thought.

Libraries were, of course, supposed to be quiet spaces. But

Catie had always known that a library was so much more than a musty old repository of books; she knew that some people thought of libraries in that way. In her mind, a library was one of the few places that still existed for the community that were a free space: a place where you could spend as much time as you wanted. Where nobody was going to kick you out for not spending enough money.

The Loch Cameron Stella Ross Memorial Library was there for everyone. When it opened its doors, anyone could come in and read, look at newspapers, use the internet and sometimes enjoy group activities like baby and toddler story time Lilian led twice a week.

It wasn't the noise level that Catie was concerned about. It was the lack of people through the door, most days. Some days the library would be busy, but most of the time, it was just the same few elderly customers who would come in to keep warm in the winter and read the newspaper, or a smattering of young mums who would come in for new books for the children. But, most people didn't come in to the library at all.

Since she had started at the library, Catie had been on a mission to improve attendance and remind people of what a great resource the library was, but the terrible website and archaic IT systems were putting a serious dent in her efforts. She had emailed a number of people in Loch Cameron that she thought might be able to help with her plans for a Summer Reading Challenge – including Hal Cameron, the laird, who had seemed enthusiastic – and had started putting some ideas together, but it was an uphill task.

How was she supposed to encourage people to use the library when the absolute basic things – finding out about what was on at the library, and actually being able to reserve books – didn't work? She had an idea for a set of online resources for the reading challenge including interviewing some authors she'd made contact with. Catie was quite excited about the whole thing, but it was never going to happen without quite a lot of help.

She poured some milk into both mugs, and returned to the issue desk where Matt was tapping away. She placed a mug next to him.

'Ah, you're an angel,' he said, and took a sip.

'I didn't put any sugar in. I can, if you want it,' she said.

'No need. Sweet enough already. Like you.' He flashed her that smile again, and she blinked. Was Matt flirting with her?

'Umm... well, I find I don't have much of a sweet tooth, these days,' she said, ignoring his comment. It couldn't be flirting. That would be a stretch: Matt was at least ten years younger than her. 'So. Any luck?'

'It's going to take some work, but I've got the issuing software and your emails back online, at least. But I'd say you need a whole new system. I haven't even looked at the website yet,' he said, ruefully.

'Oh, thank you! That's super helpful.' Catie bent towards him and looked at the screen over his shoulder. 'Aren't you clever!'

'I have my moments,' he said, his voice low. She turned her face towards his, realising the proximity of their bodies. Now, when Matt's eyes met hers, his gaze was intimate and soft. His face was close to hers; she could see his thick eyelashes, the texture of his skin.

He leaned in, towards her.

Heat intensified between them. Catie's eyes half-closed. In that moment, she wasn't thinking. Pure instinct had taken over. It had been so long since anyone had kissed her. Was it going to happen? It felt that way.

'Thanks for the tea,' he said, reaching for the mug, and bringing it to his lips.

'Oh. Umm. You're welcome,' she said, blushing so furiously that she had to turn away. She looked up to check that Skye hadn't seen, and realised that her daughter was staring straight at them both.

Why on earth had she thought that Matt was trying to kiss her?

Oh, no. Now she was absolutely mortified. *What possessed you?* she asked herself. *What is WRONG with you? This is the kind of thing middle aged men do when a hot young girl joins their office.*

What would Skye say if she thought that her mum was flirting with someone? Catie felt even worse.

'So, Hal said you had some kind of plan for a Summer Reading Challenge, or something?' he asked, behind her. Catie turned back, reluctantly. She wanted to be anywhere except here, right now.

'Umm. Yes,' she said.

'Do you need help with it? I mean, I can help. If you want.' He looked a little awkward too, and Catie felt doubly mortified at the thought that she had made him feel in any way uncomfortable just now. 'Hal gave me your email. I had some thoughts about what we could do. And he wants me to be useful, so...' He trailed off, shrugging.

'Oh. Well, that's very kind. Thank you. But we wouldn't be able to pay you, I'm afraid,' Catie demurred. The thought of having to spend more one-on-one time with Matt gave her a little tingle of excitement in her stomach, but also made her feel slightly panicky. What if another moment like the one just now happened? She didn't think she would be able to contain her embarrassment.

'Don't need paying,' he said, shortly.

'Oh. I wouldn't want to feel like I was taking advantage of you,' she said, before she could take it back. She swore under her breath. What was it about this man that made her so awkward? 'You know what I mean. Taking advantage of your time. Your good will,' she added, hastily.

'Catie. If anyone was going to take advantage of me, I'd be happy if it was an attractive woman. And a librarian.' His eyes twinkled at her obvious discomfiture. 'I mean. That's every boy's dream, isn't it?' He started laughing. 'Oh, you should see your face. I'm joking with you. I'm happy to help. And you're not taking advantage of me at all. Okay?'

Matt placed his warm hand on Catie's arm, and she broke into a grin.

'Okay,' she replied, relieved that she hadn't offended him. She certainly hadn't meant to. Presumably, Hal had assigned Matt to help her. Perhaps it was all part of some kind of community work budget. She made a mental note to thank the laird.

'Right. I can come back tomorrow, and we can look at your plans for the Reading Challenge,' he said, draining his coffee in two large gulps. 'I've got to do a video call right now, but is that okay?'

'That's fine. See you then.' Catie nodded. Matt had only been joking about the flirty things he'd said. That was good. She felt better, knowing that.

And just a little bit disappointed, the voice in her head said, quietly.

Later, as she locked up the main entrance, Skye watched her thoughtfully.

'So, how come that guy came to see you?' she asked as Catie put the keys in her handbag and tapped in the building's security alarm code.

'What guy?' Catie asked, though she knew exactly who Skye meant.

'The one talking to you earlier. He was at your computer. He was the one that showed us around the house.'

'Oh. Matt,' Catie said, breezily.

'Yeah.' Skye rolled her eyes.

'Hmm. Well, the laird had asked him to help us out with the

library's IT systems, apparently,' Catie said as they started to walk home, along the high street.

'Seemed quite friendly with you. I looked up at one point and you were giggling,' Skye said.

'I was not *giggling*. Really, Skye.' Catie tutted.

'You were.'

'Well, I didn't mean to,' Catie sighed. 'He's just some guy. I don't flirt. Who would flirt with me?'

'I don't know, but he definitely kept looking at you,' Skye said, and Catie couldn't work out whether she was unhappy about that or merely observing.

'Well, it's free to look, I suppose,' Catie said.

'Mum. You haven't had a boyfriend, like, ever. Do you think you'll ever get one?' Skye asked, suddenly.

'Do you want me to?' Catie looked at her daughter in surprise; there weren't that many occasions when Skye asked her questions, these days.

'I don't care either way.' Skye shrugged.

'I thought you wouldn't want me to,' Catie said.

'Why not? I want you to be happy.'

'Do you?' Catie said, in genuine surprise. 'Well, that's very nice. Thank you, Skye.'

'Of course. I'm not a monster.' Skye got out her phone, frowned at the screen and started tapping on it. Catie had lost her again.

She wondered what more would have come from the conversation if it had continued, but she was also secretly relieved that Skye hadn't pursued her questions about Matt.

There was nothing between Catie and Matt; they'd only met twice. The fact that he seemed to enjoy flirting with her was neither here nor there. *Was it?*

5

Catie stared at the letter in her hand, aghast. She couldn't believe what she was seeing.

Her rent was going up. And it wasn't by a small amount, either.

She couldn't afford this. Not on a librarian's salary. There was no way that she'd be able to make ends meet.

The letter was from Hal Cameron, the laird of Loch Cameron, and it informed her that, though he had been able to keep rents in Loch Cameron low and far below average for the past years, he now had no choice but to impose a rent increase for all tenants in the village.

The letter also said that, even with the increase, rents would still remain lower on average than other neighbouring areas, which he hoped was some small consolation. The letter was apologetic, but firm. Rent was going up, by more than she could afford, in two months' time.

Catie swore. Why now? Moving to Loch Cameron had been made possible by the fact that there was a local job she could do, and there was somewhere she and Skye could live that was nice, warm, spacious and homely. Being a single parent in a not-very-well-paid job wouldn't have got them anywhere near as nice a place in a lot of other towns and villages nearby.

Now, that was out of the window. She'd have to get a second job to afford the rent.

Or, you could move into Castle View for free, she thought, looking at the solicitor's letter on the kitchen counter. But she knew that Bridget had already made her feelings very clear on the matter; Catie knew that she had also emailed the solicitor to say that she was not interested in taking her inheritance, because Bridget had copied her in.

But now, it seemed that Catie had no choice. It was Castle View or trying to scrape together money with a second job, and she didn't even know where she would find such a thing at short notice.

Catie called the solicitor at the number at the top of the letter.

'John Matthews,' a man's voice answered the phone after a couple of rings.

'Oh, hello, Mr Matthews. It's Catie McGovern here. You wrote to me about Castle View,' she said.

'Ah, Miss McGovern. Of course. Thank you for getting in touch. How did you find visiting the property?' he asked.

'It was lovely, thank you,' Catie began. 'I'm sorry that I haven't called you before now. It's been... somewhat of a surprise, as you can imagine. And I think my sister has been in touch with her thoughts.'

'Yes, I received the email from Bridget,' John said, in an even tone.

'Well, the thing is, I would like to take the house,' Catie said. 'But my sister is dead against it. I know what it said in the letter about the terms of the will, but... I guess I don't know if there is some way around that?' Catie asked. 'It just seems like such a shame to say no to this amazing opportunity, but I don't know what to do if Bridget refuses to go ahead with it.'

'Mum.' Skye had walked into the lounge, where Catie was sitting on the sofa on the phone.

'I'm on the phone,' Catie mouthed.

'Mum. I need some clothes to go to the school dance,' Skye persisted. Catie frowned and waved her away, trying to listen to the solicitor on the phone.

'Hmm. Miss McGovern, you and your sister are of course at liberty to make your own decisions, but I would advise you that Castle View is a significant property interest. It has been valued. Would you like to know the current valuation of the house, if it was sold today?' the solicitor asked.

'Yes, please.' Catie swallowed a lump in her throat.

'Right. Bear with me a moment,' he said, and Catie could hear papers being shuffled. 'I'm sorry to say that I remain an old-fashioned man, and I prefer hard copy to email, where I can,' he chuckled. 'Ah. Here it is.'

John gave her the amount, and she swallowed harder.

'Can you repeat that, please?' she asked. John repeated the amount, as Catie looked at the letter in her hand telling her that her rent was going up to a level she couldn't afford.

'Goodness,' she said, quietly. She had guessed that Castle View would be worth a lot of money, but she hadn't quite been prepared for how much.

'MUM.' Skye stood in front of her, holding out her phone. On the screen was a picture of a dress with a hefty price tag. 'Can I have this? If I don't wear something like this, everyone will make fun of me.'

'John. Can you give me a minute, please?' Catie asked. She held the phone away from her ear. 'Skye. This is quite an important phone call. Can you talk to me about this when I've finished?'

'Wow. Well, that'll be never, won't it,' Skye replied, grumpily, and threw her phone down onto the sofa near to her. 'WHATEVER, Mum. Just ignore me. As usual.'

She grabbed her phone off the sofa and stalked out of the room. Catie closed her eyes and exhaled for a moment, then put the phone back to her ear.

'Sorry about that, John. Teenagers,' she said with a sigh.

'Indeed,' John said. 'No trouble. I remember what my daughters were like at that age. Now. I know what your sister has said about the house, but I'm going to give you a few more days to reconsider. I don't have to have read that email for a while, being the busy man I am, and the luddite that doesn't check his email very often, if you know what I'm saying,' he said.

'Thank you, Mr Matthews. I appreciate that,' Catie said.

'John. Please,' he chuckled. 'I hope to hear from you soon, then, Miss McGovern. Good luck.'

'Thank you. Goodbye,' Catie said, still somewhat overwhelmed by what she had just heard.

It was a lot of money. It was way too much money for her to be able to walk away from. And, even if she and Bridget didn't sell Castle View, it was a big house that could be theirs, without ever needing to be at the mercy of a landlord – and sudden, unpredictable rent hikes – ever again.

And, Castle View could be a home for Skye. It could be a home for Catie and Bridget. The thought was too appealing to say no to.

Catie picked up the phone.

'Bridget. It's me. Don't hang up,' she began, but was stopped dead by the sound of her sister crying. 'Bridge? What is it?'

'It's Dad, Catie. You've got to come home. Quick,' her sister said. 'The ambulance is on its way.'

6

By the time she had got to her parents' house, the ambulance had already arrived and her dad was being lifted into the back of it by two paramedics. She had followed him to the hospital, but she had only been allowed to look in at him through a window so far; he was too weak, and the doctors were with him. Only her mum was allowed to be in the room with him.

Skye was at school; she'd messaged her daughter to tell her what was going on, and called the school to inform them too. Skye had her own key and would let herself in when she got home. Catie planned to get home when Skye did so that she could be with her daughter, who would likely be upset.

She found Bridget waiting outside her dad's hospital room. They both looked in, watching wordlessly, as their dad was hooked up to monitoring machines.

'Hey. You okay? What happened?' Catie tried to hug her sister, but Bridget pulled away.

'He was walking up the stairs. He fell. When I saw his face, I realised it was another stroke. His mouth had pulled down on one side,' Bridget said, mechanically. 'I called the ambulance and then I called you.'

'You did the right thing.' Catie tried to reassure Bridget, but her sister was icy and wouldn't meet Catie's eyes.

'Sure. I always do the right thing,' she said, her voice devoid of inflection.

'Bridget. Come on. He'll be okay.' Catie put her hand on her sister's shoulder, but Bridget shook it off.

'Jesus. How the hell would you know that? Are you a doctor?' she demanded.

'No, I just...' Catie took a step back, feeling the anger in her sister directed at her in a sudden stab of energy.

'You just what? Can't bear not to be the centre of attention? Want to minimise the suffering of others because you can't cope with the thought of it not being all about you, all the time?' Bridget fired back.

'Bridget! That's a horrible thing to say. He's my dad too.' Catie defended herself.

'They're your parents when it suits you. You moved away and left me looking after them for years and never so much as a backwards glance. Now, you're back, and we're supposed to be holding a tickertape parade or something.'

'I don't... Bridget, none of this is helpful.' Bridget's words were deeply hurtful: Catie felt them like a stab to the chest. 'I love Mum and Dad, and I even love you, even though you're relentlessly awful to me. I'm not jealous of Dad getting attention because he's had a stroke. For goodness' sake.' She took a deep breath and stopped herself for a minute. She didn't want to say something she'd regret, and she didn't want to let the tears that she was holding inside her, break through the dam of her control.

He looked so small and helpless in that bed: nothing like the man who had carried her on his shoulders as a child; who had raced against the other dads at school sports day; who had held her in his arms and soothed her when she and her sister had had an argument.

'Look. This is an emotional time. I'm going to get a coffee, and come back in a bit. Do you want one?' she asked.

'No.' Bridget shook her head. 'I want to stay.'

'Suit yourself.' Catie sighed. She needed a coffee. And, she also needed not to be around her sister right now.

Beside herself with worry, Catie found her way down to the hospital café, got a coffee and sat down at one of the tables. It was a functional kind of place, clean and workmanlike, but hospitals had their own particular aura: you couldn't forget where you were, from the odour of antiseptic and stale bodies to the miasma of grief and anxiety in the atmosphere. Catie had hated hospitals ever since she had had to stay in one – this one, in fact – for weeks as a child.

She had fought the leukaemia; she was healthy now, and had been for a long time. But the terrible weight of such a serious diagnosis still sat on her heart like a toad. The fear was always there. That it would come back, or something else as bad. That she would be taken away from Skye. Worse, that Skye had inherited some predisposition to the disease.

So far, it seemed that she hadn't. Skye had always been healthy; she hadn't even got many colds and the usual child-hood illnesses, possessing a kind of staunch physical toughness, even though she had always been a petite, delicate little thing to look at. Catie had made sure to have Skye tested as much as she could without traumatising her daughter, but she wanted to be as sure as she could that Skye would never experience what she had.

'Hello, there.' A familiar voice broke into Catie's thoughts. She looked up to see June – one of the women who ran the weekly "crochet coven", as it was called in the village, which was a weekly meeting of middle-aged women who did crafts, baked and did a lot of fundraising for various good causes – standing next to her table. Catie knew a few of them just from having grown up in the village. In a place like Loch Cameron, everyone knew everyone in one way or another. 'Catie? I don't see you here usually.'

'Hi, June. No. I'm here with my dad. He had a stroke,' she said, trying to keep her voice steady.

'Oh, my dear! I'm sorry.' June pointed to the seat opposite Catie – a plastic bench that was attached to the table in a kind of unit. 'May I?'

'Of course.' Catie nodded.

June sat down across the table from Catie with a grateful sigh. 'Goodness. An hour on my feet these days is enough for me. Time was, I'd be up all day and think nothing of it.'

'Uh-huh.' Catie didn't want to be rude, but she didn't know if she really felt up to cosy chitchat right now.

'Your dad. Is he lucid?' June asked. 'Forgive me. As an ex-nurse, you just never really leave that part of you behind. Tell me if it's none of my business.'

'It's okay. Umm. I don't know, right now. My sister said he fell on the stairs and he had that face paralysis thing. I'm not allowed in to see him, yet.' Catie sipped her coffee, not because it was good – it was awful, actually – but because the cup would at least partially obscure her face, and she wanted to hide.

She had cried as she'd walked away from Bridget; cried, following the long, light green hospital corridors to the café. She thought her face probably looked red and blotchy, her eyes puffy and watering.

'Ah. I see. Well, they're probably just trying to work out what the stroke has actually done. It's so variable. This isn't his first, is it? If memory serves?'

'No. He had one a few months ago. That's why I moved home, to help support Mum.' Catie put the cup down. It felt like all of her insides had been weighted with sand; pulled down with worry and sadness.

'That's right. Of course. How is your mother? You know, she's always welcome to come to the community centre on

Thursdays if she wants a bit of support. Or just a bit of time out from looking after your dad. I haven't seen her in a good while.'

'Thanks. I'll pass that on.' Catie nodded.

'Well, the team here are excellent,' June said. 'He might well make a full recovery. People do, with occupational therapy, speech therapy. It really depends on what's happened in the brain.'

'It's just horrendous, not knowing.' Catie felt the tears well up in her again and she wiped her eyes impatiently. 'That might be true. But he might also... you know. Not make it.'

'Yes. That's an option,' June said, reaching across the table for Catie's hand and squeezing it. 'But we can't think like that. All we can do is wait and see. I know it's hard. I've seen strokes many times, and I know it's really upsetting.'

'Yeah. I hate this place.' Catie stared into the corridor outside, remembering walking along it with her dad, when she was recovering. The sensation of her hand being dwarfed by his was so vivid; the memory of wanting to come to the café to get a chocolate biscuit, and of nurses saying hello to her and making a fuss of her.

Little did she think, then, that all these years later, she would be waiting to find out if her dad was going to survive a stroke.

'Do you? It's sort of a second home to me.' June smiled wryly. 'I worked here a long time. I still volunteer, but just little things now. I'm too old to do the nursing part. Mostly I visit patients. Why do you hate it?'

'I was here when I was a kid. I had leukaemia,' Catie said, shortly. She wondered, suddenly, if all this was giving Bridget bad memories, too. She had often had to be at the hospital because of her sister's illness; she had been younger, so Catie didn't exactly know how much the experience had affected her. But, if she remembered any of it, then coming back to the hospital – this time, because another member of her family was critically ill – might bring back difficult memories.

'Oh my goodness! Leukaemia!' June exclaimed. 'You poor thing!'

'Yeah. It's okay. I mean, I remember it, I remember it being difficult, but I was pretty young. It was a long time ago,' Catie said the thing that she always said about her illness. It had been her standard response for her whole life: *I was young, it was a long time ago, I recovered.* But the truth was that she had never truly gotten over it, because she lived in fear of it happening again. And, her family had never talked about it. It was as if, once she had recovered, they had all entered into a consensual but unspoken agreement that they were going to forget it ever happened.

'So, you were a nurse?' Catie asked, sipping her coffee. She wanted to change the subject; she was uneasy, going back to that time in her mind.

'Aye, all my life, really. Still like to come in and help where I can.' June nodded. 'Your dad will be okay. It's amazing what they can do for strokes, nowadays,'

'Thank you. I hope so.' Catie sighed, feeling the tears rise up again. 'It's just been so stressful. And I worry about mum. How she's going to cope at home.'

'Hmm. People tend to need occupational therapy after a stroke. Maybe a carer,' June said. 'You'll have to see.'

'That's all we can do. Wait and see,' Catie echoed her. She wished she was still at home now. Anywhere but here.

'So, tell me about Castle View.' June shot Catie a compassionate glance, obviously sensing that she would appreciate a change of subject. 'I heard that you and your sister inherited it.'

'Word gets around fast,' Catie said, raising her eyebrow. She suspected Lilian, but she hadn't exactly told her that it was a secret.

'Ha. Indeed it does.' June chuckled. 'You'll have to forgive us old biddies. We like to keep abreast of events in the village.'

'I wouldn't expect anything less.' Catie tried to smile. 'Yes. It turns out that my sister and I had a great-aunt we didn't know – my dad's sister. She passed away and left us Castle View.'

'Well, it's a mystery, that house. People have always gossiped about it,' June said, thoughtfully. 'Of course, I'm old now, and having lived in the village all my life, I could tell you a few things.'

'Like what?' Catie asked.

'Hmmm. Well, you inheriting it from your great-aunt is a big piece of news, because no one knew who owned it for a long time. That's the first thing,' June began. 'It's sat up on the hill there, on its own, for years and years. People used to say it was haunted.' She looked at Catie out of the corner of her eye.

'Haunted? Is it?' Catie's eyes widened. She didn't like the idea of that at all.

'No idea, I'm afraid. More like it's old and it's got mice in the walls.' June rolled her eyes. 'Still. There were stories about it.'

'Like what?'

'Hmm. Well, I remember people talking about a man that lived there. A fellow called Frank... something like that. Now, we're talking a long time ago.' June paused, thinking for a moment. 'I'm not sure how long, though.'

'It's strange that the Camerons don't own it, isn't it? It's on Cameron land,' Catie said. 'I don't even fully understand how my great-aunt came by it.'

'I'm not sure what happened either. Odd, really, because, you're right – they do own everything else for miles around, or have some kind of interest in it,' June mused. 'You'd have to ask Hal Cameron about that. He's got a whole room in the bowels of the castle, full of local records. Stretches back years and years. Might be something in there about it.'

'Maybe. You were telling me about this Frank?' Catie prompted her.

'Yes. Now. Frank – I think that was his name, anyway – he was a bit of a character, by all accounts,' June said. 'And I don't mean that in a particularly nice way. He had a bit of a reputation for not being able to keep staff at the house – housekeepers and maids, probably. Now, I don't know exactly why he couldn't keep staff for long, but you can make a guess.' She raised her eyebrows.

'He was abusive?' Catie asked.

'Most likely. I imagine that he was taking advantage of the girls.' June pursed her lips, disapprovingly. 'Poor things.'

'How is it that you know about that, though?' Catie persisted, her brow furrowed.

'Ah. Well, there's a story that one of the maids died in what we'd call *suspicious circumstances*. And when I was a wee lassie, that was the story about Castle View. That it was haunted by the ghost of a maid in a black and white outfit – black dress, white pinny, white headpiece, you know the kind of thing.' June tutted at the thought of it. 'We used to go up there at night when we were teenagers, shin over the wall and try and get inside the house. Never could, mind you. That place was always shut up tighter than a clam. I suppose your great-aunt would have bought the house before that, but I don't know.'

'Me either. Or why she bought it in the first place,' Catie said. 'Do you think it actually is haunted? I mean, I want to move in: it's a great opportunity. But I'm not overly keen if there's some spectral maid walking about at all hours. For my daughter's sake, more than anything. She's a teenage girl. She's already a sensitive little thing. She doesn't need a ghost in the house.'

'No, no.' June cooed in a placating tone. 'I might be wrong about the haunting – I mean, all I can tell you are the tales, but goodness knows if these things are ever true. I'm sure you'll be fine. However, I expect the tale about the maid is true. Sadly, it wasn't unusual for women to endure harassment and assault as part of their jobs in the past. Men just thought women were their property. Especially rich men and their staff.' June sighed. 'That's the real horror, I'm sorry to say. Not supernatural comings and goings.'

'It's disgusting,' Catie agreed. 'Well, I hope you're right, is all I can say.'

'Let me know if you move in and do experience anything strange,' June said. 'It's not that I don't think odd things happen: that would be naive. I've witnessed plenty of strange things in my life, especially working in hospitals for most of it. But there's usually an explanation. For the times there isn't, I've a friend who does that kind of thing.' She gave Catie a mysterious nod.

'What kind of thing?' Catie furrowed her brow.

'Oh. Nothing. Probably not the time to be talking about it, dear.' June gave Catie's arm a consoling pat. 'You've got enough on your mind just now, what with your poor dad and all.'

Catie looked up to see Bridget walk into the café. Her heart sank a little, just thinking of the horrible things her sister had said to her earlier.

She's hurting as much as you are, she thought, empathising with Bridget. Now wasn't the time to take offence in what her sister said.

'Oh. That's my sister,' she said, getting up. 'I wonder if that means I can go in to see Dad now.' Nonetheless, she still couldn't understand what it was that Bridget was so resentful about; there was a sharp wedge between them that cut where it touched, and it was driving her crazy not knowing what it was or why Bridget insisted on holding on to something so painful.

She stood up and waved as Bridget came into the café, but her sister avoided eye contact and went to the food counter.

'I should go and see what's happening,' Catie said with a sigh, getting to her feet. 'She might have an update.'

'Ah. Right you are. Good luck.'

'Thanks for the chat, June. I appreciate it.' Catie gave June a sad smile.

'You're welcome, dear. Anytime.' The woman nodded. 'It's hard with sisters,' June mused, as Catie picked up her handbag. 'You know, she's hurting, too,' June said, echoing Catie's own thoughts. 'Try to remember that, dear. I know it's hard. But you must try and come together, now. For your dad's sake.'

But what if we can't, Catie thought. *What if Bridget never stops holding on to whatever it is that makes her hate me so much?*

She didn't want to say what she was thinking out loud; the fears were too jagged, too sharp to bring into reality. So, she just nodded.

And what if we lose Dad now? I don't think we'd ever come back from that. It would push us apart forever.

7

'Well, that's the last of it.' Catie stood up with her hands on her back and sighed. She'd just brought the last box of her things in from her car, and the men in the moving van had just finished bringing all their furniture in. Not that she owned a lot of it; she and Skye had rented a furnished flat in their old place in Aberdeen and, when they'd moved to Loch Cameron, Catie had bought a few new things, but the flat had the basics: a sofa, beds, a dinner table and chairs. They weren't to Catie's taste, but she wasn't in a position to do much about it on her tiny salary.

Castle View also came with furniture, she had realised, as she, Skye and Bridget walked around the rooms, removing the dustsheets that had covered various pieces for so many years – sideboards, tables, armchairs, velvet sofas, beds, dressing tables and wardrobes.

In the end, the decision to move in had happened all at once. A few days after their dad's second stroke, Catie and Bridget's mother had told Bridget that they needed her bedroom for a live-in occupational therapist for their dad. He was alive, but the second stroke had been worse than the first, and the doctors were concerned that there might be more if certain preventative measures weren't taken. Plus, he was going to need round-the-clock care, with speech and physical therapy. Luckily, there was a grant available at the hospital that would cover most of the cost and a nurse was helping Catie's mum to make the application.

So, Bridget really had had no choice but to finally assent to moving in to Castle View.

'Ugh. Now we have to unpack it all.' Bridget sneezed. 'Dust.' She rubbed her nose. 'Have we made a decision about the bedrooms?'

'Bagsy the one with the ensuite.' Skye was halfway up the staircase with a holdall in each hand.

'Go on, then.' Catie grinned up at her daughter, who whooped and skipped up the stairs. 'You go on, sweetheart. We'll come up and see what you've done with it in a bit,' Catie called after her.

'She'll like having her own space,' Bridget said, watching Skye go up the stairs.

'Yeah. It makes sense. She can be at the top of the house and have her own space away from us. God knows we would have loved that when we were her age.' Catie shrugged. 'We can share the main bathroom. The bedrooms on the floor below are still really nice.'

'Oh. Right. Good to know.' Bridget raised her eyebrow. 'Sorry. I forgot. You have to be in charge at all times, right?'

'What's that supposed to mean?' Catie felt confused at the sudden attack.

'Nothing. If you don't know by now, you'll never know.' Bridget turned away, picked up one of her suitcases and started walking up the stairs.

'After you.' Catie picked up a bag of her own things and followed her sister, wondering how on earth they were ever going to be able to live together for a whole year.

'So, listen. I'm a little bit worried about Skye,' Bridget said as they reached the first landing. 'Cat. Why don't you take a bedroom on this level and I'll go on the one above? There's a bathroom on each floor. Then we won't even have to share.'

'All right. Let me have a look around first,' Catie said, and they both walked into the first bedroom, which had a scent of mould. She pointed to a corner where the old-fashioned floral wallpaper was peeling off, and shook her head. 'Not this one,' she said, and Bridget nodded. 'What about Skye?'

They poked their heads into the bathroom, which Catie was relieved to find was pleasant, clean and reasonably modern, with fresh white tiles and a black tiled floor. A large white claw-footed bathtub sat alongside one wall, and there was a mirrored cabinet above a wide, scallop-edged sink.

'Nice,' Bridget observed. 'I hope the bathroom on the next floor has a tub like that.'

'You can borrow it if you like. My bath is your bath,' Catie said, charitably. 'What about Skye?'

'She told me she's having some problems at school,' Bridget said as they walked along the corridor to the next bedroom. This one was papered in a light blue wallpaper with a striped blue and white border at waist height. There was a pine wooden bedframe in the middle of the room, but not much else.

'Not feeling this one. Let's look at the next one.' Catie led her sister back out onto the landing. 'What do you mean, problems? She hasn't said anything to me.'

'We had a bit of a talk yesterday. She said that some of the other girls at school are a bit... unkind.' Bridget followed her into the next room, where Catie stopped and turned to look at her sister.

'Unkind?' Catie shot Bridget a concerned glance.

'Yeah. Not very welcoming to newcomers, it would seem,' Bridget said.

'Well, what's happened? Why hasn't she told me?' Catie

frowned, only half-noticing the third bedroom, which was by far the nicest. It had a tasteful rose-patterned wallpaper which didn't appear to be peeling off anywhere that she could see, a large, brass bedframe which featured pretty roses in the metal-work at the head of the bed, and there was a large, vintage French style wardrobe in the corner and a matching chest of drawers. The window overlooked the garden.

'Name calling, mostly, from what she said. You know how girls that age can be. Excluding her. But one of them pushed her, or tripped her, or something. I don't know why she hasn't told you. Well.' Bridget paused. 'I suspect it's because she thinks you won't do anything about it.'

'Why would she think that?' Catie was aghast. The thought that her daughter wouldn't trust her with something that was troubling her made her chest ache with a terrible sadness. That wasn't what she wanted for Skye: like any mother, she wanted her child to be happy. The thought that she wasn't made her instantly sad, too.

'Because that's what you do. Ignore things,' Bridget said, and cast a quick eye over the room. 'This is the nicest. You should take this one.'

She walked out, and Catie followed her.

'Bridget. I would never ignore anything that was hurting my daughter.' Catie kept her voice level, but she was horrified at the implication. As if she would ever, *ever* do anything to hurt Skye – on purpose or by omission. The thought was deeply painful.

'Catie. I'm just telling you what Skye told me. Think yourself lucky that I'm telling you at all. She asked me not to.'

'She asked you not to tell me? But I'm her mother!' Catie exclaimed.

'I know.' Bridget rolled her eyes. 'Maybe she didn't want to tell you because she thought you were going to react badly. I don't know.' She put her hands on her hips and stared her sister down. 'Maybe she comes to me to tell me stuff because she knows I'm not going to minimise what's going on for her.'

'I do *not* minimise what's going on for other people! Where is this coming from?' Catie whispered, feeling as though she had been punched in the gut. What Bridget was saying felt so radically unfair. She felt like she spent her entire life trying to make life nice for other people: she was polite and welcoming to customers at the library all day, she tried to be a good mother to Skye, she tried to be a good daughter. She had even tried to be a good sister to Bridget – over and over again – and had it thrown back in her face.

'You KNOW! Catie! Will you stop pretending that you don't!' Bridget muttered, her eyes filling with tears. 'Don't stand there and pretend to me that you don't know what happened to me! And you just stood by and let it happen, and never said anything, never did anything.' Her voice broke. 'So, excuse me if I have little faith that you're going to step in like some kind of avenging angel and help your daughter when she needs it. I'll help her. I'm here for her now, at least,' Bridget said, turned and ran downstairs.

Catie was about to follow her, incredulous at what her sister had just said, when she heard footsteps on the stairs coming down from the floor above.

'Mum! What have you done?' Skye stood at the bottom of the stairs, having obviously just heard everything. 'I can't believe you're being so horrible to Auntie Bridget,' she said, and ran after her aunt.

'Skye! I didn't do anything.' Catie reached out for her daughter as she passed her, but Skye pulled her arm away. 'Don't touch me!' she cried out.

Catie steadied herself on the thick wooden banister, feeling tears spring to her eyes. She was in shock; it had all happened so fast, and, to her knowledge, she had done nothing wrong.

Catie retreated into the rose-papered bedroom and pulled

the thick wooden door closed behind her. Then, she leaned on the wooden doorframe and started to cry.

It had felt like a gift, moving in to Castle View. A sudden blessing from out of the blue that would solve her money and housing worries all at once.

So why did she feel like as soon as she had moved in, Castle View had turned into a curse?

8

It was late and Catie was sitting up in bed reading when she heard the noise.

Thud, thud, thud.

They had finally got all their stuff into the house and settled in, but it felt like each one of them – Bridget, Skye and Catie – were all camping out in their respective bedrooms rather than spending any time together, as a family.

They had been in the house for a week already, and even though Catie had tried hard to encourage some togetherness – cooking meals for everyone so that they could sit around the kitchen table and talk, suggesting movie nights and tidying projects – Skye and Bridget were less than keen. Tonight, Catie had taken ages making a lasagne after work, only for both of them to come and help themselves in the kitchen and take their dinner up to their rooms.

Disillusioned, Catie had made a plate up for herself, put the leftover lasagne in some Tupperware in the fridge and retreated to her room, feeling sad.

She knew that it might take some time for her and Bridget to get used to living together, but she had at least thought that she and Skye would be able to enjoy their new home. But, Skye seemed withdrawn, and didn't want to talk.

Thud, thud, thud.

It sounded as though someone was stamping on floorboards far above her, or was dropping heavy books from a great height. *Thud. Thud.*

Catie frowned and put her book down, listening. There was a silence, and then it started again.

What the...? she thought, her heart racing.

Was it a ghost? It was a silly thought, but now that June had put the thought in her mind that Castle View could be haunted, she couldn't stop thinking of it. Every time there had been a creak or an odd noise when she was lying in bed at night, Catie had got goosebumps. She'd started to imagine things: things that seemed silly in the daylight, but, late at night in an old house, seemed more than possible.

She looked at the book she was reading: a vampire novel. *Maybe not what you should be reading before bed,* she thought, and put it on her nightside table.

The thuds began again, but not quite as rhythmically as before. Between the thuds, Catie thought she heard a loud cry. She jumped.

Cautiously, she got out of bed and went to her bedroom door, opening it and peering out into the hallway. It was quiet, as if whatever was making the noise had heard her and was hiding.

Pulling her robe around her – it was a chilly night, and she'd just got cosy under her feather eiderdown – Catie edged cautiously along the corridor, listening for strange noises. As she got to the stairs, there was a sudden much louder bang, and a loud exclamation of pain.

Catie ran up the stairs, this time meeting a wild-haired Bridget on the landing above hers.

'What the heck was that?' her sister asked, rubbing her eyes.

'I'd just got off to sleep and there was some kind of commotion from upstairs.'

'Maybe it was Skye. I hope she's all right,' Catie muttered, heading up the final flight of stairs that led to the top floor her daughter had requisitioned. 'I thought it was...' she trailed off, not wanting to tell Bridget that she'd thought the noise was a ghost; that Castle View was haunted.

'Was what?'

'Nothing. I didn't know what it was,' Catie said, instead.

'Skye? Are you okay?' Bridget called out, stepping ahead of her sister and jogging up the stairs.

'Skye? Honey?' Catie called out as they got to the small landing that led to Skye's bedroom and bathroom.

'Mum? What are you doing up here?' Skye's voice called out, sounding cross.

'We heard thuds, and it sounded like you were crying or something,' Catie said, walking into Skye's bedroom after Bridget. 'Goodness, Skye. What have you been doing up here?' She looked around the room, incredulous at the mess that surrounded them.

Skye seemed to have taken all the clothes out of her wardrobe and strewn them over the carpet. They weren't in any order or any sort of neat pile: it looked as though Skye had pulled them out and thrown them over her shoulders, not caring where they landed. Dirty plates and cups were interspersed with the clothes, and sewing materials – patterns, scissors and pins – covered the floor. Catie stepped carefully around them, glad she was wearing slippers.

'Nothing,' Skye replied, mulishly. Catie knew the expression on her face. She was upset, but didn't want to talk about it. That was a look that Catie had seen more than she would have liked recently.

'Doesn't look like nothing, love,' Catie said, sitting down gently next to her daughter on the bed. 'What's up?'

'Nothing,' Skye repeated. 'Go back to bed.'

'Why have you got all your clothes out of the wardrobe?' Bridget asked, stepping over a rumpled pair of jeans. 'They're going to get filthy on the floor, sweetheart.'

Skye stared at her hands for a long moment and said nothing.

'Is it something you just want to talk to one of us about?' Bridget asked, pointedly. Catie felt a sadness in her stomach at the implication: that Skye would talk to Bridget and not her. She had tried and tried to get Skye to talk to her about whatever was happening at school, but Skye had clammed up and refused to say anything. *It's all right, Mum. Don't fuss.*

Skye shook her head.

'What was the banging noise?' Catie asked, looking around.

'Boots,' Skye said.

'Boots?'

'Yeah.' Her daughter seemed not to want to elaborate further. *It's like trying to talk to Lassie,* Catie thought. *One bark for yes, two barks for no. Only, Lassie was a lot more forthcoming.*

'Why were you throwing boots around, sweetheart?' Catie took a deep breath and let it out, slowly. 'Skye. It's late. We were in bed. You can't be up here making weird noises. I didn't know what was going on.' What she didn't say was, *you frightened the hell out of me.*

'I had to clear out the wardrobe to move it,' Skye said in a flat tone, as if what she was saying was completely obvious and her mother was a complete fool not to understand.

'Right... and why did you have to move the wardrobe at midnight?' Catie asked.

'There's something behind it,' her daughter said. 'I was in bed on my phone and I noticed it. I wanted to see what it was.'

'Okay... Skye, you shouldn't be on your phone past ten at night,' Catie reminded her daughter.

'Sorry.' Skye shrugged.

'Give me the phone, please.' Catie held her hand out.

'No way. That's private.' Her daughter shook her head.

'Sweetheart. I pay your phone bill. You're under eighteen, and I have a responsibility to ensure your safety,' Catie said, tiredly. 'I just want to check the apps you're using. And, you should be asleep by now. It's a school night.'

'You treat me like a baby and it's not fair!' Skye muttered.

'I have a right to look at your phone,' Catie replied calmly.

'No, you don't, Mum,' Skye argued. Catie wondered if there was something on her phone that she didn't want her mother to see.

'Catie. If she doesn't want you to see it, you shouldn't force her,' Bridget said, and put a guarding hand on Skye's shoulders.

'Bridget. I've got this.' Catie kept her tone calm and controlled.

'Thanks for making me feel like a part of the family, I guess. Honoured.' Bridget held up her hands, making a show of letting go of Skye.

'Okay. What is it behind the wardrobe, then?' she asked her daughter, instead. 'That made you want to move it?' The phone issue could wait: it was probably better if she let the situation calm a little before asking again. Catie knew that cyber bullying was definitely a thing nowadays: maybe that was what was troubling her daughter. But she knew that she had to pick her moment: Skye was sensitive, and Catie didn't want to argue with her daughter and not get to the root of the problem.

'I don't know. Some kind of old door.' Skye held her phone protectively to her chest.

'What do you mean, a door?' Catie walked over to the wardrobe and peeked behind it.

'See for yourself.' Her daughter shrugged. Catie craned her head around further, wedging herself as far back to the wall as she could. Sure enough, what looked like a small wall safe door sat behind the heavy wooden wardrobe.

'Is that... hmm. It *is* a safe,' she said, in surprise. She had definitely never lived in a house with a safe in the wall before, but Castle View was full of secrets, it seemed. 'Bridget. Help me move this a bit.' She pushed the wardrobe, but it was too heavy for her to move on her own.

'All right, all right,' Bridget muttered. They pushed it together, and the heavy wood squeaked uncomfortably on the wooden floor, rucking up the rug that stretched under Skye's bed.

'Will you look at that?' Bridget said, as the small wall safe came into view. 'Looks like someone wanted to keep a few secrets, eh.' She raised an eyebrow. 'Did we get anything in the paperwork from the solicitor about this?'

'No, I don't think so.' Catie frowned. They had moved the wardrobe enough so that she could run her fingertips over the safe door and the lock at the edge. 'It's locked. I can't open it.'

'Wouldn't be a very good safe if you could,' Skye said, looking up from her phone from where she sat on the bed.

'Do you think there's something in it?' Catie asked Bridget.

'Maybe.' Her sister nodded. 'But we'd need a key or a passcode to get into it, presumably.'

'It looks like a key,' Catie said, squinting. 'Maybe it's been left in the house somewhere.'

'Hmm. Look for it tomorrow.' Bridget yawned. 'If there is anything in there, then it's likely just old papers and bits and bobs, otherwise the solicitor would have told us.'

'I suppose so,' Catie said, regretfully. She wanted to see what was inside. 'It's late. We should all get some sleep.'

'Night, then.' Bridget gave them both a little wave, and mussed Skye's hair affectionately as she passed by. 'Never a dull moment in this house, huh.'

'Night-night, Auntie Bridget.' Skye gave her aunt a big smile.

'Goodnight, sweetheart.' Catie hugged her daughter: Skye returned the hug, but only briefly.

'I haven't forgotten about the phone, by the way. We'll talk about that in the morning,' Catie said gently.

'Great. Goodnight, Mother,' Skye said, formally, and placed her phone dramatically on the bedside table next to her. 'Look. I've put it down. Happy now?'

'Ecstatic,' Catie sighed. 'Goodnight, Skye. I do love you, you know.'

'I know,' Skye replied. Catie nodded, and pulled the door closed behind her.

It broke Catie's heart that Skye didn't say *I love you* back to her.

She wanted to go back into the room, gather her daughter into her arms and hold her there, against her heart. She wanted to hold Skye like she used to, when Skye was a little girl and had wanted nothing more than her mother's attention. They had been so huggy and close when Skye was little. Yet, in the past year or so, all that had changed. Catie couldn't hug Skye, now: Skye would pull away or make an awkward comment and Catie was still worried about Skye being unhappy at school.

Catie knew that Skye was a teenager now, and that these could be difficult times for their relationship. Skye was becoming a young woman. It was to be expected that there might be difficult times and that their relationship would go through ups and downs. Catie knew all that, but knowing it didn't make her miss those times with Skye: the days when she could hug her and make everything better. Now, Catie didn't know what was wrong or how she could take her and her daughter back to their old selves. She hated the fact that something had been bothering her daughter at school, but she'd gone to Bridget about it instead of Catie.

As she walked back down the stairs, Catie wondered what might be inside the safe. Now that she and Bridget owned Castle View, they also owned whatever was inside it, and that included this little unexpected mystery.

Catie was desperate to know what might be behind that little metal door. Someone – Great Aunt Isobel? Someone else? – had thought it necessary to set the safe in the wall and pull a heavy wardrobe in front of it. That implied that whatever was inside it was important in some way.

Catie got back into bed and pulled the thick feather eiderdown up to her shoulders. She switched off the lamp and stared into the darkness, thinking.

Somewhere, there might be a key in the house that would open the safe. She would look for it tomorrow.

It was so clear that there was something bothering Skye, and it broke Catie's heart that Skye seemed to resist every attempt she made to try to help. Skye's heart was more closed to Catie than it had been, and that made Catie sad.

Maybe she'll just come around when she's ready, Catie thought, closing her eyes. *You have to trust that it will come good in the end. She's just going through a phase. She's a teenager.*

But what if it wasn't just a phase? What if Catie and Skye's relationship was doomed to be difficult forever, just like hers and Bridget's?

9

'Good morning, Matt.'

'Lovely day, isn't it?'

'I hope she's not working you too hard.'

Matt was back in the library with Catie, helping her with the website. It was coming along slowly, but there was still a lot of work to be done. However, that day, it had been a struggle to get down to anything because the local crochet group – locally known as the crochet coven – seemed to want to flirt with Matt almost constantly.

Catie was sure that the only witchcraft that the ladies did was gossiping, being a coven in name only. They had recently begun meeting at the library because their usual venue at the village community centre had a damp problem, so June had asked if Catie and Lilian didn't mind them coming to the library once a week. Lilian was an occasional member of the group, and Catie didn't mind having the women there at all: it made the library feel busy.

Also, the crochet coven brought tea, coffee, cakes and sand-wiches with them that they'd made, and sold them at a low price lunch offer that other people in the community liked to take advantage of. So, now, on a Thursday lunchtime, it meant that the library got quite busy with mums and toddlers – who could enjoy the picture books with some cake and a juice box for the little ones – and some of the many elderly people in the community who came down for a chat and a sandwich.

The crochet coven also brought toys for the children to play with, and Catie had seen that they were also more than happy to give newcomers a ball of wool and a crochet hook and teach them how to start something simple, like a blanket or a hat. All in all, they were a good-hearted group of women, dedicated to helping others. But, they were also quite partial to discussing the business of everyone in the village, and Catie thought that she was glad that she hadn't done anything interesting enough to become the topic of conversation.

'Sorry if they're a distraction.' Catie apologised for the women, most of whom had found a reason to come and say hello and good morning to Matt as he sat at the issue desk. 'They seem fascinated with you.'

'I have that effect on the older woman,' he chuckled, giving her an unreadable look under his eyelashes.

Oh, Catie thought, but couldn't think of a witty reply.

'It's okay. They remind me of my mum. Well, the older ones, anyway.' He looked wistful. 'I miss my mum on sunny days,' he said, looking up at the shaft of sunlight that was streaming in to the library through one of its skylights. Catie had always thought they were magical: on sunny days, sharp shards of light illuminated the dark wooden shelves, making the dust motes look like fairies, caught dancing.

'She's... no longer with us?' Catie asked, gently.

'She died when I went away to university. Hal had just graduated. Our dad was still alive, but he was never the same after that. None of us were, I don't think.' His voice was sad.

'Hal?' she asked, frowning. 'Not... Hal *Cameron*?'

'Yes, Hal Cameron.' He frowned back at her.

'The laird of Loch Cameron, Hal Cameron?'

'Ye-es,' Matt replied, patiently. 'He's my older brother. I assumed you knew.'

Oh, no.

Catie had had no idea. 'Why would I know that?' She looked around at the library, noting how all the ladies of the crochet coven had been so keen to come and say *hello* to Matt when they arrived. It wasn't just because he was attractive. It was because he was the second in line to the estate of Loch Cameron. A laird. Or, at least, heir to being the laird; Catie wasn't sure how it worked.

'I don't know. People just know. I must have mentioned it.' He shrugged.

'No, you didn't. And I didn't just know. I thought you were... I don't know. An employee of his.'

'No. Well, I'm helping him out with some family business things. Hal was keen that I was *useful* when I got back.' He made air quotes with his fingers when he said *useful*.

'Right. So you're... what. Royalty?'

'Goodness, no. Gentry.'

'Oh, like that's no big deal.' She laughed, despite her surprise.

'Well. It's not royalty. We're just a family that has lived here a long time,' he said.

'Lots of families have lived here a long time. Most of them don't live in a castle and extract rent from everybody else,' Catie commented, drily.

'That's not all we do. We look after the land. And the community. The farms, the land, support businesses, keep the historical records, host events for the village... Hal does a lot for the village,' he replied, sounding a little hurt.

'Oh, I know. I know. But you have to admit, it's a little unusual, being part of a family like yours,' she said. 'I grew up in Loch Cameron. I know how it works, and people are generally happy with everything. I get it. I just... I didn't know that was who you were.'

'My apologies. I should have introduced myself properly.' He ran a hand through his curly, dark auburn hair.

'It's okay. And I am so sorry about your mum. That's awful.' She reached for his hand. 'That was Lady Cameron. I remember her, a little, from when I lived here. I'd see her around, sometimes. She was always so smartly dressed. So glamorous.'

Matt squeezed her fingers, and then let her hand go.

'Thank you. Yes, she was very glamorous. She loved clothes and jewellery. It's okay. Long time ago now. I was sort of used to not seeing her all the time because Hal and I went to boarding school. But she was still Mum, you know? I still loved her. When I was home on the holidays, we'd sit out on the balcony on a sunny day and talk.'

'Boarding school must've been hard.' Catie thought about Skye, and even though their relationship was strained, the thought of not having her around was appalling. 'I can't imagine sending my daughter away.'

'Yes, Hal and I both went to the same school. He was a few years ahead of me.' Matt nodded. 'It was all right. I had friends there.'

'It seems sad to have to get used to being away from home,' Catie said. 'I don't know. I mean, it's not normal in my world. It is in yours, I guess.'

'I missed home. You do. We both went away to school when we were six. It's pretty young to be away from your parents. I missed Mum a lot.' His voice was sad; instinctively, Catie reached for his hand again and squeezed it. He looked surprised, but squeezed her fingers back as if to say *thank you*.

'That must have been tough,' she said, softly, releasing his grip. It felt odd to be essentially holding hands as they talked; they really didn't know each other that well at all.

'It was. I mean, you get used to it, after a while. I watched a lot of horror movies.' He shot her a wry smile.

'Wow. Did that help?' Catie chuckled.

'No. Made it worse, probably. *Poltergeist*. We must have watched that about fifty times.'

'God, that terrified me when I was a kid. When the girl gets trapped in the TV.' She shuddered.

'Go into the light, Carol Ann.' They said it at the same time, and Catie laughed out loud.

'That's such an old movie. How come you saw it when you were a kid?'

'Well, Grandma, I don't know if you know, but there were such things as DVDs in my youth. Even at boarding school.'

'I suppose so. I loved that movie.'

'I hated it. But I wound up watching it so many times. One of the boys in my dorm always put it on. Anyway, I always missed home, and Mum in particular. We were always close.'

'She must have missed you. It would break my heart to send my daughter away,' Catie said.

'You have a big heart. I can tell,' he said, looking up into her eyes. 'You know, you're really easy to talk to. I just told you all of that stuff without even knowing you that well. I'm not usually that much of an open book.'

'Oh. Thanks. I really am so sorry to hear about your mum. That's so sad.' Catie touched him lightly on the arm; it was a gentle touch of care, of a simple affection between humans. Nonetheless, he flinched as she made contact, and looked deep into her eyes.

Catie felt the blush growing on her cheeks. His eyes were so deep and serious, but so suddenly full of something more – affection? Desire? She didn't know, but she felt like she was falling into them.

'Thank you. It was a very sad time, but it was a while ago now,' he repeated, his gaze not leaving hers. 'Maybe it's because you're older. Why you're easy to talk to,' he said, and her heart sank. *Old.* The word rang in her ears. 'You know. Wise. You've had a kid. Life experience. It's very obvious,' he added.

'I certainly do have that,' she said, casting her eyes down and moving away. *Wise.* Like some kind of owl. It wasn't sexy. Not that she was there to be sexy for him, but they had had a moment, just then. There was a definite draw of energy between them. Like polarity: the two opposing ends of the battery, positive and negative, calling to each other. She didn't know what to make of it, but when it happened, she felt as though she was drowning.

10

'Anyway,' Catie cleared her throat. She didn't know what was happening between them. *Be a grown-up*, she chastised herself. 'So, I wanted to hold an event at the library, but something that people can get involved in. Summer of Reading is something I've seen at other libraries. Basically, we incentivise people to read a certain number of books in a certain time period – say, twenty books in August, or something – and if they do, they get a reward.'

'Right. What kind of reward?'

'I don't know. I mean, it could be as lame as a sticker or a certificate, or something a little more exciting. But it would be good to have something on the website that would promote it, and a place where people could list the books they've read, share them, make booklists or something.' Catie shrugged. 'I want to make it fun for people. Maybe introduce a bit of healthy competition.'

'Hmm. Okay.' Matt drummed his fingers on the table, thoughtfully. 'Could the reward be a party? You could do something fun at the library and then give something to the winners. The people who have read the most books. Like, give a certificate to everyone who reads twenty books in August or whatever. But give a book token or a cake or a goody bag to the three top readers. And we could share their reading profiles online, like, with a list of what they read, their reviews of their favourite books, that kind of thing. Make them your reading superstars.'

'Reading Superstars is sweet. It does sound quite primary school, though.' Catie smiled. 'Maybe another title. Reading Rocks. Reading Rock Stars. Something like that.'

'Well, I'll leave the creative genius to you.' Matt shot her that smile that made her want to bite her lip. 'But I'll do my best to help out. Mind you, I'm also supposed to be helping with the big wedding.' He lowered his voice, even though there was nobody else around. 'Zelda wants it how she wants it. I don't know how Hal is putting up with all of it, I can tell you.'

'Oh. Is it all a bit busy at the moment?' Catie asked politely. She had heard about the "bridezilla effect" which turned otherwise reasonable people into monsters around the time of their weddings.

'Kinda, yeah.' He ran his hand through his hair again. 'It's not that I don't like Zelda. I do. And she's really good for Hal. I get it. It's more the fact that me and Hal haven't been getting along.'

'Oh?'

'I don't want to bore you with the details.'

'It's all right. I'm happy to listen,' she said, sitting down in the chair next to his, behind the issue desk.

'Oh. Well, we've always been a bit... at loggerheads, you know? But recently... he's really disapproving of my work, and it's creating difficulties,' Matt sighed. 'Fair enough, I made some mistakes. Some gambles didn't pay off. But that's how it is, being an entrepreneur, right? That's part of it.'

'Sure.' Catie shrugged. 'I guess... I don't know enough about it. But that seems fair.'

'Yeah. Well, I came home for the wedding, and Hal's just

been on my back since I got home. Nonstop. What am I going to do about the business? What am I going to do about the family stuff? There's a lot of family businesses we have that he wants my help with. And that's cool, I am helping. But I can't do everything, right?'

'Sure.'

'And we've argued about the rent increase, too. And, meantime, it's bloody wedding this, wedding that.' He snorted. 'You'd think it was a royal wedding or something.'

'Well, it is an important event. You'd forgive them for being excited,' Catie said, gently. 'Though, I wasn't impressed with the rent increase. It made life really difficult for me. Fortunately, I had another option, but a lot of people don't.'

'Yeah. Of course. Ugh, I'm sorry about all that.' Matt exhaled. 'Things have been bad between me and Hal for a while, and it doesn't help that he really disapproved of my ex, when I was in that relationship.' Matt's expression darkened for a moment. 'Hal never welcomed her into the family. He made it really difficult for me to bring her home and spend time in Loch Cameron. I suppose I resent him for that.'

'Oh! Why didn't he like her?' Catie asked.

'I don't know. She was different to the kinds of people he's used to, or so I thought. She was American, a successful Californian woman. Glamorous. Sassy. But then he started seeing Zelda, and she's all of those things. So, I don't really get it. I thought it was just a culture clash or something. But, plainly, it wasn't.'

'Oh.' Catie watched his face as he spoke; this was clearly difficult for him to talk about, and she was touched that he trusted her to open up about it.

Even if I wanted to – which I don't, that's definitely not what I'm here for – I can't compete with that, she thought. Catie felt like the opposite of a glamorous American girl, probably with a tan and perfect hair and expensive clothes. She was just a middle-aged librarian, with messy hair in a topknot, glasses and an aged jumper with a picture of a black cat on it.

'Part of the reason I ended that relationship was because I didn't see it having a future with me, here. It wasn't the only reason, but it was definitely in the mix. So, I guess, Hal expecting me to play happy families with Zelda and prep for the wedding sits badly with me. Because he wouldn't have been half so accommodating if it was the other way around.'

'Wow. Families, huh.' Catie felt for Matt; she could tell he was upset, and she was no stranger to family dramas. 'I know how it goes. My dad's just had a second stroke. My mum's in pieces, as you might imagine. Things with me and my sister aren't good. We can't seem to stop bickering. And, apparently, my daughter is having problems at school that she flatly refuses to talk to me about.'

Catie had been desperately worried about Skye since Bridget had told her that her daughter was getting picked on by the other girls, but Skye had completely refused to talk about it at all.

'I'm fine, Mum,' Skye had said, in a monotone, when Catie asked.

'You'd tell me if anything was wrong?'

'Yes.' The monotone, again.

'The other girls being nice to you?' Catie had prompted, trying again. 'Because, if they're not, we can sort it out. But you have to tell me.'

'Oh, god! Mum! Leave it!' Skye had screamed at her, run up to her room and slammed the door.

'I'm sorry,' Matt said. 'That's a lot of stuff to be dealing with.' He looked concerned. 'I don't even know how I'd deal with one of those things, never mind all of them.'

'I know,' Catie sighed. 'Life just doesn't get easier, does it? As you get older.'

'Nope.'

'Sorry. I'm not that much fun at the moment. I'm just so worried about my mum and dad. They've organised a carer type occupational therapist to come in and look after my dad full time but my mum's not taking it well. She's always had my dad there, he was the rock, you know? And now, suddenly, he can't do anything for himself. She can't deal with it.'

'That's rough. But the therapist will probably help a lot once they're there. Fear of the unknown and all that.'

'I guess so. I just don't know how to support her. She doesn't want me to "make a fuss" which is what she says when I offer to go around.'

'She's probably just trying to protect you, though, right?' Matt said, kindly. 'She's your mum. She doesn't want you to worry.'

'But I *am* worried. I want to help.' Catie felt frustrated.

'I know. But I guess all you can do is just continue to be around, offer help, wait for her to come around.'

'You're right. We have a bit of a... strained relationship, I suppose.' Catie sighed.

'How come?' He looked at her curiously. Catie was surprised that he seemed to be so interested in all of her dull family politics.

'Oh, goodness. Long story.' She shook her head. 'Do you mind if we don't talk about it? I'm sort of up to here at the moment.' She held her hand over her head.

'Totally. I get it.' He smiled. 'I'm here if you want to chat, though. I sympathise about family stuff.'

'Thanks, Matt.' Catie felt a warm glow of gratefulness and friendliness in her heart. It *was* nice to have someone to talk to; she was overdue for a phone chat with Simran and since she'd moved to Loch Cameron she realised she hadn't really made many new friends.

'Welcome. Listen... Catie.' He looked uncomfortable, and stood up, holding onto the back of his chair with both hands as if it was a life raft. 'I wanted to... umm...' He trailed off, looking uncharacteristically shy.

'Yes?' she asked. Looking over at the crochet coven, Catie could see that more than one of the women were not very subtly watching her and Matt. *Great,* she thought. *Now we're going to be the topic of conversation.*

'I wondered... if you were free, sometime this week. Perhaps you'd like to... go out with me. In the evening. A drink, or something,' he continued.

'A drink?' she echoed. 'Like... coffee?' The question had taken her by surprise.

'Well, you can choose the drink you'd like. That's customary on a date.' He smiled, shyly. 'We can go for coffee, or to a pub or something.'

'You're asking me out... on a *date*?' Catie didn't mean to raise her voice, but she was so surprised that she couldn't help the volume going up at the end of her sentence. The women looked up, stared at her and Matt and then started murmuring to each other.

Oh, for goodness' sake, she thought.

'Umm... yes.' Matt was as awkward as she was. For a moment, Catie felt as though she could see outside herself and looked at them both, standing there, being totally awkward and adolescent with each other.

'Me?' Catie couldn't help adding. Then, because it felt so ridiculous, she started to laugh.

'Yes, you.' Matt started laughing too; it was as if it was infectious. 'Why is that so hard to believe?'

'Well... err... I guess I just wasn't expecting it,' she said. 'Go into the light, Carol-Ann!' she added, then thought, *good god woman, what did you say that for? You total nerd.* She cleared her throat. 'I mean... wake up, or something. I'm saying that to myself.'

'Okay. I don't think anyone has ever quoted *Poltergeist* to me when I asked them out before.' He gave her a shy grin.

'Is that weird? It's weird, isn't it? I'm sorry, I don't know what possessed me.' She frowned, feeling embarrassed. 'Oh, no. I made a pun and didn't even mean to.'

'Haha. That's next level punning. Well done,' he chuckled.

'Oh, I really don't think I deserve congratulations.' Catie felt mortified at the disastrous way the conversation was going.

'Catie. Do you want to know a secret?' he asked, leaning towards her, still holding the back of the chair.

'Okay.' Instinctively, she leaned back a little.

'I'm pretty weird. So. Like calls to like, maybe.' He gave her a sudden, bright grin and then wrote something on a scrap of paper on the issue desk and gave it to her. 'That's my number, weirdo. Text me later and we can arrange a drink of your choice.'

'All right,' she said, taking it. What was happening? She really doubted that she would text and arrange a date; Matt had to be joking, or something.

But what if he wasn't?

11

'Ugh. This is gross.' Skye sneezed as she opened a wall cupboard and lifted out a faded, moth-eaten blanket from a tattered box. 'It smells weird in here. What are all these black things all over the floor?' She dragged her trainer-clad foot across the floor inside the door, grimacing.

'I think those are mouse droppings.' Bridget peered over her shoulder. 'Makes sense, an old house like this.'

'Oh. My. God!' Skye yelled, backing out of the cupboard and screaming. 'MICE?! Are you kidding me?'

'Bridge. Don't.' Catie chuckled as she held out her arms for her daughter. 'Though I do have to say, those do look like mouse droppings. Hopefully old.' She peered over Skye's shoulder and grimaced. 'Anyway. Mice are cute.'

'They spread disease, Mum. They wee constantly and then walk it through the house,' Skye said, suddenly sounding much older than her teenage years.

'Well, I didn't know that. Noted.' Catie hugged her daughter and let her go. 'Come on. You can bag up the old bedspreads and I'll go in the cupboard.'

Castle View was a large house and, Catie was realising, it

seemed to have a hundred little nooks and crannies that were packed with a mixture of vintage treasures, junk and odd ephemera. *And mice, it would seem*, she thought, as she ducked her head into the walk-in cupboard and flicked on the light.

Catie, Bridget and Skye were slowly making their way through clearing out the rooms, but it was a lot of work. However, Catie was grateful that Bridget and Skye had agreed to help her: at least it was something they were doing together. Perhaps, if they started to spend time as a family, they would start to get on better.

It turned out that Great-Aunt Isobel – or whoever had lived in the house in her absence – had left a lot of stuff everywhere. This was their third day on clear up, and they still hadn't made it past the bedrooms.

'Okay. All the bedspreads will go to charity, then?' Skye asked as she held one up – a pretty, slightly faded feather down coverlet in a duck egg blue with a pattern of daisies embroidered onto it. 'This is kind of nice. Can we keep this one?'

'Make a pile for things we want to keep, a pile for charity, one for recycling and one for the bin,' Bridget suggested. 'Though, we're going to run out of room in the normal bins pretty quickly.' She was sorting through a stack of old books in the corner, crouching on her heels. 'I mean, it's going to be a bit of a challenge not to keep too much. Most of these books are worth hanging on to.' She opened a book of illustrated fairy tales and held it up for Catie and Skye to see. 'Look. Isn't this lovely?'

'Gorgeous.' Catie looked back over her shoulder. 'Quite old, too. I wonder if any of them are worth anything. Or, I could take them for the library, perhaps. If they're too frail to go into stock, we could do some kind of exhibition. I'm sure people would like to see them.'

'I'll box them up, then, and you can decide.' Bridget nodded.

Look at us, getting along, Catie thought. *I hope it lasts.*

However, she was having the nicest day that she'd had in a long time, even though the three of them were basically just cleaning. It didn't matter what they did together, she thought. It was just nice to spend time with Bridget and Skye and not bicker.

She turned her attention back to the walk-in cupboard and started opening the boxes that were stacked inside it. The first two were, as Skye had noted, full of old sheets and blankets, none of which were particularly worth keeping. She carried them out to the main room and dumped them by the door. 'These are to take to the fabric and clothes recycling,' she said, writing a post-it note and sticking it on the top box. Bridget nodded, distractedly. She was sitting on the edge of the bed, reading the fairy tale book; Catie was tempted to remind her to get back to work, but she was trying to keep things as harmonious as possible with her sister.

Going back into the cupboard, Catie began sorting through another box of stuffed toys: teddy bears that had clearly been much loved and were somewhat threadbare around the ears and paws. She wondered what to do with those· it seemed heartless to throw them away, but she wasn't sure they were good enough to go to charity. *Perhaps if they were gently washed*, she thought, setting the box to one side.

'Cate? We're going to start sorting through the ornaments on the shelves here, okay?' Bridget called out.

'Okay,' Catie called out, opening the next box. 'If anything looks valuable, google it.'

'Highly unlikely. It's like someone was hoarding charity shop junk,' Bridget called back. 'There's no rhyme or reason to it. Just tons of random cheap porcelain. Well. I don't think it's porcelain at all, actually. Just cheap, mass-produced ceramics.'

'I've got it covered, Mum,' Skye added. 'Just in case.'

The contents of the next box were quite different. Catie had been expecting more sheets, or something like tablecloths or napkins. Frowning, she reached in to the box and took out a series of notebooks covered in a mustard hessian fabric.

She opened the first one, curiously.

There was no name inside, but every page was covered in narrow copperplate handwriting.

Catie realised that the entire book was filled with poems. She leafed through the other books: there were perhaps eight of them, all the same type of notebook, covered in mustard coloured hessian, all full of poems written in the same, cramped handwriting.

'Goodness,' she murmured, squinting at the lines of poetry; it was hard to read them in the gloomy light of the cupboard. She took the first notebook with her into the room where Bridget and Skye were wrapping up ornaments that had been displayed on two shelves on the wall.

'Hey. Listen to this. There's a box full of notebooks back there, all full of someone's poetry,' she said, holding the book under the light. She flicked past a few pages where the author of the book appeared to be working through notes for a poem: there were pages of more scribbled notes, and then, the first poem, written out in full.

'Poetry?' Bridget wrinkled her nose. 'Like, they've copied it from a book?'

'No... I think this is original poetry. That someone wrote. Listen.'

Catie read the first full poem, which was titled The Taste of Grief.

> *Here is a foam of perfectly distilled grief,*
> *collected at source and aged, pressed into a*
> *gel, reduced,*
> *Enjoy its delicate flavour with difficulty. The*
> *days are short now.*

You will drink the warm wine quietly and start
        for home, pad silent in the night.
A fox crosses your path.
Here is a philtre you pressed from nightshade,
pressed and reduced, strained and compressed –
the instructions are vague he is angry you hold
        the page up to your eyes
The days are shortening.
Everyone is sad or you feel they must be, under-
        neath the crust.
You walk home slowly, under the night bridge
        that creaks.
The water is cold. Everyone is sleeping
The cabinet doors snick open, revealing under-
        whelming letters
A record of a small life. The solicitor's stamp, a
        necessary detail of chattels –

The water is cold.
The light makes it more difficult.

This is the infusion,
Pressed quiet, compressed silence.
Nightshade in my hand
Everyone will be sad but also
Everyone will forget

'Wow. That's dark.' Bridget blew out her cheeks. 'Who wrote that? It sounds like they were one step away from ending it all. From poison, it seems like.'

'I don't know who wrote it. There's not a name on anything.' Catie flicked through the book.

'Can I see?' Skye asked, coming towards her mother.

'Sure.' Catie handed her the book. 'It seems very sad, doesn't it? Someone wrote that feeling very low. *Everyone will forget.* Heartbreaking.'

'Remember when Matt showed us around the house that first time, and there were those sketches of a man, down in the study?' Skye looked up from the book. 'Do you think it was the same person that drew those, and wrote this? It kinda has the same vibe.'

'Maybe.' Catie nodded. 'It would make sense that they all belonged to someone that lived here. It suggests someone who had a lot going on, emotionally at least.'

'It's kind of... I dunno.' Bridget looked doubtful. 'I don't like it. It's so dark. What are the rest of the poems like?' She put her arm around Skye and looked over her shoulder. 'Hmm. Kind of the same.'

'It's not a bad thing to write poetry,' Skye said, holding the book protectively to her chest. 'At least the person was expressing themselves.'

'Yes. That's true.' Catie nodded. 'Well, Skye, if you'd like them, there's a whole stack more of the notebooks in a box in there. Why don't you look through them and see if you find anything interesting?'

'Okay.' Skye shrugged. 'I'll take them. Someone should have them. You shouldn't throw out something so personal.'

'You're right.' Catie went back into the cupboard and brought out the box containing the notebooks. 'Here you are.'

She was touched by her daughter's thoughtfulness. Skye could be a typical teenager: moody, introspective, snappy sometimes, but Catie was relieved to see that she hadn't lost her sweetness, too.

'Well, back to it,' Bridget sighed, picking up another sheet of newspaper and reaching for a ceramic collie from the shelf. 'And, before you ask, no. I don't think this china dog is worth anything. I'm not a hundred per cent convinced about Great-Aunt Isobel's taste, you know.'

'Hmm. In the case of that particular ornament, agreed.' Catie made a face, and both sisters started to chuckle. 'I always wonder who buys stuff like that.'

'I don't know. But as Isobel didn't really live here, it would make more sense that whoever did, bought it. And they had zero taste whatsoever,' Bridget said, picking up a ceramic clock in the shape of a house with a red roof, white walls and roughly painted brown windowpanes. 'Exhibit B.'

'Yeah. It does feel like there was some hoarding going on.' Catie nodded. 'People do it when they're sad. Maybe, at some point in their life, this person was.'

'Maybe.' Bridget shrugged. 'It's weird that we're discovering all these things about them, without knowing anything about them. If you know what I mean.'

'I know.' Catie looked at the rows of mismatched, odd little ornaments. There were more of them piled up on the floor; reams of chipped, badly coloured, mass-produced little *things*. 'It just all feels... sad.'

When she'd walked into the room, she hadn't thought much of it: just a random collection of value-less items. But now, she looked at the shelves with a new insight. Someone in this house had collected those things. Someone had wanted them. Were they beautiful or particularly tasteful? Not really. But perhaps that urge to hoard things said something about that person's state of mind. Cluttered, sad and confused, like the person who had written those poems?

'The whole house is sad,' Skye said suddenly, looking up. 'Don't you feel it? I felt it as soon as we walked in.'

'You're right,' Bridget said. 'I feel it too. Like there's a cloud over the house.'

'I guess so.' Catie was surprised to hear her sister say anything so sensitive; usually, Bridget was a lot more practical.

Not the sensitive type. 'Maybe if we clean everything out and make the house ours, it'll stop feeling sad. We can make it feel happy again.'

'Maybe.' Bridget raised an eyebrow. 'But I wouldn't get too hopeful, if I were you.'

12

'This isn't what I expected when we said we would go for a drink,' Catie said, looking around as she got out of her car. Matt had been in the car park already when she arrived, and had walked slowly over to her car as she parked.

They were in the car park of the Loch Cameron Whisky Distillery – a beautiful whitewashed old building set in the countryside just outside the village. When Catie had driven along the small winding road that led to it, there had been a high point on the road where she realised she could look down on the distillery below and see its name emblazoned on its slate roof in huge white letters.

'Yeah, well. I like to keep a lady guessing.' Matt held out his arm in an old-fashioned, gentlemanly way, and she took it. 'Be careful. It's a bit uneven underfoot just here,' he cautioned her, leading her around a pothole in the car park surface.

'Thanks. I'm surprised that you haven't laid down your cape for me to walk over,' she joked, not used to this kind of chivalry.

'Be assured that if it gets boggy underfoot, my lady will not get her shoes wet.' Matt grinned and raised an eyebrow. 'So, you haven't been here before?'

'No. I knew it was here, but never came. I haven't been back in Loch Cameron that long, and it wasn't really on my list, to be honest,' she explained as they walked into a charming courtyard filled with floral hanging baskets. Deep red poppies vied with orange geraniums for space, and boxes and planters displayed a profusion of orange, red and white roses interspersed with phlox and white daisies. 'Wow. This is beautiful!'

'It's nice, isn't it? I'm good mates with the owner, Ben, and he said we could come up and get a private tour. So, not a drink, per se, but I'm assured that we'll get a tasting as part of it. If that sounds okay?'

'It sounds very okay. Thank you for organising such a thoughtful... date.' Catie stumbled over the word.

It still felt weird, knowing that she was on a date, and, even if you set that aside for a minute, on a date with Matt Cameron, part of the family that owned Loch Cameron. Matt Cameron, who was, by all accounts, a successful business mogul, had lived in California with, she presumed, a jet-set playboy lifestyle and definitely a jet-set playboy girlfriend, or more than one, and was second in line to the lairdship.

And, he was a good fifteen years younger than her. But, in a way, that was nice. Matt wasn't a serious prospect, and Catie was allowing herself to have some fun.

She hadn't been on a date in... actually, she struggled to remember when the last one had been. She had had a brief foray into the world of dating when she'd split with Skye's dad, Greg, but it had been a disaster. There had been two – maybe three – dates with different guys, but she just hadn't been interested in any of them. One had talked incessantly about his favourite bus terminals; one had picked his nose, and the third had ghosted her after their first date.

After that, Catie hadn't felt inclined to go on any more dates, and had decided to focus on being a good mum for Skye, and on her career. That had worked perfectly fine for her but, now, she realised that she had let her love life slip for too long. Okay, she probably wouldn't marry Matt, but there was no harm in having a pleasant evening out.

She'd texted Simran to tell her that Matt had asked her out.

Am I doing the right thing? she'd asked her friend.

Of course! Go for it! Simran had texted back, sending her a number of vegetable-based emojis and laughing faces. *Tell me how it goes.*

'You're welcome.' Matt looked pleased. 'Ah, there's our tour guide now.'

'Hello, hello! Welcome to Loch Cameron Distillery, beautiful ones!' the man walking towards them called out. He was a smallish older man dressed nattily in a pinstripe waistcoat, matching trousers and a purple shirt with a cream-coloured cravat at his throat. 'My dear, I don't believe I've had the pleasure. Grenville McNulty at your service.' The man shook Catie's hand vigorously.

'Catie McGovern. Hello.' She smiled, liking Grenville's old school charm immediately.

'A joy to meet you, my dear. The second in line to the seat of Cameron, of course, I know. How are you, Matthew?'

'Fine, thanks, Grenville. Just Matt is fine.' He looked slightly uncomfortable and Catie wondered if it was the mention of his title, or the mention of his brother that was bothering him.

'I understand that you'll be having a private tour and tasting today?' Grenville gestured towards one of the main buildings. 'We're all set up for you, with a lovely guided walk through the vault too. You know, dear, our vault is Scotland's oldest,' Grenville said, with more than a hint of pride in his voice.

'Is it?' Catie enquired politely. 'I'm afraid I have no idea about whisky. I like it, but I've never even visited a distillery before.'

'Goodness. We'll have to take away some of your Scot

points, eh,' Grenville teased her. 'I'm joking, of course, dear. That's what I'm here for: to share my expertise.'

Grenville led them through a glossy black wooden door and into a large shed-like enclosure that smelt immediately as she'd imagined it would: malty and sweet. Inside, a high-ceilinged hangar-type enclosure was filled with huge gleaming copper stills. Each one was roughly the length of a car, and the shape of an oversized genie's lamp: bulbous at the bottom and tapering into a copper chimney at the top.

'Of course, every distillery is different.' Grenville raised his voice as they walked in. 'What you can smell is the fermented mash liquid being boiled in these huge copper cauldrons. They're called mash tuns. Still in their original positions, as is the waterwheel which once powered the whole distillery,' Grenville added. 'You'll see that when we go back outside.'

'It's really something,' Catie said, looking around her. 'How old is the distillery?'

'It's a family business. It's been run by a Douglas since 1785. It closed during the Prohibition years, but then it opened again in 1959 and it's been open since.' Grenville pointed to some framed black and white photos on the wall behind them that showed the copper stills in the same position, tended by men in suits from a bygone age.

'Of course, when Liz came on board a few years ago, then the company went from strength to strength.' Grenville winked at Catie. 'You didn't hear it from me, but this place was struggling before she stepped in. But now, with the new Old Maids range, they're doing so well. Opened up a café and a visitor centre, which they never had before. Missing a trick for years. And they've put me in charge of the tours,' he added proudly.

'Liz?' Catie asked.

'Oh, yes. Lovely Liz. She began as the new Sales and Marketing Director a few years back, and then she and the owner, Ben, became an item. They co-run the business now,' Grenville explained.

'She sounds fantastic.' Catie grinned.

'Oh, she is. A force of nature.' Grenville nodded. 'Very impressive. And a good soul, too. Which is so important.'

'Definitely,' Matt agreed. 'Liz and Ben are great.'

'Have you always worked at the distillery, Grenville?' Catie asked as they walked past the gleaming copper tuns. She wondered whose job it was to polish them and keep them so shiny.

'Ah, no. This is something I do in addition to the shop,' he said.

'Grenville owns a shop in the village. The Wee Dram,' Matt explained. 'Sells whisky, and other booze.'

'Well, I'd like to put it a little more artfully than that, dear boy but, yes, I am a stockist of the Loch Cameron limited editions and vintage bottles. I'm a lifelong whisky enthusiast. Set up the shop many moons ago.' Grenville beamed at them both. 'I find that the tours complement the shop, though, and it gives my sense of the dramatic a little outlet. I've really been as happy as a clam since I've been doing them.'

Grenville led them out of the hangar-like enclosure and back outside to the gardens.

'Now. If you'd like to follow me, next stop is the vault, with a nice romantic little surprise.' He led them to another building and opened a heavy-looking door that said VAULT on it.

Catie stepped through the door carefully. Ahead of her, she could just see a flight of dark wooden stairs that led down into darkness. It was much cooler in here, and she shivered involuntarily.

'Just hang on there for a moment, my dear,' Grenville said. He tapped a switch, and the stairs were bathed in light. 'I'll go down first; I'm used to it. Watch your step; the treads are a little old, here and there,' Grenville cautioned. Catie rested her hand on a wooden banister as they made their way down, very aware that Matt was following close behind her.

'It's okay. Just take it easy,' he said, quietly, and something in the timbre of his voice was both reassuring and unexpectedly erotic.

'Monks invented fermentation and distillation in this country, which I find ironic.' Grenville flicked another switch and dim lighting glowed the vault to life, highlighting a space that stretched into distant corridors, lined with barrels. 'It's so strange to think that the idea of brewing a liquid that had transformational effects was originally quite so spiritual,' he chuckled. 'Still. I expect lots of people have seen God after enough whisky.'

'I don't think I've ever got to quite that level of drunk.' Matt buttoned up his coat.

'Me neither. I'm not much of a drinker,' Catie confessed.

'Ah, well. The lady is intoxicating enough,' Grenville trilled; Catie had to laugh at that. 'Come on in. It's perfectly safe down here.' Grenville beckoned them forward. 'That's it. Now then. We're going to have a little look around, but some of the corridors are rather narrow, so you'll have to cosy up. Rather romantic, though, I always think.' He winked at Catie, who blushed.

Sure enough, as they started walking down a long, dark walkway between barrels, the space became more and more narrow. Catie was very aware of Matt's body next to hers as they walked along. She flinched as her hand brushed his in the dark, feeling a current of hot, electric energy erupt in her fingertips and trace all the way through her.

She looked up at him as they walked; the light was indistinct and dim, but she could still see Matt half-looking at her with a half-smile on his face.

'Wow,' Catie breathed. 'This is amazing. It looks like it goes on for miles. What's the oldest cask you have down here?'

'People always ask that. We have a cask just here from 1810, some from a bit closer to 1900, and then a fair few from the 1950s onwards.' Grenville stopped in front of a stack of old-looking barrels, all stamped with a faint black Loch Cameron Distillery brand that Catie could see when he held his phone light up.

'Although we can probably thank the monks for their sterling work in perfecting the art of distilling, the ancient Celts actually practiced distillation and made something called *uisgebeatha*. That means *water of life* in Gaelic,' Grenville said. 'It wasn't what we think of as whisky now, but it was a kind of alcohol made from the plants that were available. And,' he held up his finger, 'it was mainly the preserve of the womenfolk. So much so that the knowledge of fermentation and distillation was at one time believed to have been given to the women of Scotland by the fairies. So, there's a supernatural link. Proving to us all, once again, that women are the magic ones. Us men are just cloddish lumps by comparison,' Grenville chuckled.

'You won't get any argument from me there,' Matt said, his voice low and humorous. 'I was raised to revere women. I'm just grateful to benefit from their presence.'

As he said this, Matt's hand brushed hers again, and, this time, he hooked his little finger around hers. It was a tiny touch, but she felt it all the way through her like the resonance of a bell. Catie kept looking steadfastly at Grenville as he explained more about the ancient art of distillation and *uisgebeatha*; her finger entwined with Matt's felt like a delicate and delicious little secret. Neither of them looked at each other and neither of them said anything, but both of them knew.

Both of them knew the pleasure that they were experiencing, just from this tiny movement. The connection of their skin together was warm and electric, suffusing Catie with a feeling she had never felt before. It was as if Matt was surrounded by a kind of warm, masculine aura that made her heart glow and her body come alive.

She had never felt like this before. Not even with Greg, her ex, who was Skye's dad. She'd had a baby with him and she'd never felt half the chemistry she did just standing next to Matt, with just their little fingers touching.

'Well, now,' Grenville cleared his throat. 'If you come this way, I've got a few drinks set up for you now, lovebirds.' He led them towards the end of the aisle, where a table was set up with some crystal whisky glasses and a couple of bottles of Loch Cameron single malt.

Catie wanted to say, *we aren't lovebirds,* but Matt's hand in hers made her think otherwise.

'Oh! This is so cute,' Catie marvelled as she followed Grenville to the table. Matt let go of her hand as they started walking; she realised that she was sad to lose her contact with him.

'Indeed, Miss McGovern. May I pour you a dram?' Grenville enquired. 'Perhaps with a little water?'

'Thank you. Yes, please.' Catie accepted a crystal whisky tumbler that contained a generous serving of something from one of the bottles; she read the label and saw it was one of the Old Maid whiskies: The Gretchen.

'Rather smoky, this one. Named for Gretchen Ross, a real stalwart of Loch Cameron. One of the all-time greats,' Grenville sighed. 'Sadly, she passed away recently. But she's left many legacies, including this very fine drop.' He handed a glass to Matt. '*Slainte,*' he gave them the traditional Celtic toast as he held his own glass up and drained it. 'Now. I'll leave you lovebirds here to enjoy a little private time. I'll come back in a while and see how you're getting on.' He winked at them. 'Behave.'

'I don't know what he thinks we're going to do,' Matt chuckled as Grenville disappeared into the walkways. He gestured to a leather sofa that sat next to the table. 'Shall we?'

'Sure.' Catie lowered herself onto it carefully, glad that she was wearing jeans and didn't have to worry about a potential upskirt moment, as the sofa was quite low. 'It's strange to be sitting in a dark vault, drinking whisky on a black leather sofa. It's quite goth, if I'm honest.' She started to giggle.

'I like it. It's a vibe.' Matt sat beside her. 'So, did you feel like you learnt a lot about whisky so far?'

'Umm. Kinda.' Catie took another sip of her whisky and shivered a little. 'I have to admit I got a little bit... distracted at one point.' She gave Matt a sideways glance.

'You did, huh?' he grinned. 'I did too. Don't think I could tell you half of what Grenville was saying.'

'Hmm.' She took another sip of her drink. 'It's cool down here, but it is also quite... cold.' She shivered again. 'I thought I'd be okay with a jumper but it's really quite damp, isn't it?'

'Oh, I'm sorry.' Matt looked immediately chagrined. He pulled off his sweater – plain black with some kind of small image on it that Catie suspected was a subtle designer logo – and handed it to her. 'Here. Put that on Do you want to go? We can go and have tea in the café, I know it'll be much warmer in there.'

Catie couldn't help but notice that, when he had pulled off his sweater, the white T-shirt he was wearing underneath it had ridden up and accidentally exposed a toned, tanned stomach and strong chest. She gulped and looked away, feeling her pulse racing.

'Oh. Goodness. I don't want you to get cold. You'll only have a T-shirt on,' she argued.

'Please take it. I'm fine. I run hot at the best of times.' He frowned and held the sweatshirt out to her. She chose not to respond to that particular comment; anything she said about Matt being hot was going to make her blush and appear awkward.

'Well, if you're sure. Thank you.' Instead, she took the

sweatshirt and pulled it over her head: it smelt distantly of vanilla and woodsmoke. Instantly, she felt warmed.

'You're welcome.' A lazy smile lingered around his lips. 'Looks good on you.'

'Oh. Errr. Thanks.' Catie bit her lip, not knowing what to say.

'You don't take a compliment well, do you?' Matt sat back in the leather sofa and regarded her for a moment. 'I've noticed that. I don't get it. You're a really attractive woman. To say nothing of bright. Funny. Nice.'

'That's very kind of you,' Catie demurred. 'I guess I'm not used to compliments. I don't really know what to do with them.'

'Accept them and move on?' he asked, playfully. 'I guess I'm just used to a different kind of woman, then.'

'Hmm. I expect so.' Catie looked down at the cuff of Matt's sweatshirt. The memory of what Matt had said about his previous, super-glamorous American girlfriend rose up in her mind like a Gucci-bejewelled ghost. *A different kind of woman*, indeed. 'Maybe you should look for someone who's more your type,' she suggested.

'You're my type.' He gave her a curious look. 'I wouldn't have asked you out if you weren't.'

'I'm a middle-aged woman with a teenage daughter,' she replied. 'Is that your type?'

'Shouldn't you be basing this on whether I'm *your* type or not?' he shrugged. 'Seems like that would be the feminist thing to do.'

'Hmm. You're right. In which case, I suppose you'll do,' she shot back, grinning. 'So, you're a feminist?'

'Of course. Who isn't?' He raised an eyebrow.

'Well, indeed,' she laughed. 'I mean, I don't think everyone is. But I appreciate the sentiment. And the sweatshirt.' She hugged her arms around herself: it was still cold down in the vault.

'Gentlemanly behaviour and being a feminist are not mutually exclusive.' He nodded. 'Are you still cold?'

'Kind of,' she admitted.

'Come here, then.' he opened his arms, and before Catie knew what was happening, Matt had enveloped her in a hug.

She let out a surprised *oh*, and he hugged her closer.

'There,' he said, his voice deep and soothing. 'Let me warm you up a little.'

Part of Catie wanted to pull back and insist that she was fine. It was the independent part of her that had grown used to looking after herself. But, there was another part of her, a part that had longed to be held in some strong arms for a very long time, and that part – oh, that deep, hungry longing in her – that was the part that took charge now.

Catie let out an involuntary sigh, and snuggled in close to Matt's chest. She could feel his strength: he was tall, so her head rested just under his neck. He smelt of vanilla and something pleasant, resinous and masculine; whatever aftershave or products were on his skin were complemented by his own particular smell, which made the instinctual part of her want to wrap her legs around him and bury her face in his neck. He smelt *good*, like home, but a home that also made her want to lose herself in his body.

'All okay there?' he asked, his voice low, the vibration resonating against her cheek. She looked up, eyes half lidded with a combination of desire and warmth; the comfort of being in Matt's arms.

'Yes,' she replied, quietly. He nodded, and reached down, gently putting his fingers under her chin and tilting her head up to him.

'Good,' he murmured, and bent his head to kiss her.

If Catie had already felt as though she was dissolving into Matt's body before, then the kiss transported her into a new realm of bliss. She closed her eyes and sank deep into his velvety touch and the sensation of his lips on hers. His mouth was soft, and he kissed her slowly, unhurriedly, tracing the shape of her mouth with his.

Catie pressed up against him, enjoying the feeling of being held firm in his arms. A soft moan escaped her lips; she was completely hypnotised by him. She was dimly aware of her surroundings, the dark of the vault, the cold in the air, but, more than anything, she was immersed in the kiss. Lost in Matt, in the feel of his lips on hers which set off a thousand exploding stars in her body and behind her eyes.

'Oh. Miss McGovern. Excuse me.' Catie opened her eyes and saw Grenville walking towards them. 'I'm so sorry to interrupt. I'll come back.'

'Everything's fine, Grenville.' Matt looked up, his lips leaving hers; immediately, Catie felt the loss of his touch. However, his arms stayed firmly around her. 'Is it time for the next part of the tour?'

'If you're ready, my dears. But you can have longer down here if that pleases you.' He smiled warmly at them both, like some kind of approving uncle. Catie felt herself blush. She knew she wasn't doing anything wrong – she was a grown up, and she was allowed to kiss whoever she wanted – but she still felt exposed, as if she was a teenager who had been caught out.

'It is a little cold down here.' Catie looked up at Matt, who nodded.

'Oh! Yes, it can get rather dank in the vault. We should get a little heater down here for when people want to sit and chat.' Grenville tutted. 'Dear Miss McGovern. I do hope you aren't too uncomfortable.'

'I'm fine. But maybe we can go up now?' she asked.

'Right you are.' Grenville nodded. 'Follow me, then.' He led them both up the steps and back out into the daylight, which felt harsh to Catie's eyes after the shadowy dark of the vault.

'Grenville. Can you give us a minute?' Matt asked, politely, as he stepped out of the door behind Catie.

'Of course, of course,' Grenville cooed. 'I do hope you enjoyed the little tour so far. If you'd like to see more, I'm happy to finish it.'

'Thanks.' Matt nodded. Grenville sauntered off towards a part of a series of stone cottage-type buildings, one of which showed a cosy café through its windows.

'Well. That was... quite something,' he said in a low voice when Grenville was far enough away that he wouldn't overhear them.

'Umm. Yes,' Catie giggled. 'Maybe just as well Grenville came along when he did.'

'Oh. What might have happened?' He raised a questioning eyebrow.

'Goodness knows.' She smiled up at him, longing to kiss him again.

'You're amazing.' He stroked her cheek lightly with his fingertip, the sensation sending tingles into the deep core of her body.

'Thank you, but...' she broke off, not wanting to spoil the moment, but she knew she had to say it.

'But?' he breathed.

'You do know I'm a lot older than you, right? Even if we're just having fun... and this is fun, huge fun... you know that my... my body won't be the same as what you're used to. I'm not making any assumptions here. But...' she broke off. What was a polite way to say *I am not a bronzed, toned, Californian glamour girl?*

'I think you're great. Otherwise, I wouldn't have asked you out.' Matt's tone was steady, deep, sure.

'I know. It's just...' She didn't know how to say it.

'It's just what? I find you crazy hot, okay? Does that put your mind at rest?' He smiled, and kissed her gently at the edge of her mouth. She gasped, involuntarily.

'Yes... okay,' she managed to stammer.

'Good. Because I want you, Catie McGovern. I want you pretty bad, if you hadn't already guessed.' He gave her a half-lidded look of desire that left her in no doubt about what his intentions were.

'Umm... okay,' she repeated, feeling untethered from her brain. 'Oh. You should take this back.' She pulled off the sweat-shirt and handed it to him.

'Okay... thanks. I didn't expect undressing. Bonus.' Matt took the sweater and put it back on with a wry smile. 'Listen, Catie. I think you're a great girl. I'd love to see you again, if you'd give me an opportunity to organise a better date where you're not freezing to death.'

'I'd love that. You seem like a really nice guy. And any woman would be lucky to have you,' she began, trying to marshal her thoughts into something logical. 'Well. I don't mean I want to *have* you. Oh. You know what I mean.' She could feel herself getting flustered and couldn't believe it. *I am a grown woman,* she thought. *What is happening?*

'Ha. It's okay. I get it,' he chuckled. 'Come on. I think we could do with getting back into daylight. Daylight makes every-thing more rational, no?' He held out his hand for hers. 'Though I have enjoyed guiding you down into the underworld, and taking my dark pleasure with you.' He raised a rakish eyebrow; Catie felt the blush return to her cheeks.

'Does that make you Hades? And me, Persephone?' she replied. *Taking my dark pleasure* was a phrase straight out of a dark romance novel: ridiculously flamboyant and romantic. She knew he had said it as a joke, but it also just made her think about what Matt *taking his dark pleasure* with her would be like. And, that made her feel unashamedly horny.

'Why not?' He took her hand and they started walking back up to the stairs that led down into the vault. 'I think we could do King and Queen vibes.'

That sounds a hell of a lot more coupley than a bit of fun, Catie thought, glancing at Matt's face in profile. He was so handsome that she almost did a double take: the muscular neck, the strong jaw and his slightly curly hair falling on to his forehead.

'King and Queen of hell, though,' she laughed.

'I dunno. I think that's very us.' He shrugged, grinning. 'Think of the outfits.'

'Oh. I will.' She followed him out into the daylight, feeling as though something had shifted inside her heart.

Nothing had changed on the surface of things: all she had done was kiss Matt Cameron in a whisky vault, and enjoyed herself a little. But, at the same time, everything had changed. Because Catie hadn't been on a date for years and years. Despite being completely single for so long, she just hadn't been interested in finding anyone. She hadn't even been bothered about having a sex life; it wasn't like she was dead from the waist down or anything, but it just had never been top of her priority list.

And, now? She wouldn't necessarily say that everything had changed, but she did feel as though sex was a lot more of a priority than it had been. Simply put, Matt had awoken something in her that she hadn't even noticed had been dormant until now. Nobody had touched her like that in a long time. Nobody had kissed her, nobody had looked into her eyes and told her that they wanted her. Perhaps never. Not like that.

Damn. She felt alive in a way that she suddenly realised had been desperately missing from her life, and, in the same moment, sad that it had taken her until now to know it.

As she emerged into the daylight, Catie wondered if there was some small truth in Matt's joke about them being in the underworld: she certainly felt like she was being reborn into a version of herself that had lain dormant for years. *And all it took was the King of Hell to kiss me*, she thought wryly. *For me to return back to the world a woman: no longer just a mother and a librarian and a good daughter.*

Grenville led them around the rest of the distillery, talking animatedly. They walked through the bottling rooms and looked at all the packaging and advertising for the whisky, over the years. All of the buildings hummed with an atmosphere of industriousness; Catie could feel the purpose and focus that the people who had worked here had invested in their common goal. Catie liked the old stone walls, the antique machinery that was still on display – mostly, now, replaced with newer and efficient solutions – and the gleaming copper stills, which reflected a soft light around them.

Grenville explained the history of the Douglas family that had run the distillery since it opened. And, all the time, Matt held her hand. Neither of them mentioned it, but an energy flowed between them like a circuit: an energy of warmth and light and rightness that felt like home.

Finally, Grenville led them back out to the gardens that surrounded the distillery buildings.

'Well, that's the end of the tour.' He beamed at both of them. 'I hope you enjoyed it!'

'We did, thank you, Grenville,' Catie said. She *had* enjoyed the tour. It was nice to learn something new – and, being there with Matt had made it even more fun. Apart from the fact that she felt like a teenager, holding his hand, she was all too aware of his physical presence. There was just something indefinable about him that made her want to be with him, be next to him, be curled up against his chest.

'Well, when you're ready, there will be tea and cake for you in the café.' Grenville twinkled at them both and blew them a kiss. 'Au revoir, my beautiful ones. I'll just go and make sure it's set up for you.'

'Tea? Cake?' Matt looked at her expectantly, and she nodded.

'Tea and cake sounds great. But, first...' Now that Grenville had left them alone, she wrapped his hand around her waist and leaned into him, her lips finding his. She wanted another kiss; her body wanted to be close to him, and she wasn't going to deny herself, not now that she knew how it felt to kiss Matt Cameron.

'Oh, god...' he groaned, as their lips met again, and now, there was no doubt of his interest in her. This time, their kiss was deep, searching, desperate and passionate. She could feel the heat in her body instantly this time, and she could feel him reacting to her: reaching for her hungrily, pressing her into him.

Finally, he broke away from the kiss and swore under his breath, grinning. 'Catie. You're going to get me in trouble in front of all these nice people.' He still held her in an embrace, and they looked around them at a group of middle-aged tourists who were queuing up for the café and gift shop.

'Sorry,' she murmured, planting a chaste kiss on his cheek.

'Never be sorry for a kiss like that,' he said, blinking as if he was awakening from a dream. 'That was...' he trailed off, gazing at her. 'Hm. Wow. Yeah.'

'So. Tea?' She marvelled at her own composure. She had been just as transported by the kiss as Matt had: more so, even. Catie hadn't been kissed like that in her whole life.

She didn't want him to know that. It would have been embarrassing for her: for Matt to know how long it had been since she'd been on a date. And she definitely didn't want him to know that he was by far the best kisser she'd ever experienced.

'Tea.' He nodded, holding out his hand towards the café. 'After you.'

When they walked into the café, Grenville was standing proudly by a table which was set up with a plate of delicious-looking cakes – fat slices of victoria sponge with a thick layer of cream and jam, moist chocolate brownies, slices of rich fruit cake and a large pot of tea. The table was adorned in flowers. Catie held her hand to her mouth.

'Oh! It's so beautiful!' she exclaimed.

Grenville held out Catie's chair for her, and she accepted it gratefully.

'For the lady,' Grenville purred. 'Now. I'll leave you love-birds to it, but just ask at the counter if you want more of anything.'

'Thanks so much, Grenville.' Matt held out his hand. 'It's been a really great tour. Appreciate your time.'

'Not at all, not at all,' Grenville cooed, looking pleased, and shook Matt's hand. 'Enjoy your tea! It really was my pleasure.'

'Yes, thank you, Grenville.' Catie smiled warmly. 'I had a lovely time.'

'You are most welcome, Miss McGovern. And, may I say, you both make a lovely couple.' Grenville gave them both a neat little bow and made his way out of the café.

A lovely couple.

Catie felt herself blushing again, but she found that she didn't altogether mind Grenville saying it. Not that she and Matt were a couple, by any stretch of the imagination. But, it was nice to be made to feel special, and Grenville and Matt had done that.

Catie felt cherished, and she hadn't felt that in a long time. Perhaps, ever. And it was a good feeling.

13

When she closed her eyes in bed that night, Castle View formed itself behind Catie's eyelids. In a half dream, she imagined walking through the black cast iron gates and up the drive, her shoes crunching on the gravel.

This is yours, a spectral voice on the wind breathed in her ear. *Castle View has waited for you for so long.*

In her dream, Catie imagined walking through the wide, heavy front door as she had done before. Yet, now, in the space between waking and dreaming, the house seemed very different. In the night dark, the house was lit with old fashioned gas lamps, giving it a warm glow. *Welcome, Catriona,* the voice said. *Welcome home.*

As Catie walked into the entrance hall, music started to play, and a crystal chandelier that she didn't remember being there before lit up with hundreds of candles. The candlelight reflected in the crystal, refracting what seemed like thousands of flitting, glittering fairy lights over the dark green flocked wallpaper that lined the walls. The music was not modern: it sounded like a piano was being played in the next room. The tinkling melody had a melancholy tone, filling Catie with a sense of apprehension.

The house's décor was very different to how it was now. In the dream, the house seemed much older, full of antique heavy wood furniture in dark varnishes, like the colour of the floorboards she had noticed before. A tall mahogany grandfather clock with an inlaid mother of pearl design of the phases of the moon ticked ominously in the corner, and heavy green velvet curtains hung at the windows.

Suddenly, the front door swung open in the wind, and a shaft of moonlight sliced across the hall, guiding Catie's eye to a portrait on the wall.

It was a portrait of a young, bearded man. He wore trews and a shirt with a jumper over the top and a tweed jacket; it was a kind of timeless style, at least in the last hundred years or so. A falcon or some kind of hunting bird – wearing a leather hood so that its vision was curtailed – perched on his outstretched arm. The young man wore a serious expression, and there was a gravitas about the portrait that felt oppressive. Catie couldn't tell the age of the portrait: it could have been relatively modern or much older. Men in Scotland had been wearing beards and tweed jackets for a long time.

She got an uneasy feeling from it. There was something about the picture she didn't like: perhaps it was the hooded bird, which suggested some kind of attempted control of a wild thing. Or, perhaps it was his expression: there was a twist of meanness at the edge of his mouth. Whatever it was, the portrait filled her with unease.

Catriona. I have been waiting for you, the voice said. Was it a man's voice? She couldn't tell, but its tone was aggressive and hectoring: she didn't like it. Was the painting talking to her?

Who are you? Catie asked the voice, but there was no answer. Instead, one of the lead-lined windows swung open, apparently opened by the wind outside. The candles in the chandelier guttered out, and the hall was cloaked in sudden darkness apart from the candles that sat underneath the portrait.

I am part of you, the voice said, as the only remaining candlelight bathed the portrait in a spectral glow. *Help me.*

~

Thud, thud, thud.

Catie awoke suddenly to a muffled banging noise coming from somewhere in the house. She sat up in bed, disoriented.

Thud, thud, thud.

What the hell is that? she thought, blinking sleep out of her eyes and making out the vague shapes of the furniture in the dark.

Catie listened again, but silence blanketed Castle View.

Hmm. Maybe it was the dream, she thought, lying back down and pulling the thick eiderdown over her head. *Or, it's an old house, making weird noises.*

As she closed her eyes, Catie felt her body slowly relaxing again and sinking into the soft mattress. She was still only half awake, and she wanted to go back to sleep: she could feel its heaviness in her body, the pleasurable fogginess in her mind.

It was just a dream. Just a dream.

But, as she floated back into her dream space, a face swam into her mind. The same young, bearded man with intense eyes.

Catriona, he said. *Help me.*

Catie opened her eyes again, this time with her heart beating hard.

She sat up in bed again, and, this time, swung her feet out of bed.

The tiled floor under her toes was cold; Catie had brought a rug in to the room a week or so after moving in, but it didn't quite stretch to the side of the bed. She liked the look of the tiles: they looked as though they were Victorian, a tessellating cream and brown pattern that was in decent condition. But, it was cold underfoot. She shivered.

As she stood up, the noise that had woken her up originally repeated: *thud, thud, thud.* She jumped, and reached for the thick white fleece dressing gown that hung at the end of the bed.

Last time she had heard this noise, it had been Skye, taking all of the clothes and boots out of her wardrobe so that she could see what was behind it. She couldn't be doing the same thing again, surely.

Catie looked at her bedside clock. 3.41 a.m. *The witching hour,* she thought. That was what her dad said about the early hours of the morning; that time between the night and the dawn where everything was the stillest. Where the ebb of life seemed lowest.

Thinking about her dad made Catie feel uneasy and she wondered if he was all right. She hated thinking about him being so ill and not being there to look after him. This was the time of night when people slipped away; or, the time when her dad might have another stroke.

She resolved to call her mum in the morning and check how her dad was doing. They were still in the hospital while the preparations were being made at her mum and dad's house: a special medical bed with a back that could rise up to support him sitting up in their bedroom, and a room for the live-in nurse to stay in. Catie had asked how long the nurse was anticipated to stay, but her mum didn't seem to have a clear idea. *For as long as we need her, I suppose,* she'd said, bleakly.

Catie couldn't imagine what it must be like to suddenly have to completely adjust your life because your life partner – the father of your children, your husband and provider – was suddenly unable to even feed himself. The weight of grief, uncertainty and stress that her mum was going through was huge, and Catie was worried for her.

Now that she was awake, she was still spooked, but she was starting to rationalise that the thud noise might be an open window, rattling in the night wind. Or a door hanging on its hinges. Or even a fox that had somehow got into the house and might be playing merry hell in the kitchen. It was also possible that she might have been having a stress nightmare of some kind, worrying about her dad.

She sat there for a few minutes, thinking that she would fall back to sleep, but she just grew more and more wakeful.

Quietly, Catie pulled on her robe and padded out of her room. Following the stairs down, she thought about the man in the painting. In the dream, all the lights had gone out, and the painting – which didn't exist anywhere in the house that she had found so far – had been lit up by candlelight, like a sign or an omen.

But what help did he need, and why? Catie had no idea. She racked her brain, trying to remember what else it had said in the dream.

Catie couldn't say that she disliked the house: it was much bigger than anything she was used to, and the kitchen was lovely to cook in. She'd spent so long cooking in tiny little galley kitchens that it was a complete joy not to be so cramped.

However, it still didn't quite feel like home. Castle View had an odd, slightly cold and standoffish feel about it. And, now, she was up in the middle of the night, following a thudding noise that wasn't exactly making her feel secure and cosy.

She reached the wide hallway at the bottom of the grand stairway and looked around. Nothing seemed to be out of place.

Now that she was downstairs, she almost wanted to hear the thudding noise again so that she could work out where it was coming from. Almost.

Really, Catie would be happy never to hear any more

mysterious thuds in the night, *but here we are,* she thought. *Listening for them anyway. At 3.41 a.m.*

Catie walked into the kitchen. Everything looked normal. She walked into the lounge, and turned off the lamp that someone had left on. Absent-mindedly, she tidied a stack of magazines that Skye had been looking through.

Stop it, she told herself, sternly. *Or you'll find yourself cleaning in the middle of the night. It's not a good habit to get into.*

She stood still and listened for a moment. It was dead quiet: somewhere outside, an owl hooted.

It was just a dream. Catie sighed and turned back to the hallway. Back to bed. She hoped she could go back to sleep. But as she reached the foot of the stairs, there was a loud thud and a sudden, intense wailing noise. For a moment, it seemed to fill the house with a scream of pain that set her nerves aflame. *What the hell was that?* she thought, wrapping her arms around herself and feeling the gooseflesh raise on her arms and legs, under the cosy robe.

Yet, almost as soon as she had heard the noise, it stopped. Catie had no way of telling where in the house it had come from; she had thought that if she came downstairs, she would have been able to work out the direction of the thudding noise. But she was no wiser.

She waited to hear it again, but there was silence. Spooked, Catie ran all the way to the top of the house and pushed Skye's bedroom door open. Cautiously, she looked inside, being as quiet as she could in the event that her daughter was asleep. Perhaps she was having a nightmare, or Skye might have been woken up by the terrible scream that seemed to have ripped the house apart, just for one knife-sharp moment.

This time, however, Skye seemed to be sleeping peacefully. She lay in bed with one leg out of the covers and her arms in a V shape on the pillows, with her eyes closed. Catie watched her for a moment, noting the fact that she seemed to be breathing a little quickly, but, other than that, she seemed normal. Catie closed the door quietly behind her.

Passing her sister's room on the next floor, she debated knocking to see if Bridget had heard the noise, but she assumed that, because Bridget hadn't appeared, she hadn't. Catie didn't really want to wake Bridget up in the middle of the night if she absolutely didn't have to; Bridget got angry with her so easily that it just wasn't worth giving her an opportunity unless it was unavoidable.

She went back to her room and closed the door with a quiet snick. Perhaps it had been nothing. Perhaps she had just been hearing things, or was still dreaming, somehow.

She got into bed, shivering a little, and not just because of the cold.

Had she and Bridget inherited a haunted house? And, if they had, how on earth were they supposed to live in it?

14

'Oh, hey. Catie!' Matt Cameron called to her as she walked along the side of the loch. She waved; he beckoned her over to where he stood, chatting to one of the local fishermen on the deck of his boat, moored to railings at the side of the loch.

'Hello,' she said, walking over and looking up at them. 'Lovely day.'

Matt was looking as handsome as ever in a casual blue shirt and jeans, with a pair of sunglasses on his head, pushing back his hair. He had rolled up his sleeves and Catie noticed, again, his tan and the solid heft of muscle under the shirt.

Damn, he's hot, she thought.

Since their date, she and Matt had been texting back and forth. It had been flirty, but nothing too outrageous. Still, Catie had been enjoying it. It was nice to look at her phone to see if Matt had sent her a funny little GIF or a flirty message. It made a change from only getting notifications about her electricity bill or using her phone to check her meagre bank balance.

Simran approved.

Pictures please she had texted when Catie had told her about the date at the distillery. *Is he hot?*

I didn't take any, Catie replied. *It would have been weird.*

Rookie error. I want to see what he looks like, Simran had replied.

Look him up, Catie said, giving Simran Matt's full name and adding, *he's part of the Cameron family that owns the village.*

Catie's phone screen had shown a line of dots for a moment – presumably as Simran googled Matt Cameron and the Cameron family.

OH MYYYYY she replied, eventually. *You hooked a good one there!!!*

I have not hooked anything. We just had a pleasant evening Catie had replied, smiling to herself at Simran's enthusiasm.

Get him to propose her friend had texted. *I'm serious.*

Catie had sent back a laugh emoji. *After one date? That's rational.*

'It is. Catie, do you know Mick?' Matt turned to the man he'd been talking to, who waved down at her. He wore slate grey fishermen's overalls with a cream cable knit jumper underneath and heavy boots. He was probably somewhere in his late fifties, although Catie always had difficulty in estimating people's ages.

'No, I don't. Hello.' Catie waved back.

'Catie works at the library. Mick works on the boat, as you might have guessed.' Matt grinned.

'I see that. How long have you two known each other?' she called out, raising her voice slightly.

'Known this one since he was a lad,' Mick said, affectionately. 'Used tae help me on the boat when he was home fer the holidays. No' so much yer brother, eh?'

'Hal isn't into boats. I've always loved them, though,' Matt said. 'I ended up in tech, but there's a part of me that would love to do what Mick does. Alone on the water. With nature. The peace of it.' He looked wistful.

'No money in it, lad,' Mick chuckled. 'I'm not out much,

nowadays. I've semi-retired. The missus wants me home, and I don't mind. Time was I'd be gone before dawn, back late. Never saw her or the bairns.'

'I know. It's a privilege for me to come out on the boat with you, though,' Matt said, seriously. 'I always appreciate it.'

'Ah, you're welcome anytime, lad.' Mick gave Matt a hug, and Catie could see the affection between them. Matt jumped down from the boat onto the lochside beside her.

'See you soon, Mick,' he called out. Mick waved.

'Nice tae meet ye, lassie,' he called back, and she smiled and nodded.

'What are you up to?' Matt asked, nodding to the bag she carried. 'Buying goodies?'

'Yes. I just popped out in my lunch hour for a few bits, but you know how it is. You come out with a list and you go back with all sorts,' she confessed, opening her bag to show him.

It was market day in Loch Cameron, and its small, cobbled high street was teeming with people buying sugar-jewelled fruit cakes, locally grown fresh flowers and potted plants, richly hued organic vegetables and other delights. Catie loved market day, and when Lilian had reminded her that morning that it was on, she'd decided to pop out during her lunchtime to get some essentials.

Of course, she'd also ended up buying things she didn't plan for, but that was the pleasure of market day. As well as a fabulous bakery, grocery and butcher's stall, there were often extra stalls from people selling soaps and organically made cosmetics and even crystals and incense and all manner of other interesting wares. Today, Catie had noticed a new haberdashery stall and gone over to see if there would be anything interesting for Skye; she'd come away with a few metres of a cute retro cotton fabric featuring lipsticks and mirrors that she thought Skye would like, plus some bold red buttons and a couple of patterns for skirts and dresses that were on sale.

'Very nice.' He nodded. 'Are you going back to the library? I'll walk back that way with you.' He fell into step beside her.

'Sure.' She was very aware of his presence next to her, as always; it was a calm, reassuring feeling having him close by. Yet, Matt always felt... right, somehow.

'Listen. I'm glad I ran into you,' he began, as they walked along the path at the edge of the high street, alongside the loch. Catie thought, not for the first time, that you couldn't ask for a prettier view on a sunny day: the loch was so flat and glassy today that it mirrored the sky and the trees alongside it perfectly.

'Oh?'

Matt looked as though he was choosing his words wisely. 'I wanted to say that... I really enjoyed our date. Like, *really*,' he chuckled. 'I haven't had that much fun in ages. So, thank you.'

'You're welcome. Me too.' Catie was enjoying the sun on her skin as she walked along the side of the loch.

'I enjoyed us spending time together. But I also wanted to say... that's kind of all I'm looking for right now,' he continued, slowly. 'I guess you might feel like, if you started seeing someone, that you would need it to be more than that. And I understand. I hadn't thought very hard about asking you out, other than I like you,' Matt added. 'Basically I just want to be transparent about all this. I just think, you being older, you might want more than I can really give. And I want to be upfront about it. I'd love to take you out on more dates and enjoy the time we have together, but... I just want to be honest,' he finished.

'Okay.' Catie considered what he had said. 'I had a lovely time on our date too. I wasn't thinking that this would become anything in particular. Just because I'm older than you, doesn't mean that I automatically want a serious commitment from you. If I'm completely honest, it's been lovely just being a bit flirty and having someone interested in me.' She broke off, thinking about what she wanted to say. 'But, I am older than you, and I have a teenage daughter,' she replied. 'Our lives are very different. You've had this glamorous life. I'm just a middle-aged single mum, in a low wage job, trying to make ends meet. We are quite different.'

'Well, for the record, you being older is hot, and I've dated women with kids before. It's not an issue,' he replied.

'Oh,' Catie didn't know what to say. 'I always just sort of assume that men don't want to date women with kids. Unless they have their own children.'

'Not at all. If you like someone, and that's part of their life, you just take it on.' He shrugged. 'That isn't a barrier to me dating you. My ex had two kids. I still miss them.' He looked sad.

'Your ex... in California?' Somehow, the image Catie had built in her mind of Matt's glamorous ex-girlfriend didn't include her being a mother.

'Yeah. She had a girl and a boy. Eight and ten. Cool kids.' Matt nodded.

'How long were you together?' she asked, curious now about this new, previously unknown part of Matt's story.

'Five years. I thought she was the one,' he sighed, and put his sunglasses on as the sun came out and bathed the street in a golden glow.

'What happened?' Catie asked, curious.

'She wanted us to get married. I wasn't against the idea, though I was working there anyway. But then the company failed, and she had doubts about me. That I wasn't successful enough for her, I guess. Even though she's pretty successful herself. She doesn't need anyone to support her, but she said she lost respect for me. She wanted an equal. I wasn't that, apparently.' He stared off into the distance.

'I'm sorry. That seems harsh,' Catie said, gently.

'Well, she just did what was right for her.' Matt shrugged. 'I failed her.'

'I don't think that's very fair,' Catie said, surprised. 'That seems like you being very hard on yourself. Unnecessarily. These things happen. I'm sure you tried everything you could to make sure your business was a success.'

'That just shows what a good-hearted person you are. I don't think everyone thinks that way.' He paused. 'Listen. I'm not *absolutely* closed to the idea of meeting someone special and having a committed relationship again... but, I got my fingers burned last time and... I guess I just don't want to put any pressure on myself, or anyone else. Plus, it's kinda early to be having that conversation between you and me.' He frowned, and rolled down his sleeves. 'Don't you think?'

'Agreed. And I'm hugely out of practice at all this,' Catie sighed.

'I mean, I don't actually understand how you're so out of practice, or why there isn't a line of guys around the block trying to date you,' he chuckled. 'Listen. I want to make a suggestion. Hear me out. Okay?'

'Okay.' They had reached the library; Catie stopped at the door.

'Right. Well, I think we should go on another date. No pressure.' He held up his hands. 'Just a good time, okay? I think we could both do with a decent night out, a few laughs. Nothing has to happen. But we like each other's company. So, why not?' He tilted his head to one side. 'Let's just have a good time and not worry.'

'Okay. Sounds good.' She nodded. Catie enjoyed Matt's company, and she couldn't deny that there was an attraction there. She *could* do with a fun night out; she hardly went out at all.

She was surprised to learn that Matt had had a long-term relationship with a woman with children before. However, she wasn't a young, glamorous, sassy American girl. She was a middle-aged librarian with a lot of family issues. The fact that he found her attractive was some kind of odd miracle, and she didn't want to mess with it.

'Great.' He smiled, and took out his phone from his pocket. 'Ah. I need to go. Good to see you – I'll be in touch.'

He walked off, his stride brisk. Catie watched him go, wondering whether she was doing the right thing in agreeing to go out with him, even if it was against her better judgement. Where could it really go? Matt had told her that he wasn't looking for anything serious, and society seemed obsessed with telling women that they always needed to *find a serious relationship* and *settle down*. But, that wasn't really where she was.

Catie was just beginning to wake up to having fun, feeling affection and feeling alive again after years and years of being a responsible mum, working, retraining and basically making life run as smoothly as possible for her and Skye. Dating a man like Matt *felt* good, and now she wanted more. Did she *need* it to "go" anywhere? No. She had a roof over her head, a job and she wasn't unhappy with her life. But she *wanted* to see Matt. It had made her feel good, and feeling good was what she had been missing.

Was feeling good a bad goal to have? Catie didn't think it was. And she resolved to try and retrain herself – her way of thinking, her behaviour and her speech – to live more in the moment, and believe that she deserved to feel good. She knew that it was the experiences she'd had as a child – being so ill, and not wanting to be any more trouble for anyone – that made her feel, deep down, that she didn't deserve to feel good, or that she shouldn't hope for joy, because it could so easily be taken away.

You are allowed to feel good, she told herself. *You are allowed to just exist in the way that makes you happy. It doesn't have to be any more complicated than that.*

And, she walked into the library, humming a tune under her breath.

15

The next day was a Saturday, and Catie had got up late, having not slept well the night before. Despite her feeling good about herself the day before – Lilian had remarked on her good mood, in the library, after her conversation with Matt – Catie's slumber had been broken, filled with anxious nightmares of her daughter crying, shouting at her, and running away.

She had tried and tried to address things with Skye, but with no luck. Skye absolutely didn't want to talk about school, despite her having told Bridget something about not being happy.

She had gone downstairs to the kitchen to make coffee. She was brooding about what might or might not be happening at school for Skye. She was also still looking for the key to the wall safe in Skye's room, but she hadn't found anything yet. There had been a bundle of old keys in a drawer in the kitchen, but none of them had fit the wall safe. It had been quite the task to empty Skye's wardrobe again, pull it out from where it stood against the wall, try all the different keys in the lock and then put everything back again.

The dreams hadn't helped her not be worried about her

daughter. By the time she'd got up that morning, Bridget had gone out for a run and Skye had sent her a text message to say that she had taken the bus – one came once every two hours – to Loch Awe, where there was a haberdashery shop she liked to go to sometimes. So, Catie would have to wait until Skye got home to broach the subject with her again and see if she could make any headway this time.

Catie went to the postbox outside by the cast iron gate to pick up the post and breathe in the morning air. It was bright and clear outside, and just the action of being outside, feeling the sun on her skin and taking the bright, clean lochside air into her lungs helped calm her. Catie blinked in the sunlight, still amazed that she now lived at Castle View.

The view was incredible from up here on a clear day like today, when the misty *haar* over the loch had burnt off, or had never descended at all. She admired the castle for a moment, which sat opposite like something out of a fairy tale. The slate roof looked a little in need of repair, but its turrets spoke of a bygone magnificence. There was a definite grandeur to the place, with its sweeping drive, ornamental gardens and many lead-lined windows glinting in the sun. Catie had lived away from the village long enough not to take it for granted that Loch Cameron featured such an elaborate castle as part of the everyday scenery – and, one that was lived in by the current Laird. Some castles in Scotland were just ruins.

The post included a variety of leaflets for local tradespeople: a handywoman, Bess Black, was advertising her general DIY services, which Catie folded up and put in the pocket of her bathrobe: she was sure that the house had a lot of jobs to be done in it. A window cleaning service. Gutters cleared and fixed; she kept that one, too.

Last was a letter addressed to her and Bridget in a formal, old fashioned copperplate handwriting. The envelope was a thick paper stock, embossed with *Matthews and Douglas, Solici-*

tors. Catie frowned, sliding her finger under the flap of the envelope and unfolding the paper inside. She read it as she stood on the drive.

Dear Catriona and Bridget,

If you are reading this letter, then it means that Mr Matthews of my solicitor, Matthews and Douglas, has forwarded it to you as part of my instructions.

You have had my first letter, setting out the overarching instructions for Castle View and what I require you to do to complete the inheritance.

Now that you have moved into the house, I have a new task for you.

There is a small anteroom off the bedroom at the top of the house which can only be accessed with the key you will find in this envelope. Inside that room there is a chest containing some belongings. The chest is not locked.

I realise that you both may only have the faintest of idea about me and what I achieved in my life, and that will be revealed to you in time. In this chest you will find some items that I always meant to return to their original owners: however, this proved difficult, for reasons that may or may not become clear during this process.

I would like you to return them for me. I am unsure if, by the time you get this letter, the recipients will still be at the address I knew, but if they are not, then some forwarding address may perhaps be found: The Blossoms, Half Moon Lane, Loch Cameron.

With thanks,

Your great-aunt Isobel

Catie re-read the letter, getting used to the odd feeling that her great-aunt was speaking to her directly from beyond the grave. She and Bridget's lives had changed so much since getting the first letter, it felt like fate, or perhaps Great-Aunt Isobel, was directing them.

Now, there was more mystery. *How exciting!* Catie thought, turning back to the house. It wasn't every day that anyone received instructions to locate a mysterious chest. She wondered what was in it, and why it had been so important to Isobel that she and Bridget return its contents to its owner.

Life had certainly been eventful since they'd all moved into Castle View, and it didn't look like it was about to get any less eventful anytime soon. *Bring it on,* Catie thought.

16

'Perfect timing.' Catie looked up as Bridget jogged up to the gate.

'What is?' Her sister frowned at her.

'We got another letter from the solicitor.' Catie walked back to the gate and let Bridget in, then handed it to her to read.

'No way!' Bridget grabbed the letter and read it excitedly.

'So, do you want to come and find this chest with me, then?' Catie exchanged an excited look with her sister.

'Wow. This is some real life detective stuff, huh.' Bridget broke into an unexpected grin. 'Yes. Okay! Let's do it! Just let me get a shower first. I'm too sweaty to be able to concentrate on all this Miss Marple malarkey.' Bridget strode past her and into the house. Catie, smiling to herself, took the key out of the fold of cardboard that was also inside the envelope, and followed her into Castle View.

∼

'Jeez. This hasn't been opened in a while. I thought it was an airing cupboard or something,' Bridget muttered as she pulled at the wooden door. It was painted white, like the walls around it, but the paint was thick and Catie thought that it obviously hadn't been opened for a long time. The paint had probably stuck.

The door was actually in the hallway outside Skye's new bedroom rather than in the room itself, as Isobel's letter had suggested.

Catie slotted the key in the lock and turned it. The key itself was one of the old-fashioned, ornate cast iron kind, and there was an audible click as the lock freed. She turned the handle and pulled, but nothing happened.

'Oh.' She frowned, and tried again. Nothing.

'Have you unlocked it?' Bridget pushed her to one side and tried the door, but was met with the same resistance.

'Of course I unlocked it,' Catie said, patiently. 'You just saw me do it.'

'I saw you wiggle the key around.' Bridget turned the key back, locking the door, and then unlocked it again, and pulled. Nothing happened.

'Let me try again,' Catie said, but Bridget's mouth was a stubborn line.

'No. I've got it,' she muttered, tugging at the door again, but it didn't budge. She swore under her breath.

'*Bridge.*' Catie knew that her sister had always been impatient. A door that wouldn't open was like a red rag to a bull.

'Fine.' Bridget rolled her eyes and stood to one side. 'Because obviously you're so much stronger than me.'

'That's not what I meant.'

'Whatever.'

Catie tried the door, ignoring Bridget's tone, but she couldn't budge it either.

'We'll have to do it together. Pull.' She nodded to the handle, and Bridget placed her hand over Catie's. Together, they pulled, and the door creaked open. Both sisters were flung backwards with the suddenness of the door opening.

Bridget swore again, but Catie caught her eye and started to giggle.

'It's not funny. That could have been really dangerous,' Bridget muttered, but a smile lurked at the edge of her mouth. 'Come on. Let's see what's inside.'

Catie felt around inside the cavity – she wasn't sure if it was a room or a cupboard until she found a light switch and flicked it on.

The letter had called it an *anteroom*, and though Catie had only the faintest of ideas as to what an anteroom actually was, she guessed that the large, walk-in cupboard she was looking at, qualified. Inside, there were two free-standing rails of clothes, mostly hung with zippered garment bags and covered in plastic sheets. There were a number of cardboard boxes, festooned with spider webs, and a large wooden chest.

Bingo.

Catie knelt by the chest and fiddled with the clasp. As the letter had said, it wasn't locked, and she managed to open it after a couple of tries.

'Cate. Check out what's under here.' Bridget had gone straight to the rail of garment bags and started unzipping them. 'Look. Fur coats. Suits. I bet there's all kinds of treasure in here.'

'That's cool.' Catie nodded, but she was laser focused on what she was supposed to find in the chest.

She turned the light on her phone on and pointed it at the inside of the chest; even though they had turned the light on, she wanted to make sure that she wasn't plunging her hand into a spider's nest or something similar.

Inside, there were a number of odd bits and pieces: books, a few pairs of old high heels that she took out and held up for Bridget to see. *Surely these aren't what Isobel wanted us to return to someone in the village,* she thought.

Then, under the shoes, there was a white cardboard box. And the box was labelled – in a similarly antique-looking copperplate style of handwriting as on the front of the envelope they had received that morning – *For Catriona and Bridget.*

Catie's heart started beating more quickly. It was so strange, seeing their names on the box. How long had it sat there, waiting to be found? How long had Great-Aunt Isobel had this plan – to leave them both the house, and make them unravel her little mysteries?

This was the box that the letter had meant. But what was inside?

Carefully, she took out the box and sat back on her heels.

'Bridget. Look,' she said, holding up the box for her sister to see.

'Oh, wow.' Bridget raised an eyebrow when she saw their names written on the box. 'Go on, then. See what's inside.'

Carefully, Catie pulled off some aged rubber bands that were holding the box closed and put them to one side. She opened the box.

Inside, a framed pencil portrait stared out at them. Catie frowned, taking it out: she knew that face, but she couldn't place it for a moment. Then, she remembered.

'I know this guy. I mean, I don't know him. But there are some sketchbooks down in that weird study, off the kitchen. I swear they have drawings of this same guy in them.' She held the drawing up to the light. 'Yes. I'm sure it's him.'

'Huh. I didn't see those,' Bridget said. 'Who is this guy, then? And whose books were they?'

'I don't know who he is. And I don't know who owned the sketchbooks. Whoever lived here before us, I guess.' Catie shrugged. 'Me and Skye found them when we got shown around the house. Before we moved in.'

'Oh. Okay.' Bridget hunkered down next to Catie and

looked into the box. 'What else is in it? It might help us find out more.'

'Right. Hmm. Okay.' Catie nodded and propped the portrait up against the edge of the chest. 'Well, there's also a book of poetry. Siegfried Sassoon.' She handed the small, green leather-bound book to Bridget, who opened it to the title page. 'One of the war poets.'

'It says, To Simon, with love forever. F. Three kisses,' Bridget read aloud. 'Who is Simon? Or F?'

'I don't know,' Catie confessed. 'Maybe one of them is the person in the portrait, though.'

'That would make sense,' Bridget admitted.

'There's nothing else in here except some pressed flowers. Hard to see what they were originally.' Catie peered into the box. 'I don't really want to take them out because they'll fall apart in my hands.'

'So, the letter said we need to take this stuff to a certain address?' Bridget looked at the flowers in the bottom of the box. 'Hmm. Tulips, maybe. But they must have been in there for years and years.'

'Yes. The Blossoms, Half Moon Lane. Where's that?' Catie frowned.

'I think it's one of those little side streets at the far end of the high street. I'll look on a map.' Bridget got out her phone and paused for a moment, looking at the map app. 'Yeah. Here we go. Half Moon Lane. It's that little tiny lane near to that lane that leads up to Gyle Head. Maybe three houses on it.'

'Oh, right. I sort of remember, but I never had any reason to go up there.' Catie nodded. 'Well, we should deliver this to The Blossoms, then. See if anyone there knows this guy. No time like the present. We've both got work tomorrow.' Catie shrugged. 'We'd better do as Great-Aunt Isobel commands.'

'Otherwise what? She'll haunt us?' Bridget scoffed, but

Catie thought that maybe wasn't the most unlikely thing in the world, after all. Clearly, Isobel had a firm agenda when it came to Castle View. *I wouldn't put anything past her*, Catie thought.

~

They found Half Moon Lane where Bridget had said it was: off a country lane that led up to the new housing development on Gyle Head. Half Moon Lane hadn't been developed, and sat off the fields that led up to the new houses.

Yet, as they turned the end of the tiny road – barely wide enough to get a car up it at all – Catie stopped in her tracks.

'Oh,' she said, and turned in surprise to Bridget, who wore the same expression.

'Ah,' Bridget echoed her sister. 'I guess people still lived here the last time Isobel checked.'

'But not now.' Catie started walking up the little lane to the first of three derelict buildings. They were just walls now, and not complete walls at that: the roofs were gone from all three little cottages, exposing the insides to the elements. Nothing was left inside; the brick was blackened throughout, and the little gardens beyond had run wild.

'Fire. Must be.' Bridget pushed the half of a wooden door open that remained on one house and peered inside. 'I wonder when it happened. Strange that no one's done anything about it. Especially with the new development.'

'Hmm. Very strange,' Catie agreed. 'There's no way of knowing which one is The Blossoms. Not that it matters, I guess. There's no one here to give this stuff to. I wonder who did live here? That it was so important for us to give the picture and the book to?'

'Well, we could find out.' Bridget put her hand on the blackened brick and stared up at the teetering walls. 'People would know. The Laird would know. There's records up at the castle about who's lived where. The laird's the landlord for pretty much everyone, right?'

'That's a good point. I wouldn't have thought of that,' Catie admitted. 'I could ask the laird's brother. He's been helping me at the library.'

'Has he, now?' Bridget gave her an imperious look. 'I've heard about that.'

'From who?' Catie crossed her arms over her chest in a protective gesture. She didn't like the thought that she might be the subject of local gossip, even though there was nothing to gossip about.

'My friend Kathy. She saw you at the library, canoodling with the guy.' Bridget raised an eyebrow. 'Care to comment?'

'I was *not* canoodling,' Catie protested. 'I was working.'

'Hmm. That's not what Kathy said,' Bridget said. 'Nice work if you can get it.'

'Well, I'm telling you, and I'm your sister,' Catie said, giving Bridget a bright smile.

'Fine, fine. Whatever you say, lover girl.'

'Oh, for...' Catie swore exasperatedly under her breath. Bridget laughed.

'Come on, Cat. I'm just teasing. I don't care what you get up to. Probably overdue, to be honest. A bit of fun at last.'

'Oh. Right. Well. It's nothing, really,' Catie muttered. 'Anyway. Matt or Hal Cameron might be able to help us find out more about who lived at The Blossoms.'

'Fine. Ask them, then.' Bridget shrugged. 'Now, if you'll excuse me, I have an appointment with the sofa and a bag of crisps. I've done my exercise for the day. And you need to talk to your daughter, may I remind you. She needs to talk to you.'

'I know. Easier said than done, though,' Catie sighed. She turned away from the burnt-out buildings, holding the cardboard box to her chest, protectively. There was something disappointing about coming here and finding these houses:

disappointing and sad. There was an air of desolation here that mirrored her own sadness about Skye.

What had happened at Half Moon Lane? And how did it relate to the picture, the book of poetry and the desiccated pressed flowers that Great-Aunt Isobel was so keen to return to its former residents?

17

'Catriona, dear. I don't have much time to chat,' her mum said at the end of the line. Her voice was tense. In fact, Catie had been trying to get her mum on the phone for ages with little success, so she was relieved that Barbara had finally taken her call.

'I know. I just wanted to know how you're doing. And how dad is,' Catie said. She could hear noises in the background: voices and beeping noises. 'What's going on there?'

'Your dad is having more tests. And the physical therapist is here,' her mum whispered.

'Oh. How's that going?' Catie asked.

'All right,' her mum said, noncommittally.

Skye came to stand next to her as she spoke on the phone.

'Tell Grannie and Grandpa hello from me,' she said. Catie nodded, and went to wrap her arm around her daughter, but she pulled away.

'Skye says hello,' Catie added.

'Oh. Is she all right? Say hello from us.' Catie's mum's tone brightened when talking about her granddaughter.

'Okay, I will... listen, Mum. I know all this is hard for you, but I wanted to say, I'm around to help. Whatever's needed. I can come round and clean, cook, whatever,' Catie offered.

'I don't need you to do that, dear,' her mum said.

'Mum. Just accept help, for goodness' sake,' Catie said.

'Don't be rude. The most help you can be to me is trying to make a go of things, living with your sister. Goodness knows I need her out of the house to make room for everything for your dad now,' Barbara snapped. 'Wait a minute.' There was the sound of her putting her hand over the phone and talking to someone for a moment, then a shuffling as Barbara passed her phone from hand to hand.

'Right. I've stepped out for a minute,' her mum said. 'It's quieter out here.'

'Okay,' Catie said. 'Listen, Mum. I just want to help.'

'You don't know what all this is like for my nerves,' Barbara said. 'It was bad enough when you were small. That stress, that we might lose you – that about killed me. But I had your father, and he was my rock. And now, he's not my rock anymore,' her voice wavered.

'I'm sorry –' Catie began, but Barbara cut her off.

'Listen, Catriona. When you were ill, it almost ruined this family. I don't think you know the impact it had,' she said. 'This is bringing it all back. I don't know how I'm going to cope, and I don't know what you can do to help except stay out of my hair. I need to focus on your father,' she continued, and Catie felt the steely reproach of her mother's words stab into her heart. *I ruined our family*, she thought. *But I was only a child.*

'All right... well, I guess I'll check in again tomorrow,' Catie said, knowing that what her mum had said was desperately unfair, but also knowing that she wasn't herself. This was a stressful time, and for as long as Catie could remember, her dad had been the one to hold the centre when any of them needed support.

Now that the centre was gone, none of them knew what to do.

'You don't need to,' Barbara said. 'Nothing will have changed.'

'Mum. He's my dad. I love him,' Catie said. Her mum sighed.

'Yes, I know,' she said. 'But you're both grown-ups now, dear. I can't be there to hold your hand through everything. Someone needs to hold *my* hand.' Her voice cracked. 'And, if I'm being completely truthful, dear, I don't wonder that this all isn't a delayed reaction to you being ill when you were small. That poor man. He held onto it for all those years.'

Catie knew that her mum was hurting, and that she wasn't thinking straight. Catie had literally just offered help and support, but her mum couldn't see it.

Catie closed her eyes and stopped walking, taking a moment. Her mother couldn't see that Catie and Bridget needed support as much as she did; she couldn't see anything apart from her own grief. Had she always been like this? Catie wondered. It was hard to know; for so many years, it had always been her dad that had been the one Catie had gone to with a problem, or for a talk. Her mum was always there, but in the background, making dinner, doing the housework, always subtly reminding her daughters that their dad had to get up for work in the morning, that they shouldn't take up so much of his time. Like a dragon, greedily protecting its hoard.

'Mum. That's really not fair.' Catie tried to keep her voice level, but the accusation was awful. She knew, rationally, that it was completely unlikely for her dad's stroke to be caused by something that had happened such a long time ago. And yet the idea took hold in her mind, wrapped in the guilt she still held for her own illness.

'I just haven't got the energy for you right now, dear,' Barbara said, and Catie's heart shrank yet again. 'You took all I had when you were a child. Stand on your own two feet now. There's a good girl. Now, I have to go,' she said, her tone brisk.

'All right, Mum.' Catie's voice broke; what her mother had said had hurt. 'I'm offering to help you,' she added, but her phone screen went dead.

So much for trying to be the good daughter, she thought. She missed her dad. She had been so terribly worried about him, and, instead of reassuring her, talking to her mum had made it so much worse. Now, it seemed that she wasn't allowed to help or even be present at her dad's bedside, and it was all her fault for something that she had been a victim of, years ago.

Catie knew that her mum was stressed out, grieving and even possibly having a nervous breakdown, but it didn't make what she'd said any easier to hear.

I don't wonder that this all isn't a delayed reaction to you being ill when you were small. That poor man. He held onto it for all those years.

Catie had never managed to let go of her guilt for being ill. She had also never stopped worrying that the leukaemia might come back. What her mum had said was cruel. But there was a part of her that believed it. She couldn't help but worry, what if her illness was responsible for some kind of long-term stress that had made her dad have two terrible strokes?

18

'Well, the way I heard it, young Matt's come home under something of a cloud,' June said as she added hot water from a silver urn into a large stainless-steel teapot. The crochet coven were in residence again at the library like they were every Thursday at the moment.

Catie was walking past, pushing a trolley of books that needed to be re-shelved. She carried on with what she was doing, but stayed in earshot. Her curiosity had been piqued at the mention of Matt's name.

'Oh, aye?' another woman – Catie knew her name was Sheila – was laying out a pot of cutlery on the trestle table they'd put up for refreshments.

'Indeed. Seems that the laird's not happy with him frittering away the family money.'

Catie watched as Sheila took a cup of tea and a cheese sandwich from a tray covered in cling film and put it on a paper plate. She started shelving books, so it wouldn't look like she was eavesdropping.

'Where was he, again? America, was it?' Sheila asked.

'California, I believe. Silicon Valley,' June replied, pulling her lips tight. Catie guessed from her expression that she didn't approve of the home of the "tech bros". Matt had told Catie at the Inn that he'd been working in app development. But she hadn't known that there was some kind of issue between him and Hal over the family money.

'Nice.' Sheila raised an eyebrow. 'I would nae mind all those palm trees an' white beaches. Make a change from the driech weather here.'

'Hmm. Well, I can see that. But I'd prefer Loch Cameron to Los Angeles, or wherever he was,' June said. 'I heard from Anna, the housekeeper up at the castle, that Hal is absolutely livid about the money.'

'What money?' Sheila asked. 'The Camerons've never been short o' a bob or two.'

'Well, I don't know the ins and outs of the family finances, of course. And nowadays, I hear that the salmon farming's doing very well, as is the nursery,' June said. 'But there's been some problem about Matt using family money to invest in his business...' June lowered her voice, though Catie could just about still hear her. 'It all went under. He lost all of it.'

'No!' Sheila put her hand to her heart. 'What a shame! The poor lad.'

'Yes. Though I can understand if Hal's none too impressed, especially with an expensive wedding coming up.' June sniffed. 'Anna said that it's not the first time Hal had to bail Matt out, and he's not happy. *At all*.'

'Well, companies do go under,' Sheila said, fairly. 'That's no' necessarily the lad's fault. I'm sure he did all he could.'

'Well, it's not the first time. That's the thing, Anna said,' June continued. Catie felt more than a pang of sympathy for Matt, as his life was being dissected in some detail by the ladies – especially when he wasn't around to present his own version of events. 'No, she says the thing that Hal's really angry about is apparently Matt made a series of quite unethical investments and choices with his businesses, and this is just the icing on the cake.'

'What d'ye mean, unethical?' Sheila took a bite out of her sandwich and smiled at a young mum who had come in with toddler twins in a buggy.

'I'm not sure exactly, but I suppose companies that Hal disapproved of in some way.' June shrugged. 'I'm not an expert. I can tell you about the health service, but some of these corporate jobs just go over my head.'

'Hmm. Me too, when it comes tae computers,' Sheila said. 'I hope it's not too much money he's frittered away, then. What a *scandal*.'

Catie thought that Sheila sounded positively enthusiastic about the news rather than scandalised. She imagined that the Loch Cameron rumour mill would be in full swing with this story very shortly, if it wasn't already.

However, Catie wasn't about to judge anyone: she too had a dysfunctional relationship with her sibling, and she too had apparently come to a point where they had a shared asset that they both had to care about, despite the fact they didn't get on very well.

'Catie, dear. How are ye?' June waved at her, and Catie nodded, hoping it wasn't obvious that she'd been eavesdropping on their whole conversation.

'Hi, June. Fine, thanks. Hi, Sheila.'

'We saw ye flirtin' wi' the laird's young brother the other day. Ye absolute scoundrel.' Sheila nudged her and giggled. 'How's that goin'?'

'It's not really going anywhere.' Catie had no intention of discussing what might or might not be *going on* between her and Matt Cameron with the worst gossips in the village. 'We're... just friends.' She thought that vagueness was probably the best way to go.

'Hmm. Lovely lookin' lad.' Sheila raised an eyebrow. 'If I

was single... and a wee bit younger, I'd give it a try.'

'Sheila. Behave yourself!' June tutted, amusedly.

'Agh, ye cannae blame a girl fer dreamin',' Sheila giggled. 'Now. Excuse me, ladies. I said I'd help Kathy with a tricky bit o' a pattern on her throw.' She pointed to Kathy, a girl with black and white two-tone hair and tattoos who was sitting frowning at a colourful crocheted blanket. *Ah. Kathy,* Catie thought. Bridget's friend. She would have to be extra careful what she did and said if Kathy was in the library, if everything was going to go back to her sister.

Not that I have anything to hide, she corrected herself.

'So. How's things up at the house? And with your dad?' June asked as Sheila sat down beside Kathy. 'You've been in my prayers.'

'Have you? That's kind. Oh, well, it's going,' Catie sighed. 'Not very harmoniously, but we're there. And dad is improving slowly. Thank you.' Catie liked June: she was no-nonsense, but she was kind. If June said that she'd remembered Catie in her prayers, then Catie knew she meant it.

'Not very harmonious?' June prompted her.

'Oh, you know. We're not really getting on,' Catie sighed. 'And the house... I don't know. It feels unwelcoming, somehow.'

'Oh. I'm sorry to hear that.' June frowned.

'Hmm. I heard strange noises. In the night,' Catie said, aware that she probably sounded mad. But she felt that she could trust June. 'A thudding noise. And I had a funny dream.'

'About?'

'A voice. Telling me that I need to help him. A man. A sense of dread.' Catie made a face. 'I know it sounds mad.'

'Not mad at all, dear,' June mused. 'If you recall, when we spoke before, I was suggesting that you might need a house clearing, up at Castle View,' she added.

'What do you mean, house clearing? It's not cluttered.' Catie frowned.

'No, I mean, a priest comes and blesses the house if it needs it. You know. Exorcisms and the like. People don't talk about it, but it happens more often than you'd expect.'

'Exorcism?!' Catie laughed out loud. 'It's not a horror movie! It's just an old house.'

'I know. But, as I say, you witness a lot of strange things, working in a hospital for all your life. I've known Kevin for many, many years now. He was the hospital chaplain, and we had a couple of occurrences when we had to get Kevin in to clear spaces. An operating room once, and a couple of times, rooms where people had died.' June looked reflective. 'I saw ghosts a few times. You're going to, if you hang around places where people die. It's just the way it is.'

'Well. I didn't expect to be having this conversation today,' Catie said. 'I can't say I've ever thought about it much.'

'Hmm. Just life and death, dear. It is what it is.' June looked philosophical. 'As I say, I've seen a lot of it, one way or another. And if you decide you need a bit of help at home, then let me know. I'll put you in touch with Kevin. Really, the nicest man.' She patted Catie's hand.

'All right. I mean, I don't think I will, but... thanks.' Catie felt more than a little surprised at the turn of the conversation, but there was something about June's reassuring manner that made her think, *well, maybe it wouldn't be the worst thing in the world for someone to come around and sort the house out. If it can be sorted.*

Catie knew that real life wasn't like a movie. It was so much less glamorous; she didn't for a moment think that anyone was going to get caught behind the TV screen or start spewing ectoplasm from their mouth like the horror movie she and Matt had joked about.

There are more things in heaven and earth than can be dreamed of in your philosophy, Catie thought, quoting Shakespeare. *Sometimes, life is just weird.*

19

'So, this area is personal to each user, and they can see all the books they've borrowed here,' Matt said, pointing to a boxed-off area on the screen in front of them. 'They can see any fees due, pay them online, reserve books, audio and ebooks, and then there's this social function.' He clicked into a different section. 'I made a kind of chat room type function where people can swap book recommendations, leave each other messages, message you with questions, that kind of thing. You said you wanted to help improve people's social experience in the village. Help them to connect.'

He looked up at her and brushed his hair out of his eyes. *Gosh, he's beautiful,* Catie thought. His eyes were a deep blue, and there was something so soulful in them when he looked deep into her eyes. Matt had a way of making eye contact that felt like it slowed the world down.

Catie pretended to have been looking at the library bulletin board for a moment, and then re-focused on the screen.

'It looks great.' She nodded. 'We'd have to teach some people how to use it, and not all the village are online at home. Especially not the elderly. But it will help a lot of people.'

'Thanks. I'm pleased with it so far. Still a lot to do, though. How's your Reading Rocks project going?'

'It's good. With your help with the online portal, I think people will enjoy it. I've been telling customers and quite a lot of them are looking forward to it. They're surprisingly competitive about it,' she chuckled. 'Old Mrs Carstairs was vying with her friend Marjorie about how many books they thought they could read over a month the other day. And the primary school are going to get the kids involved too.'

'That's awesome.' Matt looked at a handwritten list of notes on a pad next to him. 'I need to talk to you about making an app. And maybe starting a library newsletter for members. You can use a newsletter marketing tool for that.'

'I wouldn't know where to start with that.' Catie pulled a face.

'I'd show you. It's not difficult,' he grinned.

'Even for a slightly confused, middle aged librarian?' she teased.

'I can't see one of those anywhere here.' His smile widened. 'I can see a very attractive woman, though.'

'Errr... okay. Thanks,' she said, hating the fact that she was blushing furiously.

'You're welcome,' he chuckled. 'Sorry. Was that inappropriate, as we're at work?'

'A bit, yes. But I don't mind.'

'It sort of slipped out. I'm sorry. You just have that effect on me.'

A slight blush now covered his cheeks, which amused Catie. She liked the fact that she evidently made Matt feel as off-balance around her as he made her feel in his presence.

'Listen. Can I ask you something a bit off-topic?' She thought it would be a good idea to change the subject. 'Does your brother keep local records up at the castle? Like, if I wanted to find out who had lived somewhere at a certain point. He could find out for me?'

'Err... yeah. There's an archive in the basement.' Matt nodded. 'What do you want to know?'

'Oh, it's this thing with the house.' She sighed. 'Our great-aunt's sent us this letter with instructions to give something from the house to this person in a particular house in the village, but when me and Bridget went to find the house, it had burnt down.'

'How has she sent you instructions? From beyond the grave?'

'Via her solicitor, silly. It was a letter she had asked him to send once we had moved in. I want to know who did live there so I can find them.'

'And obey your dead aunt's wishes? So gothic.' Matt shot her a shy smile. 'Yeah. I mean, I'd imagine there would be some info up at the castle. But I'd think that the gossip mill in Loch Cameron would be able to tell you quicker. You know. Dotty, at the Inn. Dotty knows everything that's ever happened in Loch Cameron. I'm pretty sure she'd remember a fire.'

'That's a very good point.' Catie mulled the thought over. 'You're right. I'll ask her.'

'Happy to help. If you want to come and have a look around the castle archive, though, you're welcome to.' He scuffed the tip of his shoe on the ground. 'I'd be happy to show you around. It's a nice old place really. The gardens are pretty, this time of year.'

'Okay. Thanks. I'll let you know how I get on,' she said, shyly. She liked Matt. She liked that he was helpful and thoughtful. 'I forget that you're... you know. The lord of the manor.'

'Ha. The younger laird. Less of a thing.' He shot her a shy smile. 'But... the offer's there. Come and I'll show you around. If you like. No pressure. We could have tea.'

'That would be... very nice,' Catie replied, cautiously.

'Let's say tomorrow after work, if you like. I don't have any plans,' he said, still sounding a little shy.

'Oh. Umm. Sure.' Catie felt herself blushing, and hated it. She cleared her throat. 'Well. I should get on.' She waved a hand at the almost empty library. 'Busy, busy.'

'Tokyo at rush hour has nothing on this.' He nodded, sagely. 'Okay. I'll leave you to it. Until tomorrow, then. I guess I don't need to tell you where the castle is. We'll have tea, then?'

'Okay. Tea,' Catie agreed, and watched him as he picked up his jacket from the back of the chair, pulled it on, revealing a glimpse of toned torso underneath his T-shirt. She blinked. 'And, yes. I know where the castle is.'

'See you there.' He gave her that shy smile again, and Catie smiled back. It was easy to smile at Matt. It was easy being around him. She hadn't felt that ease in a very long time.

20

'Well, my memory isn't what it was, dear. But I do remember the fire,' Dotty said, lowering herself slowly into a chair by the fireplace. 'Ah. That's better. You know, I broke my leg a year or so ago and it's taken forever to heal. I'm old, that's why.' She rolled her eyes, signalling the fact that she had little patience for aging. 'Time was when I'd have been fine after a week.'

'I'm sorry to hear that. Can I get you anything? A cushion?' Catie hovered next to the pub landlady as she settled herself into her chair.

She had popped into the Inn to see if Dotty knew anything about the fire on Half Moon Lane and found the landlady more than happy to take a break and reminisce.

'No, no. I'm fine, dear. Sit yourself down.' Dotty waved her to the chair opposite and Catie sat, obediently.

'Now, then. Yes. The fire on Half Moon Lane.' Dotty leaned her head back against the back of the upholstered chair and closed her eyes for a moment. 'It was some time back. I was, what? In my thirties. A young slip o' a thing. So that's about forty years ago,' she began.

'Okay. A long time for those houses to remain derelict after the fire, then,' Catie said, surprised. 'I don't remember them from when I was a kid. But then I suppose I was ill for a lot of the time we lived here, and when I was home, I wasn't allowed out to play very much.'

'Aye, right enough.' Dotty nodded. 'I do remember your mum being so worried about ye. I wouldae been tearin' ma hair out if it had been my wee lassie was so ill.' Dotty opened her eyes and smiled warmly at Catie. 'Still. Nice an' strong now, eh?'

'I think so.'

'Good. Now, The fire. Aye. It was a mystery. I dinnae think anyone ever found out for sure what happened, but it took all three houses out on that lane. The families got out in time; people said it was a chip pan fire, but I dinnae think that it was. Tragic, really.'

'What happened to the families?' Catie asked.

'The laird re-homed them, as I recall. This was Hal's father, Donald.' Dotty frowned. 'I dinnae especially remember where they went, but it would've been elsewhere in the village. He was good like that, and they were his tenants. The McPhersons, they were one of the families,' she mused. 'Now, I remember that because I was friends with Emily Hyland and she was friends with Anne McPherson, the wife. And I remember Emily tellin' me all about how Anne had tae wear donated clothes because all of hers were ruined in the fire.'

'I wanted to know who lived at The Blossoms. Do you remember that? Or the names of the other families on that street?' Catie asked.

'I cannae remember the particular names o' the cottages, I'm afraid.' Dotty shook her head. 'But I think another family was the Emersons. Sad, after what happened tae the son, Simon,' she tutted.

'What did happen to him?'

'Oh, he died in an accident. Terrible, it was. Young fella.

Whole life ahead of him. Fell intae the loch. Just one o' those freak occurrences.' Dotty sighed. 'Even sadder then that his family lost their house in the fire. Course, that was some years after.'

Simon Emerson. The name *Simon* tugged at Catie's memory, but she didn't know why.

'Hmm. Anything else you can tell me?'

'Eh. Not really, dear. Always wondered why the houses never got repaired or replaced. Cleaned up, even. But they've been there, burnt out, all these years. I thought that new developer that did Gyle Head – thought he'd have done somethin' with them. But no.' Dotty shrugged. 'Sad, really. Could be a nice place tae live if there was a new house built there.'

'It would,' Catie agreed, remembering Half Moon Lane: it was quiet, rural, right on the edge of the village. But it had a spooky atmosphere; as if it was haunted. 'Do you think the laird would know more? Seeing as he's the landowner around here?' she added. Matt had offered to look at the castle records for her, and she was intrigued to know what was up there.

The name *Simon* rang in her memory, and it was annoying her. There was a connection there. But, to what?

'Aye, he might.' Dotty nodded. 'Hal has always taken an interest in the village an' its history. There might be a reason those cottages never got knocked down. Ask him, lassie. See what he says.'

'All right. I will. Thanks, Dotty.' Catie smiled.

'You're welcome, hen. Loch Cameron's full o' secrets,' Dotty sighed. 'Sometimes it feels like a heavy burden, knowin' most o' them. But it turns out even I don't know them all.'

21

Catie pressed a buzzer on the frame of the large entry way to Loch Cameron Castle and waited, listening to the old-fashioned bell echo into the cavernous space beyond.

She had no real idea what she and Bridget were doing here. Matt had asked her to the castle for tea and to look at the archive. She'd expected to go on her own, but when she'd mentioned it to Bridget, her sister had insisted on coming too.

'It's not like it's an everyday occurrence, to be asked to a castle for a social visit,' Bridget had said, breezily. 'I've been dying to get up there and have a nose around. And Great-Aunt Isobel sent that letter to both of us. She wants us both to investigate the mystery.' She sprinkled her fingers in the air as if she was spreading fairy dust in it. 'So, I'm coming. It's not like it's a date.' Bridget stopped for a minute and pulled on a cardigan. 'Wait. Catie, is it a date?'

'No, of course not.' Catie made a face, like that was the most ridiculous idea she'd ever heard. Of course, she was being disingenuous in saying that, because Catie had wondered, privately, if it was. Matt had said, when they'd last talked about it, that he wanted to take her out again, after their time at the distillery. She hadn't been sure if he was serious, but when he'd asked her at the library, he had seemed to be quite nervous. Which wasn't necessarily how anyone got if they were suggesting they meet a friend for tea.

A woman flung open the heavy wooden door and grinned at them.

'Hey! You must be Catie. Come in, come in.' She stood aside and ushered Catie into the large stone-walled hallway. 'Be careful of the swords. I'm always snagging my sweaters on them,' she tutted, good-naturedly. 'I never thought that would be a sentence I'd say, right?' she laughed, and held out her hand. 'Hey. I'm Zelda. Hal's fiancée.'

'Hello, Zelda. This is my sister, Bridget,' Catie said. 'And it's lovely to meet you.' Catie shook the American girl's hand. 'Congratulations on your engagement, by the way! You must be so excited.'

'Oh, *am I?*' Zelda shook her head in wonder. 'Bridget! Good to meet you too.' She shook Bridget's hand.

'I hope you don't mind me tagging along. It was too good an opportunity to pass up: a private visit to the castle. I mean, I've come before, on the May Day party a few times, and when we were kids, we came on a school trip. But never like this.' Catie was surprised at her sister's fawning; Bridget wasn't usually someone to make a fuss about anything really. *Who knew that Bridget was a secret fan of the Loch Cameron gentry,* she thought.

'Oh, not at all, but I have to tell you girls. Organising this wedding is no joke. I haven't slept in weeks.' Zelda rubbed her eyes in an exaggeratedly owlish way. Catie laughed. In fact, Zelda looked absolutely gorgeous, even though she was dressed in a baggy beige tracksuit, her long poker-straight black hair up in a high ponytail.

'It'll all be worth it,' Catie reassured her. 'I mean, I've never been married. But I can imagine the wedding's going to be amazing. Not everyone gets married in a castle.'

'Oh, I know, babe. I know.' Zelda shook her head in wonderment. 'Really. I am gratitude journaling like you wouldn't believe.'

'Hey. Catie. Sorry. I was on the phone.' Matt Cameron jogged down the corridor towards them, giving Catie an awkward wave. He was dressed in a white shirt and light blue jeans; it was a simple outfit but, again, Catie was struck by his wholesome good looks. *Like an off-duty Hugo Boss model*, she thought wryly to herself. *Thank you, God.*

'Matt. Don't leave your gorgeous guests waiting,' Zelda said, a little archly. 'Not very fitting for a laird. Most ungentlemanly.' She raised a playful eyebrow at Catie and Bridget.

'Yeah, well. Thanks for stepping in, Zelda. I'll take it from here.' Catie detected a tension in Matt's voice, even though his expression was open and pleasant. 'Hi. I don't think we've met? I'm Matt Cameron.' He held out a hand to Bridget, who shook it warmly.

'Bridget McGovern. I'm Catie's sister,' she said.

'Bridget was keen to come up and look in the archive too. I hope that's okay,' Catie said, a little apologetically, but Matt seemed unfazed.

'Of course! You're most welcome, Bridget,' he said, giving her a bright smile.

'Okay. You guys have fun. I've got to run. Meeting about flower arrangements.' Zelda saluted them both and slung an expensive-looking handbag over her shoulder before striding out of the front door. The noise of it closing reverberated through the house.

'Shall we?' Matt held out a hand, beckoning them forward, and led them down an impressive, oak-panelled hallway and into a large drawing room. Catie caught Bridget's eye as she took in the oxblood leather sofas, the walls lined with leather-bound books and the vast stone fireplace at the centre of the room. Bridget gave her a wide-eyed look.

'We're actually out on the patio.' Matt gestured towards some tall glass doors that were open at the edge of the room. 'Go through. I'm just going to get something from the cupboard here.'

They followed where he pointed and walked out onto a sunny patio overlooking Loch Cameron Castle's stunning ornamental gardens.

'Wow.' Bridget stood like a lovestruck cartoon deer, gazing out at the view. 'This is... wow. How the other half live. Right?' She turned to Catie, lowering her voice.

'It's lovely,' Catie said as she sat down at a glass-topped rattan table on which a plentiful tea had been laid out. 'I wouldn't mind having my breakfast out here once in a while.'

Matt walked through the open patio door, holding another place setting of the fine bone china carrying the Cameron clan logo, and setting it down on the table: bright white with the logo in black and gold. Catie immediately realised what she'd just said.

'Sorry. I didn't mean... I was just...' she trailed off, feeling embarrassed.

'Catie was just saying that she'd love to have breakfast here one day,' Bridget repeated, with a mischievous glint in her eye. Catie narrowed her eyes at her sister and mouthed *shut up* when Matt looked away.

'Oh. Well, we must make that happen one day,' Matt replied, pouring aromatic, amber tea from a white china teapot into three fine bone china cups.

'Bridget is making a joke,' Catie interjected. 'She thinks she's hilarious.'

'I'm delighted to meet your sister. Bridget can give me all the gossip about you.' He raised an eyebrow.

'There isn't any.' Catie gave Bridget a death stare. 'This all looks amazing, Matt. Thank you.'

On the table, a plate of coronation chicken sandwiches jostled for room with a cake stand piled high with golden, freshly-baked scones and generous pots of ruby red raspberry jam and thick cream.

The fact that Matt had go to get an extra place setting wasn't lost on Catie. He had only laid out two cups, two saucers, two plates; he had only expected her.

Well, that's because he only asked me, and I didn't tell him I was bringing Bridget, she rationalised. And that was all true, except, Catie had the feeling, looking at the table, that Matt had made quite an effort with it all, and maybe he had intended this to be a date, after all.

He had rolled up the sleeves of his white shirt; Catie tried not to notice his tanned, muscular forearms underneath.

'You're very welcome.' He sat down and helped himself to a sandwich.

'This is really delicious. Probably the best sandwich I've ever eaten,' Bridget said, sitting down and helping herself.

'I feel like a princess,' Catie said, taking the cup of tea that Matt handed to her. She'd said it before she could stop herself. 'Oh. You know what I mean. It was a turn of phrase.' Catie felt a blush steal onto her cheeks.

'You're welcome, my lady,' he replied, that now familiar shy smile tugging at the edge of his lips. 'The scones are good. The housekeeper makes them fresh.'

'It's wild you have a housekeeper.' Catie shook her head.

'I'd love a housekeeper.' Bridget was stuffing a sandwich into her mouth; her words were slightly muffled. 'Of course, the house used to have one, before we moved in. We didn't get to keep her, though, apparently.'

'I know. I mean, I had a maid service in LA. And I often had a caterer help out for dinners, events, that kind of thing. So, it's not that different, I guess. This is a big place. You need help with somewhere like this. As it is, Hal has a skeleton staff, to be honest. In the old days, there was a whole team: drivers, maids, butlers, the lot.' He sipped his tea.

'No, I know, it makes sense. It's just a whole other life, really.' Catie looked around her. 'I just can't imagine growing up in a castle.'

'I guess it's weird.' Matt took another bite of his sandwich.

'It's bloody lovely,' Bridget said. 'Cate. We might actually get on if we had to share a *castle*. We'd never have to see each other.'

'Hmm,' Catie said, smiling thinly. Bridget was really annoying her, but Matt didn't seem to mind.

'So, you wanted to look at the archive?' Matt turned to Bridget.

'Yeah. If that's okay.' Bridget leaned forward to take a scone, and cut it in half with her knife. Which, Catie noticed, was solid silver and also bore the Cameron monogram. 'Just to satisfy our mad great-aunt, and this one.' She pointed to Catie with the knife. 'If there's something not tidy and *just so*, she can't leave it alone. We got told to do something, so heaven forbid she doesn't do it.'

'It's fine. And, I get that. Attention to detail is a good quality.' He grinned. 'I wouldn't be able to leave that alone, either. Such a mystery!'

'Is it possible to find out who lived on Half Moon Lane some years ago?' Catie asked, deliberately ignoring her sister. 'The letter said that we had to return some items that we found inside the house to someone who lives there, at a house called The Blossoms. But we walked down there, and the houses aren't there anymore. So there's no way of knowing who the family that lived there was. I talked to Dotty at the Inn about it and she had an idea but I'd like to know more.'

'Of course. Let's go down there now, if you like.' He stood

up. 'We can come back for more scones. I'll cover them over.' He placed a glass cover over the scones and draped some napkins over the sandwiches.

'Oh. Right.' Bridget looked crestfallen, but Catie stood up, ready to go. She was more eager to investigate the mystery than she was to eat scones, even if Bridget was more interested in eating cake with a fantastic view.

The sisters followed Matt as he led them through the grand drawing room behind the patio, into a long hallway and down some stairs at the end of it. They emerged into a narrow, cold corridor below stairs, and followed Matt to a room that led off it. Beyond, Catie could see a larder hung with hams and with racks of bottles, and hear a radio playing; she glimpsed what looked like a large kitchen at the end of the corridor.

'Here we are.' Matt flicked a switch, and a bare light flickered on, illuminating a small room lined with glass-fronted cabinets. 'Should be able to find what we need fairly easily.'

'Wow. This is amazing.' Catie looked around her with interest. A large oil painting of an old-fashioned sailing ship on a choppy blue sea hung over a heavily singed cast iron fireplace. Most of the cabinets were piled up with old leather books and large ledgers.

In the centre of the room, three chairs sat around a wooden table. Catie guessed that was so people – the laird, mostly, she thought – could sit down and look at the old records, or indeed contribute to them, if that was still done. She imagined him writing in longhand, some kind of beautiful penmanship, probably.

'Not as flash as upstairs,' Bridget observed, bluntly.

'No, it's all very basic below stairs,' Matt agreed. 'It used to be all servants' quarters, the laundries, the store rooms and what have you. Now, then.' Matt went to one of the glass-fronted cabinets and opened it. 'Ummm. It's been a while since I was down here, but let's have a look. I think there are records here about the tenancies. That would show names and addresses. What did you say? Half Moon Lane?'

'That's the one,' Bridget said, standing behind Matt. While he was busy looking at the shelves, Bridget looked him up and down and gave Catie a thumbs up, mouthing *well done*. Catie frowned furiously at her sister and willed her to behave herself.

'Hmm. Okay, try this one.' Matt handed Catie a ledger, which she opened and started to peruse.

'Here we are. Oh, wow. The Emerson family *did* live at The Blossoms.' Catie nodded, running her finger down a page of handwritten entries. The lines were organised by surname, then the address, but there wasn't much deviation on the page for Half Moon Lane: it appeared that its residents hadn't changed much in the years before the houses had burnt down. 'Dotty mentioned the Emersons. I think the son, Simon, was somehow connected to someone at Castle View. There are several drawings and a book of poetry that my great-aunt wanted us to return to the people in that house.'

'That's strange. Did she say why?' Matt's brow furrowed.

'No. But Simon Emerson died in an accident, according to Dotty.' Catie frowned. 'It just seems like there's something missing from this picture. Like, there was a lot of tragedy for the families on that little street. Was Simon's accident related to the fire, somehow?'

'Maybe. Hang on.' Matt held up a finger and went back to the cabinet. He flicked through some other files and notebooks, and then pulled out a dark blue book with a police constabulary logo embossed on it. Loch Cameron Police, it read.

'Yeah. I thought we had these in here somewhere.' He nodded with satisfaction. 'Back in the day, the local station used to send their log books up here after five years, because they didn't have room in the station to keep them. They're kept here in case anyone needs to consult old records. Not that anyone ever does. Until now.' He raised a wry eyebrow, and Catie grinned.

'What, there aren't a lot of cold cases in the sprawling metropolis that is Loch Cameron?' she asked.

'Oh, what, Gotham City out there? Ha.' He opened the book and flicked through it. 'It's hard to know when the fire happened. Do you have any idea?'

'Dotty says it was years ago. Thirty or so.' Catie stood up and went to look over his shoulder.

'Right... okay. It's a different book, then.' He replaced the one in his hands with a similar tome and started flicking the pages. 'Okay. Hmmm. Fire, fire... Half Moon Lane. Oh, look. Here it is!' He tilted the book towards Catie, and read the entry aloud.

October 7th, 1990

Fire reported at multiple properties on Half Moon Lane. The fire began at The Blossoms and spread to the two neighbouring cottages. Fire crew in attendance put out the fires after several hours. All family members were safely evacuated.

Investigated as suspicious. Two men sighted at the scene by an elderly neighbour and resident of Moon Cottage, a Miss Maggie McKie. Miss McKie reported seeing Simon Emerson of The Blossoms "hanging around" in the lane when the fire started. She claimed to have seen another, unidentified man with Emerson, who she described as tall and bearded.

Emerson when questioned said that he was out at the time of the fire, and that he suspected it had been begun by a chip pan. He had been telling his mother it was dangerous for some time. Emerson denied that he had been accompanied by another man, and had gone for an evening walk. When he returned, the houses were on fire. No-one could corroborate his story.

However, despite door-to-door investigation and inter-
viewing a number of members of the community, no-one else
apart from Miss McKie seemed to have seen the second man.
Considering that Miss McKie is elderly and, on subsequent
conversations with the investigating team, that she also
observed that she "knew" the fire was going to happen because
of "ill omens" such as a dead crow on her doorstep, and the
milk going sour, Inspector Craigie dismissed her testimony and
closed the case.

'Wow!' Catie was agog, listening to Matt read the police
record aloud. 'That's all very odd, isn't it?'

'I mean, it probably was an accident. I remember those old
chip pans. They were lethal,' Bridget said.

'But... it seems like there might have been something else
going on. I mean, it's weird that Simon Emerson was suspected
of being involved in the fire. And then he had a fatal accident.
Right?' Catie thought aloud.

'That is kind of weird.' Matt nodded. 'I mean, it might just
be a coincidence, of course.'

'But what if it wasn't?' Catie looked up at Matt's deep blue
eyes. 'What if there's some mystery that I have to uncover about
Simon Emerson? And there's a link to Great-Aunt Isobel?'

'I don't know, Catie. But it is certainly intriguing.' He held
her gaze for a moment, then looked away. Catie had the sense
that when Matt said *it is certainly intriguing*, he didn't necessarily mean the house fires. She cleared her throat, remembering that Bridget was there.

'Listen. I forgot to ask you, but being up here has reminded
me. When I was up in my daughter's room a couple of weeks
ago, we found a wall safe behind her wardrobe. It looks like it
takes a key – it's not a modern one. Do you know where I
might find a key for it? I don't know how well you know in the
house, but I thought it was worth asking,' she said, keen to

dispel any sense of romance that might have just arisen between them.

'Oh. Right, umm, I don't know offhand, but I'll have a think. Have you looked in that bowl in the hall? The crystal bowl on the hall table? I feel like I saw some stuff in there,' he said. 'And I can ask Hal if he has any old keys for Castle View. Since we've been looking after it for a while.'

'I looked there, I think, but I'll look again. And, thank you,' she said, feeling awkward. They had got into the habit of being quite flirty with each other, but it felt wrong to be doing that around Bridget.

'You're welcome.' He nodded, and gave her a long, appraising look. Catie felt the blush stealing to her cheeks once more.

'Well, we should get back,' she said, picking up her handbag and looking inside it as if she had forgotten something. But, really, it was just a way to appear more casual than she really felt. 'Can we get a copy of this, or something?' She held out the police report.

'Sure. I'll get Anna to make one while we finish our tea,' he said, tucking the police ledger under his arm.

'Thank goodness. I'm craving another scone.' Bridget pushed her chair back and stood up. 'You happy now, Cate? Feel like the mystery's been solved?'

'Not entirely, no. But I feel like we're on the way to it.' Catie followed them both back out into the dingy below stairs hallway. She was fairly sure that whoever had done those drawings of Simon Emerson had been in an intimate relationship with him. The poetry book seemed to indicate that even if the sketches didn't. And, the police report had said that Simon was seen with another man before the fire – they had gone out for a walk.

So, who was this mystery man? What did Isobel know? And what was she trying to get her and Bridget to find out?

As Bridget and Matt walked ahead, chatting freely, Catie felt her phone vibrate in her handbag. The ring tone was loud and insistent and echoed off the walls around her.

Catie opened her bag and looked at her phone, seeing that it was the school's number on the display. She swore under her breath.

'Hello?' she answered warily. Getting a call from school wasn't good: they rarely called with pleasant news.

'Ms McGovern? This is Ms Barrington, I'm the headmistress at your daughter's school. There's been an incident. Could you come in to get Skye, please?'

There's been an incident. Never words a parent wanted to hear.

'What's happened? Catie asked, her heart pounding.

'I'm afraid that Skye has been involved in a fight with some other girls,' Ms Barrington said, smoothly. 'Best if you just come in.'

'All right. I'll be there as soon as I can,' Catie answered, and the line went dead.

Her stomach closed in a knot; her chest clenched in pain. *Skye.*

'Bridget!' Catie ran to catch her sister up; Matt was leading her back up the cramped stairs that led to the ground floor. 'We have to leave. Now.'

'What's up?' Bridget frowned.

'It's Skye. Some trouble at school. A fight,' Catie panted; the stress was making her feel out of breath.

Bridget swore under her breath.

'Okay.' She followed Catie to the grand entrance hall.

'I'm so sorry that we have to leave,' Catie apologised to Matt. 'It was so kind of you to have us here. But this is a bit of an emergency.' She shrugged on her jacket which she had left on the coat rack.

'Not at all. I hope she's okay.' Matt looked concerned. 'Let me know, okay?'

'Sure. Thanks.' Catie practically ran out of the castle, grateful for the fact that she and Bridget had decided to be lazy and bring her car instead of walk from the village. Her heart was beating hard with panic, and her face had drained of all colour.

Please, please, please don't let my baby be hurt, she prayed, fervently, as she got in the car. *Please make sure Skye is okay.*

22

'Thank you for coming in.' The headmistress of Skye's school welcomed Catie and Bridget into her office and directed them to some comfortable seats in a mid-blue woven fabric on the opposite side of a small, bland coffee table. 'I'm Ms Barrington, the head.'

'That's okay. We were just really worried to hear from you,' Catie said, trying to be polite, but her heart was hammering in her chest. When Skye had been little, when the school called it might be because she'd taken a tumble in the playground or had a temperature. Those were fairly non-worrisome things: the usual childhood issues that could be resolved with a cuddle, a plaster or a little paracetamol and a day under a blanket on the sofa.

Being called into your daughter's secondary school because she and some other girls had been fighting was in a whole other league. Nothing like this had ever happened before, and Catie's stomach had been in knots for the whole journey here.

Skye sat in a more formal wooden chair that looked like it belonged at a dinner table. Her hair, which had been in a neat plait that morning for school, had been half pulled out of the braid and straggled onto her shoulder. Her clothes looked rumpled and a bruise was starting to rise on her cheek.

'Oh my goodness. Skye!' Catie ran to her daughter and took her face in both hands, studying the damage, then hugged her close. 'Are you all right?'

'I'm fine,' Skye said, mulishly.

'You're clearly not fine, poppet.' Bridget frowned, following Catie into the office and putting her hand gently on her niece's shoulder. 'Who did this to you? I'll have their guts for garters.'

The headmistress cleared her throat.

'Well, I don't think that's a helpful strategy,' she said, neutrally. 'Shall we sit down?'

They sat.

'Right. Skye. Why don't you tell us what's been going on?' The headmistress turned to Skye, who refused to make eye contact with anyone.

Skye said nothing; her lips pressed together tightly and stress emanated from her in waves of discomfort, but she didn't say anything.

'Skye?' Catie asked, gently.

'I don't want to,' Skye said.

'Well, it would be better if we heard it from you,' the head-mistress continued, patiently.

'I've got nothing to say. I had a disagreement with some of the other girls. It happens,' Skye said, folding her arms over her chest.

'Well, it seems to have been quite a significant disagree-ment.' The headmistress was sitting in the remaining blue fabric chair facing Catie and Bridget, and now she leaned forward and poured some water into one of the glasses that were on the coffee table. 'The information I have is that you were involved in a fist fight, with name calling and hair pulling with two other girls in your year.'

Skye shrugged again and said nothing.

'Skye!' Catie was shocked. 'How could you? What happened?'

'I don't want to talk about it,' Skye repeated.

'I've been asking and asking you. For weeks. You told Bridget something was wrong at school but you wouldn't tell me.' Catie felt like tearing her hair out, she was so frustrated.

'Babes, you have to talk about it,' Bridget said, quietly. 'How did this start? When did it start? Because you've been withdrawn for a while. Your mum's been worried about you. So have I.'

Skye didn't reply for a long moment, and then whispered, 'Months.'

She looked out of the window, but Catie could see that she was biting her lip so hard that it was white.

'Skye? Are you being bullied?' Ms Barrington asked, gently. 'You can tell us. This is a safe space. If you have been bullied, I will address it. The school has a zero tolerance policy for bullying.'

'They just wouldn't leave me alone,' Skye said, quietly. 'I didn't know what to do. They were just always following me around at first, making fun of me because I was new. Because I didn't have the right kind of bag and shoes. Then it got worse.'

Catie flinched; Skye had asked her for a new school bag and different shoes, but she'd refused, because money was tight. She hadn't known. She'd thought that it was just a teenage girl being fashion obsessed.

'What happened? How did it get worse?' Bridget asked, gently. 'It's okay, Skye. You didn't do anything wrong.'

Skye paused.

'They stole my coat. And then when I got it back it was covered in paint. Tripped me up. Slapped me. A couple of times they...' she sighed. 'They held my arms behind my back and twisted them. It really hurt. And just constant name calling and...' she stopped, and started to cry. 'It was horrible and I didn't know what to do.'

'Why didn't you think you could come to me?' Catie asked, aghast.

'You've got so much going on with work, the new house, whatever. I didn't think you'd want to hear it,' Skye said between her tears.

'But I asked you, Skye! I knew something was wrong! These girls were trying to get you involved in fights! You should have said something!' Catie cried out, frustrated and heartbroken at the same time. She got up and enveloped her daughter in a deep hug. 'Darling Skye. I love you. I never want you to be hurt. Ever.'

'You and Auntie Bridget are always fighting,' Skye said, muffled.

'Skye. Don't talk to your mum like that.' Bridget chastened her niece, and Catie looked up in surprise. It was rare – or, actually, it never happened – that her sister took her side against her daughter. 'She loves you. We both love you and we care that you're being bullied at school.'

'I'm sorry.' Skye started to cry then, deep sobs of grief, and Catie held her tight to her chest.

'You have nothing to be sorry for. Nothing at all,' she said, determinedly. 'I will not let another day go by and have you miserable. I will end this now,' she said, firmly, and fixed the headmistress with a steely gaze. 'Ms Barrington and I are going to sit down and sort this out right now. Aren't we, Ms Barrington?'

Catie's tone was controlled and calm, but she was furious that anyone could have hurt her little girl without her knowing.

'Certainly, Ms McGovern.' The headmistress nodded. 'Perhaps you'd like to go with your aunt, Skye, and wait outside. I'll talk to your mother.'

Bridget and Skye got up; Bridget put a protective arm around her niece's shoulders.

'I'll take Skye home. We'll see you there,' she said.

'All right. Thanks.' Catie shot her sister a thankful expression. For the first time in longer than she could remember, she could feel what it was like to be supported by her sister. And it was a nice feeling.

23

When she got home from the school, Catie found Skye and Bridget watching TV.

'Hey. What are you watching?' She gave her sister a wary look.

'Just one of those home renovation shows,' Bridget said, in a calm tone. 'We had sandwiches. We didn't know if you'd want any.'

'No problem. I can make something.' Catie stood in the doorway, unsure of what to say. 'Skye. Are you okay?'

'Yeah,' Skye replied in a monotone.

'I had a long talk with your headmistress. She seems good,' Catie continued.

Skye didn't reply or look up from the TV.

'She's said she'll monitor the situation,' Catie added.

'That's good, isn't it, Skye?' Bridget said, gently nudging her with her elbow.

'Great. Thanks,' Skye said in a dull tone.

'Skye. Can we please talk about this?' Catie sat down gingerly at the end of the sofa and put her hand gently on her daughter's socked toes.

'What do you want me to say? We talked about it earlier.' Skye put her arm over her face. 'Leave it, Mum.'

'Umm. No, Skye. I can't just leave it.' Catie frowned. 'This is serious. These girls have been bullying you! It's not okay! I'm really upset about it. I'm upset that you didn't tell me it was going on.'

'I'm sorry you're upset,' Skye said, sulkily. 'But I'm the one that's got the bruises, so...'

'I'm sorry that they hurt you.' Catie had heard some of what had gone on in her meeting with Ms Barrington, but she had suspected that wasn't the full story. 'Was there... anything else that happened? Apart from what you said earlier?'

'God, Mum. What do you think? They're just going to slip me notes that say, *what ho, old girl, you're looking a little off par today*? Yes. They kicked and punched me. Tripped me up. As well as what I said. I can't prove most of it.' Tears sprung to Skye's eyes and she wiped them away with her sleeve.

'Skye. I'm so sorry.' Catie tried to hug her daughter, but Skye pulled away and stood up.

'It's not your fault,' she said, but her face was white with misery, and Catie felt the gulf between them widen. She'd thought, in the headmistress's office, that there had been some kind of connection between them, but it seemed that whatever wall had come down between them temporarily had gone straight back up again.

Skye wasn't willing to let her mother in and Catie didn't know how to reach her.

'Skye. Please let me help you.' Catie reached out a hand for her daughter, but Skye got up and walked out of the room.

'Skye!' Bridget called after her.

'I'm going to my room,' Skye said, looking back at both of them. 'I just need some space. Okay?'

'All right.' Catie sighed, and watched as Skye walked into

the hallway. They both listened to her footsteps get more distant as she ascended the stairs.

'Well. That was quite a day,' Bridget said, raising her eyebrows.

'Yes, it was.' Catie closed her eyes and pinched the bridge of her nose; she could feel a headache coming.

'Do you want to talk about it?' her sister asked.

'I don't know what there is to say. We'll have to watch what happens at school. I mean, I don't want to move her, but I could, if it doesn't improve. I had high hopes for that school, but...' she trailed off. 'I don't know what to do.'

'Well, it was good that you went in,' Bridget said, a little abruptly. She had a strange expression on her face, as if she was holding back a lot that she wanted to say.

'Bridget, I am Skye's mother. Naturally I was going to go to school if they called me.'

'Yeah. Forget I said anything. What do I know? Just the interfering aunt, I guess.' Bridget's eyes had filled with tears.

'Bridget. What's wrong? Why are you being like this?' Catie wasn't sure whether her sister was just upset because of what had happened at Skye's school, or whether there was something else that was upsetting her. 'It's been a tough enough day. Please, if you've got something to say, just say it.'

'I don't have anything to say. Goodnight.' Bridget walked out of the room; Catie heard her treading up the old wooden staircase, and her heart ached.

'Bridget...' Catie called after her sister, but Bridget didn't stop.

She hadn't meant to upset her sister, though she wasn't entirely sure how she had. It had been such a horrible day, and now Catie had managed to make it even worse, without knowing how she'd done it.

Alone, she finally let herself cry.

It seemed unbelievable that Skye would have been suffering

with something as bad as the bullying she was experiencing at school and not have said something.

Catie felt like the worst mother imaginable. She'd sensed that something was wrong, but she'd thought that Skye was just being a normal teenager: moody and wilful. But Skye was being bullied, and carrying around a terrible burden that she had kept from Catie. And that made Catie feel totally and utterly dreadful.

It was even worse that it seemed that Bridget was the one that her daughter wanted to go to when she was sad or scared; Bridget had told her that Skye was being picked on by the other girls, but Catie hadn't done anything about it. She'd tried, but Skye had pushed her away. And that broke Catie's heart: to think that her daughter clearly didn't trust her.

Skye had asked for new trainers, and Catie had said no. She'd asked for the expensive dress when Catie was on the phone to the solicitor, and Catie hadn't had the spare attention to give her, or realise why she was asking. She'd thought that Skye was just after something new because it was trendy, not because she was getting picked on at school for being *poor*.

They *weren't* poor. Catie had a job, though admittedly it wasn't extremely lucrative. And, now, they had Castle View, which had given Catie a degree of financial security she could never have expected. But, the girls at school who had been picking on Skye didn't care about Castle View. They just cared that Skye didn't have the right trainers, the right bag or the right coat. Skye was the new girl, and they had sensed something about her that didn't *fit in*.

And they had made her life hell, just because of that.

The very thought of what Skye must have been enduring made Catie's heart feel hollow. She wiped her eyes and stared into the darkness, feeling hopeless.

She'd met with the headmistress now, and made it clear that any more aggression towards Skye would be unacceptable. But, she couldn't be with Skye every minute of the day. She couldn't be at school with her. How was she supposed to ensure that Skye wouldn't be a target for those girls anymore?

Her phone buzzed; she looked at the screen. It was a text from Matt.

Hey. Is everything okay with Skye?

Fairly okay. I'll tell you about it when I see you she replied.

It was good to see you today. I was actually planning on asking you out again on a proper date. A walk, maybe? We could take a picnic somewhere.

It's not the best time right now she replied. Organising a date with Matt was the last thing on her mind right now. *Let's talk about it next time I see you. Okay?*

Okay he replied, immediately. *Sorry if it's a bad time. I just don't want you to think I don't like you, or don't want to ask you on a date. Because I do. Very much.*

Catie looked at the text for a long moment, then switched off her phone screen. Right now, a date was the last thing on her mind, and she didn't need another reason not to be there for her daughter. Skye was her priority now.

She walked to the kitchen window and looked out, wondering what to do.

All she could do was be there for Skye, and hope that her daughter would open up to her more. She'd monitor the situation at school and check in with Ms Barrington regularly. And she'd be absolutely as present as she could for Skye – and buy her the damned trainers. She would buy her anything she wanted if it made her daughter happy. She just wished that Skye would let her in, and allow Catie to love her again, like she used to.

24

Catriona. Catriona! Help me! I am trapped here.

Catie dreamt that she was standing outside Castle View, outside the cast iron gates, looking in.

In front of her, a man was pacing around the house. His slumped posture and general mien suggested hopelessness; he was wailing and wringing his hands. His clothes, hair and beard were dripping wet.

Catriona. Catriona! Help me! I am trapped. I have been here so long. It wasn't my fault! It wasn't my fault! he cried out, running to the gates and gripping them with both hands.

He began shaking the gates violently, screaming.

Catriona! Please! Please help me!

She woke, sitting up in bed, her heart pounding.

From above her, the now-familiar thudding started. Catie got up, pulled on her robe and ran up the stairs to Skye's bedroom.

Her daughter lay in bed, asleep, but the thudding noise was louder. It was *here,* whatever it was. In this room.

No. Not here. Not Skye.

Catie's fear dissolved, and was replaced with the protective fury of motherhood. She grabbed Skye's school hockey stick that stood in the corner of the room.

The thudding intensified. It sounded as though it was coming from behind the heavy wardrobe. *Thud, thud, thud.*

'Mum?' Skye sat up in bed, rubbing her eyes blearily. 'What's going on? What time is it?'

'It's late, sweetie. There was... a noise,' Catie said, holding the hockey stick aloft and looking around her with wide eyes.

'Mum! What's happening? You're acting crazy!' Catie could hear the fear in her daughter's voice and went to her, dropping the hockey stick and wrapping her daughter in her arms.

'Baby. I'm so sorry.' She tried to calm herself, but her heart was beating wildly and she realised that she was panting: from the panic and exertion. She stroked Skye's hair, taking some deep breaths. 'I heard that thudding noise again. And... I just felt like... I should protect you. That's all.'

She didn't want Skye to know that she thought there was a malevolent presence in her bedroom. She didn't want her daughter to be upset at all, but she had panicked and now Skye thought Catie was some kind of maniac. Despite not wanting to worry her daughter, she had succeeded in doing exactly that.

This has to stop, she thought, wildly, her eyes scanning the room to reassure herself that the man from her dream wasn't standing in the corner of the room. *I can't go on like this. There is something in this house and it won't leave us alone.*

'What the hell is going *on* up here?' Bridget stood in the doorway, rubbing her eyes. 'Guys. It's 3 a.m. Have mercy.'

'I think we have a problem,' Catie said, looking up. 'But I think I know what we can do about it.'

25

'I never told you, but since we moved in, I've had quite a few strange experiences,' Bridget said as they waited for Kevin, the hospital chaplain.

After the fraught night when she had run up to Skye's room and threatened whatever it was that was in the house with her daughter's hockey stick, Catie had asked June from the crochet coven for the number of her hospital chaplain friend. She remembered her mentioning it when they'd talked at the hospital: at the time, she'd thought it sounded absolutely ridiculous. Now, she was ready to accept whatever help she could get.

Catie was making a pot of tea and looking in the cupboard for a milk jug; she'd already put some cake on a plate on the kitchen table. 'Like what?' she turned and looked at her sister. 'You didn't say.'

'You didn't tell me about the thudding noises and the weird dreams until I found you brandishing a hockey stick in Skye's room the other night.'

'Fair. I didn't.' Catie sighed and picked out a packet of biscuits from the cupboard. 'These too? Or is that too much?'

'How would I know? I don't know what's usual for an exorcism. Isn't it supposed to be holy water, not tea and cake?' Bridget shrugged.

'I don't know either!' Catie exclaimed. 'It's weird we're doing this at all.'

'I know, but it's worth a go, right? We have to try and put this thing to rest, whatever it is. And if June recommends this guy, then...' Bridget trailed off. 'Well, we might as well.'

'What strange experiences?' Catie prompted her sister. More than anything, she was relieved that they were communicating. After their argument, the night after being called in to Skye's school, they had maintained a tense silence for a week or more. Catie wasn't sure what had changed, but Bridget seemed to be talking to her again.

'Oh. Weird dreams. About a man with a beard, stamping around the house. A few times I woke up and I thought I could hear someone walking around.' Bridget looked embarrassed.

'Why didn't you say anything? That's similar to what I heard. Thuds in the middle of the night.'

'Dunno. I don't believe in that kind of thing. I just thought, it's an old house. Nothing to worry about. Or it was a funny dream. I've always had weird dreams,' Bridget said.

'It would have been pretty helpful to know I wasn't going completely mad,' Catie replied, laying the biscuits on a plate.

However, she was oddly grateful that Bridget was going along with this craziness at all. In fact, her sister seemed strangely supportive, which was completely unlike her.

The buzzer from the gate rang, loud and harshly in the hallway.

'Oh! That must be him.' Catie jumped.

'Calm down. You're like a cat on hot bricks.' Bridget rolled her eyes; Catie ignored it. Her sister still annoyed the hell out of her, and she supposed she always would. She still doubted that they could make a year of living together.

They both went to the door; Catie pressed the button that

opened the heavy cast iron gates at the end of the short drive, and she and Bridget watched as a small, ordinary looking man approached the house.

She didn't know what she'd been expecting, but it wasn't a man wearing a SCOTTISH RUGBY bobble hat, blue jogging bottoms and a grey hoodie under a thick blue coat. He was possibly in his sixties, chubby with a grey beard that was still hanging on to a couple of black stripes. As he approached the front door, Catie stepped out to meet him and held out her hand.

'Kevin? Hi. Thanks for coming. I'm Catie and this is my sister Bridget,' she introduced them.

'A pleasure. Misty, this morning, isn't it? The haar's down,' he remarked. The fog that could often lie over the loch would sometimes lift in an hour or two and be burnt off with the sun, but some days it might blanket the whole village in thick fog for the whole day.

'Yes, it's thick today. Come in. I've made tea.' Catie stood aside and welcomed him in.

'Well. It's a treat to see inside Castle View,' Kevin said as he walked into the wide hallway and took off his bobble hat. 'I never thought I'd be invited in, and it's been such a mystery for so long, eh?'

'Apparently so.' Bridget took his coat and hung it up on an antique wooden coat stand next to the bottom of the stairs. 'I think I was dimly aware of it when we were kids, but the whole thing about there being rumours and stuff kinda passed me by.'

'Ah, yes, plenty of rumours.' Kevin nodded. 'I have to admit, in my line of work – that is, the house clearances, which isn't what I do most of the time – I always wondered if the rumours were true about it being haunted.' He followed Catie into the kitchen.

'Tea?' She gestured to one of the chairs at the kitchen table, and Kevin sat down.

'Lovely. Thank you.'

'Help yourself to cake.' Catie cut some slices of the fruit cake and put a side plate – one of the blue and white patterned set that had been in the kitchen when they'd moved in – in front of him.

'Don't mind if I do,' he said, taking a thick slice. 'Thank you very much. Cake is always appreciated.'

'Most welcome. I got that one at the bakery stall in the village. Have you been?' Catie asked, pouring tea into one of the matching blue and white cups and saucers. 'Milk?'

'Just a splash. Thank you. Ah, yes. That's a lovely stall. I quite often get one of their granary loaves. And their brownies are to die for.' Kevin chuckled and patted his tummy. 'As you can see, I tend to indulge rather more than I should, but, as I always say – life is for living.'

'Indeed. Cake is one of the great pleasures of life,' Catie agreed. She was making banal chitchat, but she was using the time to assess Kevin and feel him out a little. Talking about nothing in particular was a great way to get an insight into someone's energy, Catie always thought. She often had these little, apparently meaningless chats with customers in the library and they served a good purpose. You subtly could check in with people that way without ever having to ask them difficult questions.

'So how does all this work?' Bridget cut into Catie and Kevin's exchanging of pleasantries. Catie shot her a disapproving look. 'Sorry. I don't mean to be rude. I'd just quite like to know. We haven't done anything like this before,' she added, in a more conciliatory tone.

'No, no, you're right to ask.' Kevin took a sip of tea and placed it gently back in its saucer. 'What do you want to know?'

'June said she knew you from the hospital. You're the chaplain there?' Bridget asked.

'I was, back in the day. We worked together about ten years.

Now I mostly do counselling for those that need it, but I'm more or less retired.'

'How do you become a hospital chaplain?' Catie asked, out of genuine interest. 'I don't think I've ever met one before. Though I had to stay in hospital when I was a kid, so I wonder if I saw one then.'

'You may have done. That would probably have been before my time, though. I was a normal vicar before making the move to chaplain.' Kevin nodded. 'Was it a serious illness?'

'Yes. Leukaemia.' Catie exchanged a look with Bridget.

'Oh, dear. You poor little poppet.' Kevin tutted. 'Well, you seem all right now, so I trust that the Lord led you towards healing.'

'Yes. I've been clear many years,' Catie said, shortly. She still found it hard to talk about.

'Hmm. That's good. I wonder if you still think about it, though?' Kevin took a bite of cake and looked at her, keenly.

'Umm... Yes. I do. I worry that it might come back,' Catie confessed.

'Do you?' Bridget sat down opposite Kevin and poured herself a cup of tea. 'I didn't know that.'

'I don't like to talk about it,' Catie said, feeling uncomfortable. 'It's just a silly fear.'

'It's not, hon. You were really sick. You could have died.' Bridget reached for her sister's hand across the table. 'There's nothing silly about that. But you know it's not coming back, right?'

'I *don't* know that. You don't either,' Catie said, quietly. 'But that's not what we're here to talk about.'

'Okay, but we can talk about this later.' Bridget frowned.

Catie gave her sister a direct stare that said *can we not talk about this right now?*

There was a brief silence. Kevin cleared his throat.

'Well, to answer your previous question, the resident

hospital chaplain might well have counselled your parents when you were young. You're sort of there to help people out in matters of faith at those crunch times that can sometimes occur in hospitals. Challenging times. Tests of faith. And quite often we'd talk to people who weren't religious at all, or people who have a different religion to yours. We had a team of four – I was the Church of Scotland person, I had a Muslim colleague, a Jewish colleague and an interdisciplinary faith colleague at the time, but any of us would talk to anyone if needed. You're still there to be a support to people, if they want it. That's where counselling skills come in handy,' Kevin said.

'Wow. It's the sort of thing you never really know about. Until you need it, I guess,' Catie mused. 'Sorry. I just... I want to stay focused on what we're here to do today, if that makes sense. Not talk about the past.'

'I understand. But I'd happily have a chat to you another time about any past issues that are still troubling you,' Kevin said, kindly.

'All right. Maybe.'

'Fine. Now. As to the house clearance.' Kevin finished his tea and tapped his fingers on the wooden kitchen table. 'I was trained as a Church of Scotland Minister in the basic exorcism techniques. Which is basically prayers and holy water,' he added. 'People don't really think that's something that we do, but it is. You'd be surprised how often you get asked to do this kind of thing. And, as June may have mentioned, there were a few times in the course of my hospital chaplaincy that I was required to... clear a space, as it were.' He steepled his fingers together.

'We've got something that likes to make noises in the night. Thuds. Screams. That kind of thing. Will that get rid of it? Prayers and holy water?' Bridget raised an eyebrow.

'Quite possibly. I seem to remember that you have a teenager in the house, too? A daughter?' Kevin asked.

'Yes. I actually wondered whether she was doing it at one point, but it was a coincidence. She was up in her room throwing her stuff around,' Catie said.

'Interesting.' Kevin nodded. 'So, I still use the basics I was taught back at theological college. But I have added a few things to my repertoire since then. The benefits of working with some incredibly wise and talented multi-faith professionals over the years,' he chuckled. 'So, we can see what we see, and I'll do what's necessary. But,' he held up his finger, 'I would say that sometimes, it seems to be the case that teenagers – especially girls – tend to spark the recurrence of spirit activity in houses that may have long been dormant. I've seen it a few times.'

'Like that film? *Poltergeist*?' Catie thought of the movie she and Matt had joked about, and both confessed to watching multiple times.

'Oh, right. Yes, exactly.' Kevin nodded. 'I mean, that was a little sensational, of course. But the principle applies. Teenagers are very sensitive. Quite often, when there are phenomena in a house, or it just feels wrong and something's off, it's more psychological than anything particularly external. The mind – and energy – is a powerful thing.'

'Are you saying that it might be Skye? Doing all this?'

'Possibly. Completely unconsciously, most likely. Or, sometimes the energy in a house is just a little off. There might have been something bad that happened here; someone might have been depressed here over a period of time. And people pick up on it, if they're sensitive types. Has she been upset at all?' Kevin asked.

'Umm. Yes, she has, actually,' Catie said with a frown. 'It's odd that you should mention it. She was being bullied at school. We only just found out.'

'Ah. Well, that's likely affecting things. And you moved into the house about the same time?'

'Yes. I think so. Nothing weird happened until we moved in

here, though. But I also had quite a few dreams about a man. I don't know who he is,' Catie added, frowning. 'Bridget has dreamt about him too.'

'Ah.' Kevin got up. 'All right. I'll go and have a bit of a walk around and suss the energy out a bit, but I'm going to do a general blessing and releasing of old energy, and we'll see where that gets us.'

'All right. Should we just stay in here, or come with you, or...?' Bridget asked.

'I'll have a potter about, and I'll likely do the blessing at the foot of the stairs,' Kevin said. 'That's where it feels like it needs to go, just from my sense of it so far. But you said there was thudding coming from somewhere upstairs. So, I might do something up there too,' he said. 'You're welcome to accompany me or enjoy your tea. I don't mind.'

'No way. This I have to see,' Bridget exclaimed. 'I'm coming. Cate?'

'Umm... I guess so.' Catie pulled a face; the whole thing made her slightly anxious but she knew it had to be done. 'Let's do it.'

26

Our Father, who art in Heaven, Hallowed be thy name...

Kevin was standing at the foot of the stairs, praying.

Bridget stood next to Catie, watching eagerly.

'What do you think will happen? Do you think, like, stuff will explode, float around, that kind of thing?' she whispered, not taking her eyes from Kevin.

'I should hope not. There's already so much DIY to do on this place.' Catie rolled her eyes. 'Really, Bridget. Nothing's going to happen. I mean, some nice prayers can't hurt. That's about it, right?'

'You don't know. There's definitely something in this house. I feel it.' Bridget shivered.

'Hmm. I think that's your overactive imagination, but sure.' Catie didn't disagree with her sister, but she was – what? Putting on a brave face, perhaps. After all, there had been the dreams, the thuds in the night. Yes, some of that had turned out to be her daughter, but that didn't explain the other nights when Catie had definitely heard things. On those nights, Skye had been asleep. Catie had checked.

However, what Catie really couldn't get over in that

moment was the fact that Kevin was so *ordinary*. In films and TV she'd got used the idea that exorcism – when it happened – was performed by bearded men in frock coats in period dramas or by Catholic priests in black robes, driving the devil out of teenage girls and armed with sizeable crucifixes.

Catie had never for a moment imagined that a fleece-wearing, middle-aged retired hospital chaplain would be the one to do something like this. And she had no idea what would happen – if anything.

Kevin had a bottle of water with him, and as he began a different prayer – Catie thought she remembered hearing it before, a psalm, maybe – he opened it and started sprinkling water around the room.

O God, almighty and eternal, every place is subject to You Who are present everywhere filling all things. You, who accomplish Your Holy Will, be attentive to our entreaty. Be the protector of this dwelling so that, here, no evil will have power to resist You but that by the co-operation and help of the Holy Spirit...

Kevin went into each room, sprinkling the water and reciting prayers.

'I'd expected them to be in Latin or something,' Catie whispered to her sister as they remained at a respectful distance.

'Cat. He's not a Catholic. It's not the Middle Ages.' Bridget shrugged. 'Reckon it all hits the same way, right? There must be this kind of ceremony in all kinds of cultures, and therefore languages.'

'I expect you're right.' Catie watched as Kevin walked up the main staircase. She could hear from the creaks on the ceiling above them that he was standing in the middle of the first hallway. He raised his voice now, and they could both hear what he was saying without any problem at all:

Visita, quaesumus, Domine, habitationem istam, et omnes insidias inimici ab ea longe repelle: Angeli tui sancti habitent in ea, qui nos in pace custodiant; et benedictio tua sit super nos semper. Per Christum Dominum nostrum. Amen.

'See? Latin.' Catie nudged her sister. Bridget shrugged.

Throughout Kevin's blessing of the house, Catie had felt nothing apart from a simple curiosity.

But, suddenly, she felt a shift. It was as if there had been a constant hum in her ears that had just stopped, and replaced with sudden quiet. She darted a look at Bridget to see if she had felt it, but her sister was scrolling on her phone and seemed oblivious.

Catie could hear the prayers continue from above her head. Now, Kevin was moving around the rooms, his voice muffled.

As she looked around, she remembered the version of Castle View she had seen in her dream.

In the alternative Castle View, she remembered that the house was lit with old fashioned gas lamps, giving it a warm glow. A crystal chandelier hung above, lit with hundreds of candles. The candlelight reflected in the crystal, refracting what seemed like thousands of flitting, glittering fairy lights over the dark green flocked wallpaper that lined the walls.

She remembered the heavy wood furniture from her dream; the tall mahogany grandfather clock with an inlaid design of the phases of the moon. She remembered the heavy green velvet curtains.

And, as she turned to the far wall, she remembered the portrait that she had seen in her dreams.

A young, bearded man in a tweed jacket. A hooded falcon or some kind of hunting bird perched on his outstretched arm. Catie had dreamed of it. But she suddenly realised that she had seen that painting in real life, and it wasn't in the house. It was in the library, of all places: on a wall at the end of one of the library stacks. The library had a number of old paintings in it, which went with its Arts and Crafts décor. But, Catie had forgotten the painting until now.

She couldn't deny what she'd dreamt: a voice, asking for help. But, maybe, her brain had supplied a convenient image to go with it: a face she had seen elsewhere, and subconsciously remembered.

> *Lord, enter graciously into the home that belongs to You; construct for Yourself an abiding resting-place in the hearts of Your faithful servants, and grant that in this house no wickedness or malicious spirits may ever hold sway. Through Christ our Lord. Amen.*

Catie could hear Kevin's voice now, loudly. She could hear him ascending the second set of stairs and making his way into Skye's room at the top of the house.

'It's done.' Kevin nodded, calmly. 'The house is cleansed. And I think I found the source of that thudding noise.' He pointed to a tabby cat that bolted down the stairs, past them all, jumped wildly onto the sofa and started to purr. 'This little madam was hiding behind your daughter's wardrobe. There was a racket going on when I went up there, so I pulled it out a little and there she was. There's a loose floorboard back there, I don't know if you saw it. She's likely got some way in and out because she doesn't look like she's been trapped up there. But she's obviously been trying to get past the wardrobe without much luck.'

'Oh, my goodness!' Catie cried out in relief. 'So, Castle View wasn't haunted after all?'

'Oh, I don't know about that. There was definitely an energy here,' Kevin said, sagely. 'But I wouldn't say a haunting, per se. A real haunting is fairly rare. But, houses can hold on to sadness, like I said. Someone was sad here for a long time. And angry, I'd say,' he shrugged. 'But I think we've said goodbye to all of that now.'

'Right.' Catie nodded, though she didn't have to be told. Catie *knew*. Whatever the presence was that had lived in Castle View for all this time, it had gone. 'Thank you, Kevin. We appreciate it.'

'You are most welcome, dear,' Kevin replied, looking keenly at Catie. 'Do you feel better?'

'I do, actually,' Catie said, surprised. 'The house feels... lighter.'

'Aye. And you have a task still to do, I think.' He nodded, thoughtfully.

'Yes. I think so. Though I'm not sure what,' she admitted. 'How do you ...?' she trailed off.

'You get an inkling, when you've done this kind of work long enough.' He shrugged. 'Sometimes, in cases like this, the spirits – the presences, energies, if you like – in a house might have been dormant a long time. And then they get activated when someone new moves in that has a bit of sensitivity or openness to them. You and your daughter, I'd wager. Possibly all of you.' He glanced at Bridget.

'And of course, if there's a family connection, that also comes into it. Other cultures believe that our ancestors remain with us and watch over us. They're with us in our DNA, of course; that's the most logical explanation. But I personally have come to believe that they can stay with us as guardians, sometimes.' He walked back into the kitchen and retrieved his coat from the back of the chair.

'You think... the presence in the house. It was guarding us?' Catie frowned. It certainly hadn't felt like a protective spirit. If anything, it had freaked Catie out more than once.

'No. But it's linked to you, and it wanted your help,' Kevin said, pulling his SCOTLAND RUGBY knitted hat back on and doing up the buttons of his coat. 'I would advise keeping an open mind if ideas come to you in the coming weeks. Anything about the people that used to live here. Finding out more about them. Finding out their stories. If that avenue opens up, I would say, follow it.' He gave them a kind smile. 'There might still be something that needs a release.'

'All right.' Bridget's tone was dubious. 'So, what do we do now?'

'You should both eat and drink something. Keep a window open. Have a salt bath if you're concerned. But you should both be fine now. It's done. This house is blessed now.' Kevin gave Bridget a reassuring pat on the shoulder. 'But of course, any problems, let me know.'

Catie went to the tap, poured herself a glass of water, and drank half of it. 'Thank you, Kevin. We really appreciate your time. Can we pay you?'

'No, no.' He held up his hands in an open gesture. 'I don't need paying. If you'd like to do something, make a donation to St Benedict's Hospice.'

'Of course. We'll do that. Thank you.' Catie nodded.

'Well, I'll leave you to it, then.' Kevin gave them both a gentle smile. 'No rest for the wicked. And, by that, I mean it's the Six Nations this afternoon, so I'm off to the pub to watch Scotland v Italy.'

'Ah. Good luck.' Catie smiled.

'Luck is what you make it, dear,' Kevin chuckled, as Catie opened the kitchen door and stood aside so that Kevin could make his way out of the side of the house. 'And I feel that the three of you have a lot of luck ahead of you. But, you must follow the signs, and your intuition.' His expression darkened for a moment. 'There was a heavy energy in this house. It's gone, but there's something about this family... a legacy... something. Something remains to be done.'

'I felt that too.' Catie rested her hand on the doorknob, looking out at the afternoon mist. The haar hadn't lifted off the loch all day, and the atmosphere outside was ominously grey.

'Hmm. Indeed.' He pressed her hand for a moment, and gazed at her, though not in her eyes. It felt as though Kevin was looking just above her head, at something only he could see. 'A legacy. Even though the presence is gone... it wanted me to tell you that. A story. That's what I got.'

'All right.' She smiled, a little awkwardly. 'Thank you.'

'Pleasure, dear.' He waved, and walked out towards the heavy iron gates. Bridget had gone into the hallway to press the button to let him out; slowly, Catie watched as the heavy iron gates turned on their hinges with an aged creak.

A story. A legacy. But whose story? she wondered, as the gates closed behind Kevin. Whose legacy was still waiting to be told?

27

'Hey. Can you give me a hand?' Catie was hanging up some posters advertising Reading Rocks outside the library when Matt approached, just in the nick of time. 'Hand me that stapler, just there? Thanks.' He handed her the library's ancient, heavy-duty metal stapler and Catie stapled the edge of the sign to a ribbon, then tied the ribbon to a useful bit of stonework outside the library entrance.

Reading Rocks was almost upon her, and Catie still felt like she had tons to do.

They hadn't texted any further since the night of the house cleansing. Catie hadn't quite known what to say, but she had thought about going on a date with Matt quite a bit, and come around to the idea that it would be a nice thing to do.

Since the house clearance, everything had just felt a lot *lighter*. Catie had been getting on better with Bridget, and she seemed to have fewer anxieties in herself. The night before, knowing that she was going to see Matt today, she realised she was looking forward to seeing him, and looking forward to the date he'd mentioned: a picnic sounded lovely. She felt like she could definitely do with some light-hearted fun right now.

When he'd mentioned it before by text, she hadn't been in the right place to really follow it up. The next day, she'd texted Matt to say that she'd catch up with him when she next saw him at the library.

'Looks good. Not long till the big launch, eh.' Matt shielded his eyes from the midmorning sun and smiled up at her. 'Here. Let me help.' He held up his hand and guided her back down the ladder she was standing on.

'Thanks. This thing is ancient. We should probably get a new one, it's wobbly as a blancmange.' She grinned as she stepped down carefully, trying to ignore the delicious feeling of Matt's hand on hers. 'How are you?'

'Enjoying hearing the word "blancmange" dropped casually into conversation, for one thing.' He grinned back. 'Going back in?'

'Yeah. It's just me today. Lilian has an hospital appointment.' Catie apprised the sign above the library. 'Looks all right, doesn't it? I've put some up around the village, left some posters in shops and stuff. Hopefully it gets people interested.'

'I'm sure it will. You've worked really hard on this. It's going to be great.' Matt followed her inside the library, where Catie had put up colourful bunting and made displays of exciting new books. 'The site just needs a bit more tweaking and then it'll be up and ready.'

'When will it be done? By the end of the week would be perfect.' She went to the kitchenette and flicked on the kettle. 'Tea?'

'Coffee, if you have it. And if you need it by the end of the week, then it will be done by the end of the week, milady,' he said.

'Have you heard? There's been a petition in the village. About the rent increase.' She busied herself, making the coffee. 'It's there on the counter.'

In fact, Sheila had brought in the clipboard and asked to leave it at the issue desk so that people could sign it.

'What?' Matt frowned, and turned back to the desk. He picked up the clipboard which held a number of pieces of paper, all with lists of signatures. He swore under his breath. 'I didn't know this was happening. So, like, what kind of increase was it? I thought it was just going to be five per cent or something.'

'No. It's way more than that.' Catie frowned. 'I thought you and Hal talked about it.'

'We did.' His expression was dark. 'But... I didn't know it was this bad. I didn't realise...' he trailed off.

'I told you before, Matt. I told you that if I hadn't been lucky enough to inherit Castle View, Skye and I would have been screwed.' Catie turned to face him, a cafetiere in her hand.

'Right. I know you did. I guess... I don't know. I didn't realise this was as big of a thing as it is.' He bit his lip.

'Well, it's not your fault. It's something Hal has to sort out.' Catie shrugged. 'It's him that decided to turn into some kind of money-grabbing landlord. Sorry. I know he's your brother. I always thought he was a good guy, but this is just... disappointing,' she added.

'Hmm.' Matt looked as though he was going to say something, but pursed his lips and said nothing. There was a silence.

Maybe I shouldn't have said anything, Catie thought. She felt bad for him; she knew she was putting him in a difficult position. But, Matt was a Cameron, after all: the wealthy landowners of the village. There was always going to be a "them and us" situation if she talked to him about this kind of thing. Blood was thicker than water, as the saying went.

'Actually, there was something else I wanted to tell you,' he said, leaning awkwardly against the kitchenette door.

'Oh?' She poured milk into a mug and smiled, warmly.

'I'm going back to California.'

The words rang in the silence of the library.

That was not what she expected him to say. Catie's throat felt suddenly thick and heavy as an insecure feeling took hold of her heart.

'What?' she asked, faintly.

'Yeah. There's a business opportunity there.' The tone of his voice said that he knew it was a shock; knew that this was unexpected.

'California?' she repeated. 'But... I thought... there's the wedding, and Reading Rocks... and...'

'I'll have finished the platform for you by the time I go. I'm off at the weekend,' he said, not meeting her eyes. 'I'm sorry that we won't have time for our date, after all,' he added.

'That's okay,' she said, belying her feelings. It wasn't okay, but she'd be damned if she said it. 'And the wedding?'

'I have to leave,' he repeated, mulishly. 'When an opportunity happens, it's not going to wait around for some wedding.'

'But... It's not just *some wedding*. It's your brother.' Catie tilted her head in surprise. 'You're really not going to go to? They'll be so disappointed.'

'Catie. With all due respect, that's my business. Not yours,' Matt said, suddenly cold.

'Right. Sorry.' She turned her back to him and made herself a mug of tea. The change in his manner was so abrupt that it shocked her.

'My ex has a startup and she's asked me to invest and consult. It needs a lot of intensive presence in the first phase,' he said, in the same cold tone. She turned around to face him.

'Your ex?' She thought immediately of what he had said about her, once: she was glamorous, beautiful, vivacious. A knife twisted in Catie's stomach.

Why? she thought. *He isn't yours. He never was. You just went on one and a half dates, that was all.*

But, somehow, the thought of Matt leaving the country to

be with his glamorous, beautiful and vivacious ex-girlfriend made her feel ill. She had finally allowed herself to go out with Matt Cameron, and now he was abandoning her to go to America.

'Yeah. Angelica.'

Angelica. Even her name was beautiful. Catie's stomach clenched uncomfortably.

'Right. What kind of business is it?'

'Media. She's got some big investors interested. It could be the thing I've been waiting for,' he said, and she thought she could detect a sense of awkwardness in his voice.

'Oh. Well, good luck with it.' Catie painted a smile on her face and turned to face him. 'Thanks for all your help with Reading Rocks. It seems like very small potatoes compared to a media empire. But we appreciate it, nonetheless.'

'It's not small potatoes. I really enjoyed helping you out with that,' he said, in a quiet voice. 'I've really enjoyed getting to know you, too, Catie.'

'Hmm. Yes, it's been nice,' she said, businesslike. She didn't want to reveal her feelings at all; it was best if Matt just disappeared off to California and they never saw each other again. She could think of him as a fond memory of a flirtation with a younger man. That was all.

That's all, she told herself, sternly. Even though there was a part of her that had wanted more.

'I'm sorry that it worked out like this. I thought I'd be around for longer.' He sounded regretful. 'I really did want to see where it went, between us. I feel like, though, with you and me, it's just been... things didn't align. I don't know. Wasn't meant to be, maybe.'

'There wasn't really a you and me,' she said, with a horrible ache in her heart. 'Don't worry about it.'

'Okay.' His eyes met hers for a long moment. 'Well, for what it's worth, I'm sorry.'

'Sure. Well, I'd better not keep you,' Catie said, far more breezily than she felt. 'I'm sure you've got things to do before you leave and I've got a lot to catch up on before the launch.'

'Catie... I wish things could have been different,' he said, looking chagrined.

'But they weren't,' she said. 'Goodbye, Matt.'

28

'Listen. I could really do with a cup of tea about now.' Catie took a deep breath, and let it go slowly. She had got home at the end of what felt like a long day in the library and found Bridget in the kitchen.

'Fine. I'll make it.' Bridget took the teapot to the sink, drained what was left, shook the wet tea leaves into the food caddy and began making a new pot. 'What's going on? You've got a face like a wet Wednesday.'

'Thanks.' Catie sat down and reached for a biscuit; she ate it in two bites and reached for another. Immediately, she felt the sugar taking effect, restoring her energy a little.

'It's nothing,' she sighed. 'Just stupid stuff.'

'You don't want to talk about it?' Bridget continued what she was doing; her tone was level.

'Not really,' Catie said. She hadn't opened up to her sister about Matt at all, and it felt strange to talk about it now. But, at the same time, she was desperate to share her feelings with someone. And then she thought, *oh, for goodness' sake. You're being exactly like Skye. This is what was so frustrating when she did it. And you're a grown adult.*

And so, screwing up her bravery, Catie said, 'It's a guy.'

'I see.' Bridget raised an eyebrow. 'Matt?' she added, not missing a beat.

'How did you...?' Catie trailed off.

'Who else was it going to be? Kevin the vicar? Come on.' Bridget gave her a hard stare. 'It was obvious.'

'How was it obvious?!' Catie exclaimed.

'Oh, please. The way you looked at each other when we went up there. I was a bit sick in my mouth.' Bridget made a face. 'He obviously likes you.'

'Anyway, it doesn't matter now. He's going back to America,' Catie said, weakly.

'Oh, Cate,' Bridget sighed. She set a mug of tea in front of her sister, and then enveloped Catie in an unexpected hug. 'I'm sorry.'

'It's okay. Nothing really happened between us. But, I thought... I don't know. I thought it might,' Catie said, into Bridget's shoulder: she was surprised by her sister's show of affection.

'I'm sorry, Cate. That sucks. You haven't liked anyone since Greg,' Bridget said.

'I know. I... I really liked him.' Catie fought back tears, pulling away from the hug. 'I dunno... I finally felt like I was allowing myself to have fun, and enjoy life a bit more. I've been so bloody *responsible* for so long, and suddenly, here was this fun, hot guy who wanted to bring a little bit of joy into my life. We got on so well. He made me laugh. He was so sexy. And *nice*, you know? I don't think I've met anyone like him before. Ugh.'

'I'm sorry, babe. That's rough.' Bridget sighed and shook her head. 'Love sucks.'

'Well, I'm not sure it was love, but, yeah. I agree with the sentiment.' Catie rubbed her eyes. 'I didn't think you ever worried about me. I didn't think you cared.' Catie picked up a biscuit. Bridget placed the pot of tea on the table between them.

'What's that supposed to mean?' Bridget asked. 'You're my sister. I love you.'

Catie stared at Bridget for a long moment. 'Bridget. You know as well as I do that we haven't said that to each other in a long, long time,' she said, finally. 'That things have been... tense... between us, forever, really.'

'I know. But I still love you.' Her sister sat down and looked at the wall. She looked as though she was trying to find the words for something. 'I... this is hard to say, Catie.' She took a deep breath. 'But I think I have to tell you. I think... it's something to do with the house clearance, or something, but I feel like something has shifted and I... I *can* finally tell you this.'

'Tell me what?' Catie frowned, worried about what Bridget was going to say. It sounded intense.

'There's something that you never knew.' Bridget bit her lip anxiously. She picked up the teapot and poured tea into both of their cups.

'Knew what?' Catie asked, taking the cup distractedly. 'Knew what, Bridget?' she persisted.

'Whatever. It doesn't matter.' Bridget's voice wavered: Catie could tell that she was holding back tears.

'Well, it does matter, clearly. I can hear that you're upset,' Catie replied, patiently. 'Please tell me.'

'It was a long time ago,' Bridget said, letting out a long sigh. 'It doesn't matter. I shouldn't have said anything.'

'No, Bridget. I can't forget it. I won't.' Catie laid a hand on her sister's arm, but Bridget shook it off.

'Let it go, Catie!' Bridget spun around to meet her sister's eyes; Catie saw that her eyes were brimming with tears. Her sister looked terrified. 'Please!'

'Bridge. What on earth is wrong?' Catie felt deeply

concerned now. There was obviously something that was really troubling her sister, but she had no idea what it could be.

'I... I can't tell you.' Bridget looked downcast. 'It's too hard.'

Catie took both of her sister's hands in hers, and looked earnestly into Bridget's eyes. She took a deep breath.

'Bridget. Please. You're my sister, and despite the fact that we haven't managed to agree on anything in the last twenty years, I love you. I've always loved you and I always will. Please let me help you.'

Bridget stared back into Catie's eyes for a long moment, not saying anything. Catie wished in that moment that she could read her sister's thoughts. However, she could read Bridget's emotions: she could feel the pain resonating through her sister's body as if it was her own.

'I love you too,' Bridget said, quietly. 'But there's something I've never forgiven you for, and it's been eating me alive for years.'

'What? Tell me. I'll fix it. Please, Bridge.' Catie hadn't called her sister Bridge for almost as long as she could remember, and the impact of that old nickname made her sister's eyes widen. It took Catie back a long, long way, into their childhood. 'I know it was difficult for you, when I was ill. I know that I took up all of the attention. I know that Mum and Dad probably didn't have a lot of time for you then. But I couldn't help that. We were just children,' Catie said, gently.

She knew that it wasn't her fault that she had been so ill. She had had leukaemia; it was horrible luck, but it had arrived completely out of the blue.

The first time, the treatment seemed to work, but then the leukaemia had come back, three years later.

She had been six, the first time: her sister was four. When it came back, Catie was nine, and Bridget was seven. And that second time was what really scared Catie: the sudden realisation that this peril could return at any time, whenever it wanted to. Before then, her child's perception had been that being ill was just something that happened to you, and then you got better and you were never ill with that same thing again.

Learning that there were some things that could go away and then come back – things with teeth, that could kill you – was terrifying.

The first time, Catie had been too young to really realise much of what was going on. She'd been old enough to know she was ill, and she remembered feeling weak, and feeling pain. But, she had also been in the misty fug of childhood, and much of it was forgotten, after.

Catie had felt guilty for being ill; particularly when she was older. Guilty for demanding so much attention. She had never wanted to be ill; had never asked to be the special one. And in the years after it had gone, even when she was officially in remission – when she had resumed her life, gone to secondary school, re-entered the life of a tween with all its attendant friendship dramas and the life of a teenager opening up in front of her, a fragile rose of possibility – all that time, and to this day, the thought that the leukaemia might return had haunted her.

'I know that you couldn't help being ill. God, don't you think I know that? I never blamed you for that. It wasn't your fault, and I hated it when you were ill. I hated seeing you in that hospital bed, so weak, wired up to those machines. I hated that disease.' Bridget shook her head.

'Well then, what is it? Tell me.' Catie squeezed Bridget's hands. 'Bridge.' She repeated the childhood name she had called her sister, as if it was a magic charm that would unlock whatever secrets Bridget was holding so deep within her. 'I don't want you to be sad. Please talk to me.'

Bridget looked at her feet. She didn't say anything for a long time, but Catie continued to hold her hands, hoping that somehow the love that was flowing through them would help her sister have the strength to talk.

'When you were ill the second time, Mum and Dad sent me away to school. Do you remember that? It was for a year. Brown Hill Academy for Girls.' Bridget finally met her eyes. 'I was seven. It was a boarding school.'

'I remember. I didn't want them to send you away,' Catie said, truthfully. She hadn't wanted Bridget to go, but their parents had been adamant. They had said that Catie needed the space to recuperate; that they needed to focus on her recovery, and that Bridget would be happiest at a place she could get the support and structure she needed.

'I didn't want to go,' Bridget said, her voice choking up. 'And... I never told them, or you, but I hated being away. I was so lonely. Brown Hill was supposed to be this caring place, I think Mum and Dad chose it because it had all these great ratings for pastoral support or something. But the truth was that the girls were savage, there. Maybe they had behavioural issues, I don't know. In retrospect, they were probably sent there for similar reasons as me. Their families needed some respite, they didn't have time to look after them properly, so they thought that sending them away would be the best option. Like, it would give us stability, or something. It didn't.' Bridget's face crumpled.

'What happened there?' Catie asked, dreading what her sister was going to say, but needing to hear it. 'Tell me.'

'I was bullied. Terribly.' Bridget let out a long breath. 'So, when I found out that the same thing was happening to Skye, I couldn't stand the thought of it. That's why I wanted to support her. Talk to her.'

'And why you were so upset with me. You didn't think I was protecting her,' Catie said, the pieces of the puzzle falling into place in her mind. 'Was that why you were so angry with me, all these years?'

'Yeah. And with Mum and Dad. I know that it wasn't your fault. But it was just a lot to deal with. It was bad enough that you were ill. I loved you so much. You were my big sister. You were everything to me. But then I got sent away and I had to fend for myself with these... these girls who were intent on making my life a misery.' Bridget started to cry. 'Cat. I'm so sorry. I should have told you.'

'Oh, darling. Please, never be sorry for that. Or anything.' Catie pulled her sister into a tight hug. 'I'm just appalled that you coped with that, all on your own, and never told anyone. That must have been so hard. I'm heartbroken for you.'

'It was horrible. I thought I would have to stay there forever. I thought you were going to... to... *die*.' Bridget's voice broke, and she sobbed onto Catie's shoulder. Catie felt the violence of her sister's grief shake her body, but she held on tightly.

'I am so sorry that you had to experience that. Mum and Dad shouldn't have sent you away,' she said. 'And I'm so sorry that I was so ill. I missed you when you were away. They wouldn't let me do anything but write you those postcards. Do you remember those?'

'Yeah. They were a lifeline. I'd get phone calls from Mum and Dad, at the beginning. But Matron said that the school discouraged excessive home contact, as it made us sad and less able to concentrate on school life. So, they stopped calling so much. I'd hear from them about once a month. And we were told to sound cheerful when parents did call.' Bridget stood back and released herself from Catie's arms.

'Probably they were thinking about the image of the school, or something. No boarding school wants parents dealing with weeping kids at the end of the phone. I guess when you send your kids away, you have good intentions, and once they're gone, you want to think they're happy. And children are hard-wired to please their parents. I got the message, loud and clear, that I was expected to be happy. So, I made sure I sounded happy. But I cried myself to sleep every night. Nobody came. Nobody ever came to help.'

'Oh, Bridge. I am so, so sorry.' Catie felt a fist of grief clench its fingers in her chest, as if it was catching her heart and her lungs in its fearful grasp and crushing them.

'It's okay.' Bridget wiped her eyes with the back of her hand. 'Well. It's not, but there's nothing we can do about it now. It happened. Fortunately, I didn't have to stay there forever, and you didn't die.'

'But it ruined our relationship, Bridge. Because you were so hurt. And I understand that. I would have felt the same,' Catie said. 'I just wish I had known. I wish you would have said something. I know that Mum and Dad would say that, too.'

'I know. I have to talk to them.' Bridget let out a long breath. 'I just always thought... it was better left in the past, you know? When I got home and you were better, they were so keen to have a new start. It was all about the future, and I could see that they so desperately wanted to be happy. They wanted us to be happy.'

'So, we played happy families for them.' Catie nodded. 'I felt the same. Because I'd been so sick, twice, I always felt like I'd been enough of a burden. I never wanted to be a problem.'

'Me either. But I was so angry. And I guess I took it out on you, because I couldn't take it out on them. I don't know why. I just felt like I couldn't.'

'I get it. I understand.' Catie sighed deeply. 'Wow. This was a lot, huh.'

'Yeah.' Bridget gave a wry laugh. 'Sorry for being a fuckup, I guess.'

'Same,' Catie chuckled, wiping her eyes. 'And, we're not. We just had to deal with some big stuff when we were kids. And, as much as I love Mum and Dad, they should have talked to us about all this. Or sent us to therapy or something.'

'Yeah, maybe.' Bridget shrugged. 'But people didn't do that, then. We just had to deal with things.'

'But we didn't. I don't think anyone does, not on their own,'

Catie said. 'Especially not when these things happen to you when you're a child.'

'You're probably right.'

'Wow. I think that's the first time I've been right in at least thirty years.' Catie chuckled. 'God. Never mind tea. I could do with a drink. What about you?'

'Could murder a glass of wine.' Bridget nodded. 'I think we deserve it.'

'You're right. I think we're allowed.' Catie got up and went to the cupboard. 'Let's start as we mean to go on. From now.'

'What, tipsy?' Bridget followed her. 'I could do that. Just slightly toasted every day for the rest of our lives. We could be those mad old sisters up in the house on the hill that everyone avoids.'

'Well, though I am invested in that idea.' Catie got a bottle of red wine out of the cupboard and two wine glasses. 'I was thinking more that we could make a new start, here in the house. As friends.'

'Friends, huh. I suppose it could work.' Bridget shrugged. 'Friends that drink together, stay together.'

'You won't get any argument from me.' Catie poured wine into each glass and brought them back to the table. 'Bridge. I missed you.'

'I missed you too, Kaybear,' her sister said, wiping her eyes. Hearing her sister's pet name for her was the thing that pushed Catie over the edge: she started to cry.

29

'Ladies. Welcome.' Hal stood in front of the grand stone fireplace in the drawing-room Catie remembered from her previous trip to the castle. However, today, the mood was more sombre than Catie's visit here with Bridget. There was still tea, in the same Cameron clan bone china as last time – and a plate of chocolate biscuits – on the low coffee table in front of the sofas where she and the crochet coven sat, but they weren't here for scones today.

'Thanks for making the time to see us, Hal,' June said. She was always elegantly dressed, and today she wore a long rose-pink knitted cardigan over a matching long knitted dress. She wore a cream-coloured scarf tied over her short grey hair and a statement burnished gold necklace glowed against her dark brown skin. 'We are here to submit this petition on behalf of the village.' She handed him a bound sheaf of papers which, Catie knew, contained the names and signatures of almost all the inhabitants of Loch Cameron.

'We know that you've got the weddin' comin' up, Hal,' Sheila added. 'An' we really dinnae want tae cause ye any unnecessary stress. We are happy fer ye. But we cannae stand by while the whole village suffers over this rent increase.'

'Thank you,' he said, gravely, taking it and turning its pages. 'I appreciate you comin' to me, and for bein' so honest.'

'You know we are nothing but honest, Hal,' Mina, another member of the crochet coven, said, a little archly. 'Quite how you thought you could increase the rents by the amount you have, across the board, and not have the whole village up in arms, I don't know.'

'It wasnae somethin' I had much choice about,' Hal sighed, and ran a hand through his hair. 'I'm sorry. But I purposefully kept the rents down for as long as I could. Rent has been lower than market rate in Loch Cameron for some years. Significantly lower.'

'So, why did you have to put all the rents up?' Catie asked. Like everyone, she was mystified. 'Why now? What changed?'

As she sat there, her phone flashed. It was a message from her mum. Panicked, Catie picked it up and read it.

Just wanted to let you know that Dad had his first session with the speech therapist today and it went really well. Jane, the new carer, has moved in and she's already doing wonders. When you have time, pop by. We'd love to see you.

Catie's heart had started to race, ready to hear bad news. Her mum never got in touch unless something had gone wrong, and any conversation that Catie had been able to have with her over the past few weeks had been fraught.

This text, by contrast, was a huge relief to receive.

I'm so happy to hear that Mum, Catie wrote quickly. *I'll give you a call later.*

Thanks. I'm sorry if I've been difficult recently her mum replied. *It's been stressful with your dad. I think I said some things to you that I didn't mean, and I want you to know that I love you very much.*

Catie felt emotion choke her throat.

Thank you. I love you too she wrote back.

It was the first time in a very long time that Catie's mum had told her she loved her. Catie made an effort to focus back on where she was, but it was an emotional moment.

'Well, basically, the Loch Cameron estate – that's what I look after, as Laird – has a certain amount of money an' business interests. Most o' that is invested. An' the upkeep o' all the property, the local infrastructure, the castle, it all costs. A lot,' Hal began. 'Now. Some years back, the estate invested in some tech businesses that we were assured would be safe. My brother, Matt, oversaw those investments. An' they did do well. Good news for Loch Cameron. So, when Matt came tae me after that and asked fer investment in his own tech business out in America, I said yes. Because he's my brother, but because he also showed a lot of good business acumen in those previous choices.'

'You're saying that... you lost money because of *Matt*?' Catie asked, catching up with the conversation. So, the gossip she'd heard was, in essence, correct.

'Aye,' Hal sighed. 'So much that I had no other option but tae look at increasin' the rents.'

'Couldn't you have sold one of the Cameron businesses?' June asked, eyeing Hal beadily. Catie thought that, as lovely as June was, she wouldn't ever want to get on her bad side.

'Isnae that simple.' Hal shook his head. 'If we sell the salmon business or the nursery, it'd mean we'd slash future income. That would then threaten the village in just the same way.'

Catie thought of Matt, when they'd spoken about the rent increases. He had seemed surprised at the severity of it. Had he not understood the repercussions of his actions? He'd said that he and Hal had disagreed about the decision, but the way Matt had said it, he made it sound as though it was Hal who had just come up with the idea, and Matt that had disagreed.

Now, Catie was learning that was very much not the case.

'When you say you invested in Matt's company, and it lost money – was that just bad luck? I mean, investments are always a gamble.' She was trying to give Matt the benefit of the doubt.

'My husband Sanjay and I run our own company. We have investments. We have managed not to lose large amounts of money,' Mina interjected, frowning. 'Investments are not a gamble if companies are managed well. I think what Hal is saying is that his little brother did not manage his business very well at all.'

'Aye. That's about the size of it,' Hal sighed. 'I trusted him an' I didnae ask tae see the financial plans. I was stupid. I wouldnae do it again, but Matt's family.' He looked sad. 'I didn't think anythin' would go wrong.'

Catie was furious. She felt deceived. She would never have gone out with Matt or even given him the time of day if she had known the truth: that he was some kind of rich playboy wastrel, investing the family money in his own shaky business concerns.

'So, what are you going to do about this, Hal?' June prompted him. 'There are many village residents who won't be able to make ends meet. It's going to make life significantly more difficult for them. There is strong public opinion about this.'

'I know,' Hal admitted. 'An', as I say, I am grateful tae you all for coming up here to talk about it. I don't know yet how I will solve the problem, but perhaps selling one of the Cameron businesses is the only way. You have my word that I will put it right.' His voice was low and gravelly.

Catie believed that Hal cared about the problem they had put before him; Hal Cameron was a sincere, honest person. She could see that, and she knew that was his reputation. But it was one thing for someone to say they would do something, and quite another for a problem of this magnitude to be solved.

'All right, then, Hal,' June said, echoing Catie's thoughts.

'We do trust you. But you have to stay in touch with us about this. We won't just be fobbed off with well-meaning platitudes.'

'Oh, I know that you won't.' Hal nodded. 'You have my word, ladies. I'll be in touch soon.' He stood up. 'Now, if you'll excuse me, I have a wee mountain of tasks tae do, wi' the weddin' comin' up, an' no' least all o' this to sort out. I'm sure you understand.'

'Of course.' June stood up, beckoning the rest of the group to do the same. 'Thank you for your time. We appreciate it.'

'We are looking forward to the wedding!' Mina tapped Hal's arm as he guided the group of women out of the room and into the wide hallway towards the main entrance hall. 'Is Zelda very excited? We can't wait to see her dress. Have you seen it?'

'Ach, no. All under wraps.' Hal chuckled, being the perfect host and chatting to Mina and the rest of them as he walked them out. Yet, Catie could detect a tension under his pleasant manner; Hal was worried. Matt had left his brother with a horrible problem to solve, and Matt had disappeared off to America with apparently no care for what he had left behind him.

It didn't look good. And it was making Catie doubt her own instincts: how could she have liked Matt so much when he was capable of this? What he'd done was so unkind, immature and irresponsible, that it took her breath away. She had thought that Matt was a good guy. She'd liked him. A lot, if she was being totally honest with herself. And, now? Now, she just thought she'd had a lucky escape.

'I'm sorry...' she said, quietly, to Hal as he ushered them all out. 'I know this wasn't your fault. I... I thought Matt was better than this.'

'Ah, Catie.' Hal lowered his voice so that the other women couldn't hear. 'He is. I've always believed in my brother. This was... just a mistake. We all mistakes, from time to time, eh? Dinnae think too badly of him for it.'

'It's hard not to,' she confessed.

'I know. But I also know he thought a lot o' you. Don't be too hard on him, eh,' Hal repeated, as Catie walked out of the front door. 'An' I'll see you an' the family at the weddin', I hope?'

'Of course.' Catie nodded, smiling as Matt closed the heavy main door to the castle behind them all.

Matt had *thought a lot of her*, apparently. But not enough to consider staying in Loch Cameron and not running off to California at the first invitation from his beautiful ex-girlfriend.

Catie sighed. Whatever she had had with Matt, it was over now. And she was sad about it, but there was nothing she could do, apart from be grateful for the reminder that he had given her: that it was okay to want a little joy and affection in her life, and to welcome it when it occurred.

She followed the other women onto the gravel drive, thinking that even if Matt had royally messed things up in Loch Cameron, then he had at least still given her a gift. That was the way to see it. He had given her the gift of pleasure, and she would remember that in her life going forward. She might even re-join a dating app. Matt wasn't the only man in the world, after all. Catie could find other dates, and enjoy at least some of them.

'You all right, hen?' Sheila asked as Catie climbed into the passenger seat of her car; she had offered to drive Catie back down into the village. 'I noticed you became a bit distracted when we were in there. Something on your phone.'

'I'm fine.' Catie cleared her throat. 'My mum texted me. She was telling me that my dad had his speech therapy and it had gone well. He had a stroke,' she explained.

'Ach, I know. June told us that she had a chat tae ye at the hospital. Poor fella. I know your mum and dad, of course.' Sheila reached across and patted Catie's hand. 'We've been takin' food up tae them. Casseroles, curries, pies, that kindae thing.'

'Have you?' Catie did a double take. 'I had no idea, Sheila! That's so kind!'

'Of course, hen. That's what we do.' Sheila waved her hand as if to indicate that it was nothing. 'Your poor mum doesnae want tae be cookin' as well as everythin' else that's goin' on.'

'I'm amazed she let you,' Catie confessed. 'She wouldn't let me or Bridget help at all. I've been trying, believe me.'

'Ach, I can believe it.' Sheila chuckled. 'But it takes a ballsy woman tae argue with me an' Mina. We didnae give her much choice.'

'Oh. I see.' Catie laughed. 'Just turned up and thrust a casserole dish into her hands, eh.'

'More or less.' Sheila drove away from the castle, and Catie watched as it grew smaller in the rear view mirror.

'We did the right thing, goin' up there, aye. Hal had tae know how people feel,' Sheila said, as she guided the car down the long, rhododendron-filled drive.

'I absolutely agree.' Catie turned towards Sheila. 'I'm glad I went. I'm glad we told him.'

'Aye. Me too.' Sheila shot her a grin. 'The coven has tae stick together, eh. An' protect the village. It's what we're here for. Tae keep the powers that be on track, an' hold them tae account.' She patted her hand on the steering wheel, as if to emphasise her point.

'Is that what the crochet coven does? I thought it was a lot of cake and gossiping,' Catie replied, a twinkle in her eye. 'And casseroles, apparently.'

'Aye, there is that, too,' Sheila chuckled, as she stopped at the tall, wooden gates at the end of the long gravel drive, waiting for them to open onto the road beyond. 'But it's all in a good cause. Community cohesion.'

'Right,' Catie chuckled. 'I must remember that.'

'You must, dearie.' Sheila nodded sagely. 'Otherwise, what

else is there? We've got your back. No one has tae suffer in silence in Loch Cameron. We willnae stand fer it.'

'It's funny, isn't it?' Catie mused. 'Gossip is such a negative term. But you're right. It's not a bad thing for people to share news, talk, make sure people know what's going on. I see it at the library, too. People get so lonely. They need community.'

'The word gossip is only negative because it's traditionally women that do it.' Sheila pursed her lips as she drove back to the village, over the narrow blue-painted bridge that spanned a narrow point of the loch. 'I seriously believe that we're providin' a service. We care. We've always cared.' She looked thoughtful for a moment. 'An' the thing about middle aged women is, we dinnae give two hoots about speakin' up if somethin's wrong.'

'That's true. It's a good thing,' Catie agreed.

'An, might I say, dear,' Sheila added, looking over meaning-fully at Catie in the passenger seat. 'The other good thing about bein' a middle-aged woman is tae have the wisdom tae be able tae enjoy a good thing when it comes along an' be secure enough in yourself tae know that whatever happens, you've got your own life tae live. That young man, the laird's brother – I know ye had a likin' for him. But ye mustn't dwell on him leav-in'. There'll be another one along directly, if that's what you want. Believe me. No shortage of men in the world. Sometimes I wish there was.'

'Thanks, Sheila,' Catie said, quietly, as they pulled up outside Castle View. 'I appreciate it.'

Was she sad about Matt?

Yes.

Would she survive?

Also, yes.

She'd been through so much in her life already that being disappointed over a man ranked fairly low in the scheme of things. But, still, she was sad about it.

And maybe it's okay to be sad, she thought. *Just like it's okay to feel whatever happiness you felt when he was around. Maybe all life is, is feeling our feelings.*

Ugh, she thought, a little playfully, *feelings suck. But, I guess I'm glad I have them.*

'Ah, you're welcome, dear. See you at the library, eh. Remember. Plenty more fish in the sea, aye. If you've a mind tae go fishin' in the first place,' Sheila called after her as Catie got out of the car.

Catie waved as Sheila pulled away. It felt good to be a part of the community of Loch Cameron, and today had been a good reminder that, despite whatever happened in her love life, there was a network of friendship available to her in the village. And that, in itself, was a valuable treasure.

30

'I'm delighted to announce that Reading Rocks is now open!' Catie exclaimed, standing on a chair in the middle of the library and blowing a whistle that Lilian had brought in.

There was a round of applause from the attendees: not a bad turnout, Catie thought, as she surveyed the room. A number of the crochet coven had come to support the launch, plus a group of children from the primary school, Dotty from the Loch Cameron Inn, Fiona, who ran the local fashion boutique, and the local hairdresser. Plus, there was a smattering of some of Loch Cameron's elderly residents: Catie suspected that they might be in attendance mostly for the free food, but that was okay by her. The library was an important part of the community; a place for everyone.

'So, for the next month, we challenge you all to read as many books as you can, and register your reads online! If you haven't seen the page on the library website yet, Lilian and I can take you through how to register,' Catie explained. 'And, we have hard copy booklets that can be filled in, if you don't have internet access or would just prefer to do it the old-fashioned way,' she added, smiling. 'The people who have read the most books at the end of the month will get a book token – and, of course, the satisfaction of having read lots of brilliant books.'

She smiled, happy that her project was finally going ahead. It had been a lot of work, but Catie was proud of it. The online portal all worked beautifully and she'd had posters, bookmarks and reading log books designed up and printed with some extra money from the laird. There seemed to be interest in the project from the village, which was all that she had really wanted: to inspire people a little, encourage them to engage with the library more, and to enthuse people about reading again.

Mentioning the Reading Rocks online portal made Catie think about Matt: it was his hard work that had made it happen, and she was grateful for his help. Regardless of him leaving so suddenly – and even though she had learned about Matt's part in the rent increase – she remained grateful for his help. He had listened patiently, made her what she wanted, tested it, tweaked it when it wasn't quite right. As well as sorting out all the library's IT systems for good. Since Matt had started helping out at the library, the issuing software hadn't crashed once.

'Help yourself to food and drinks,' Lilian added, from the back of the room. 'All generously donated by our Thursday crochet group. And have a good look around the library – come and choose your first books for the challenge!'

There was a cheer, and Catie stepped down from the chair. She looked up to see Hal Cameron making his way through the crowd.

'Catie. Hi,' he said, holding out his hand. 'Sorry I'm a wee bit late. I wanted tae come down an' support Reading Rocks.'

'Oh, hi, Hal. Thank you, that's very kind.' Catie shook the laird's hand.

'Of course. I'm a big reader myself, so I know how important stuff like this is. An' I'm so glad we've got someone like you tae make the most of the auld place. I've always loved the library. Used tae come here when I was a bairn.' Hal looked around fondly at the dark wood shelves and the beautiful carved wood decorations that Catie and Lilian had taken time to polish with beeswax. 'It's lookin' lovely. Well done.'

'Thank you. I appreciate it. And thank you for the budget for the materials, and for Matt's assistance,' she said. 'Despite everything, he was a huge help. I wouldn't have been able to get Reading Rocks off the ground without him.'

'You're welcome.' Hal nodded, though Catie could see that the mention of his brother made him slightly uncomfortable.

'Is there... any word, from Matt?' she asked, cautiously.

'No.' He smiled at her, kindly. 'I'm afraid that's my brother. He does this sometimes. Disappears. He'll be back at some point, but...' Hal sighed. 'Matt finds it hard tae be home, I think. Since we lost our parents, but particularly our mother.' He looked sad. 'They were very close. I dunno,' he sighed. 'I wish he was gonna be here fer the weddin', but... Not tae be, I guess.'

'I'm sorry, Hal.' Catie nodded, her chest aching. She had really tried not to think about Matt since he'd left, but it was hard. She missed him, despite everything.

'Ye have nothin' tae be sorry for.' Hal gave her a warm smile and reached into his pocket. 'Anyway. I also wanted tae give ye this, since Matt said ye were askin' if we had any keys for Castle View. Ye have a wall safe, I think he said?' He handed her two old-looking silver keys with ornate ends. 'This is all I have, apart from the main keys tae the house. They were in a box in the store room where my father kept things related tae the various properties.'

'Oh! Thank you, Hal.' Catie had been so busy with Reading Rocks recently that she had forgotten the wall safe. She'd looked everywhere for the key and found nothing. 'That's great.'

'Welcome.' He nodded. 'Anyway, I should get back, I just wanted to show my face, and give ye the key. Weddin' prep is intense right now,' he chuckled. 'We've got a gang o' Zelda's

American friends flyin' in tae stay at the castle today, so it's all hands on deck tae get the rooms ready.'

'Oh, my. Good luck!' Catie said, raising her eyebrows.

'Aye. An' we'll look forward tae seein' ye at the weddin, I hope?' he asked, kindly. 'I know that it might be a wee bit strange, wi' Matt no' bein there? I know ye had dated a little. But we'd still love ye and the family tae come. We've invited yer mum and dad, if they feel up tae it.'

'I'm planning on coming, with my daughter and my sister,' Catie said. 'They're really looking forward to it. I don't think I have a choice not to come, to be honest. And I don't really know if Dad will be able to make it, but it's really kind of you to invite them,' she added.

'Ha. Right ye are.' He nodded. 'Well, the whole village is invited. So, they're more than welcome, if they want tae come.'

'Thanks, Hal. That's really nice of you,' Catie said. 'Can I ask... did you come to any conclusions about the rent increase? When we came up to the castle, you said you were looking into it...' she trailed off, feeling a little rude for asking. But it was important. *I have a right to ask,* she thought. *I care.*

'I'm sortin' it out.' He nodded. 'Can't say too much right now, but should be able tae update everyone soon.'

'Okay.' She turned the key over in her hand. 'Thank you, Hal.'

'Nae bother.' He smiled, and made his way out of the library, stopping to greet the children on the way and say a few words to Sheila, Mina and June, who were busy making teas and handing out cake.

Catie wondered what Hal *sorting out* the problem of the rent increase was going to look like, but for now, she had to think about Reading Rocks. She slipped the keys that Hal had given her into her pocket, and made her way to the issue desk, where a queue was forming.

~

Later that evening, after she'd made dinner, washed up and done all the usual housework tasks she did at the end of the day, Catie reached into her pocket, remembering the keys that Hal had given her.

She found Bridget and Skye in the lounge, watching TV. Since they'd had the house blessed by Kevin, things between them all had become far more harmonious. There were far more evenings now when all three of them would watch a movie after dinner or spend time together rather than disappearing to their respective bedrooms. Plus, they now seemed to own a cat, which Skye had called Fluffy. Catie had applied flea medicine, fearing that it might be feral, but it seemed happy being a pet. She'd fitted a cat flap to the kitchen door and now Fluffy could let herself in and out when she wanted, without making a noise in the hole in the wall behind the wardrobe in Skye's room – which Catie had now closed off.

'Hal gave me these. Shall we try the wall safe?' she asked them both.

'Oh, my. I can't believe you're still trying to open that thing.' Bridget rolled her eyes, but then she saw the look of excitement on Catie's face and her expression softened. 'Okay. Come on, Skye. Let's go. I can tell Mum's excited.'

Catie noticed her sister's kindness, and it warmed her heart.

Skye lifted Fluffy from her lap and set her down on a cushion.

'Actually, I'm quite curious to see what's in it,' she said, grinning.

Catie was so relieved that her daughter seemed to be happier recently. Catie was keeping in close touch with Ms Barrington at Skye's school, and there hadn't been any more incidents since she and Bridget had gone in. Skye was opening up more, talking about her worries as and when they came up rather than stewing about them alone in her room, and she'd made a couple of new friends that were also interested in fashion.

After they emptied Skye's wardrobe enough to move it again, and had shunted it away from the wall safe, Catie tried the first key. It fit the lock, but it wouldn't turn. She tried a couple of times with no luck.

'Damn,' she muttered. Her shoulders slumped. If neither key worked, then the wall safe would stay closed forever.

Catie realised, with the prospect of never knowing what was inside it, that she *really, really* wanted to know.

Although Kevin had "cleared" the house, there were still a lot of questions left in Catie's mind. Why had Great-Aunt Isobel left clues for her and Bridget to follow around the house, and what had really happened with the fire on Half Moon Lane?

'Bad luck. Try the other one,' Bridget said, encouragingly.

Catie fit the key into the lock. The second key fit, as the first one had, but, this time, when she turned it, there was a reluctant – but definite – feeling of the key turning.

The wall safe door swung open.

'Oh my goodness! I can't believe it!' Bridget exclaimed. 'What's inside, Cate?'

Catie reached inside the safe, her heart pounding.

31

If Catie had imagined that the wall safe was full of bundles of cash, expensive jewels or the deeds to a luxury yacht, she would have been disappointed with the single envelope that she retrieved from it.

But, Catie hadn't imagined any of those things. She wasn't by nature materialistic. She had never dreamed of vast wealth and international fame. She had always just wanted to be happy.

She had just been curious. And, when she and Bridget had received the second letter from the solicitor, it seemed all the more true that Great-Aunt Isobel had secrets that she wanted the sisters to uncover. Was this another one?

Catie showed Bridget and Skye the envelope. It was plain, white and ordinary: there was nothing written on it at all. But Catie could feel that there was something inside it.

'Open it, then!' Bridget cried. 'This is so mysterious. It's like living in an Agatha Christie novel.'

'I'm opening it! Be patient,' Catie chuckled. She shook the contents into her hand.

A folded piece of paper fluttered to the floor of Skye's bedroom, and another key.

'Dear lord. Another one?' Bridget exclaimed. 'We should open a locksmith or something.'

Catie bent to pick up the piece of paper.

'This one looks different. It doesn't look like a door key, and it's not as pretty as those,' Skye said, pointing to the key that was still in the lock of the wall safe.

Indeed, the key was flatter than a normal door key, with deeper indentations. Catie turned it over in her hands, but there were no markings on it.

She opened the note and read it aloud.

My dear girls,

If you have found this key, then you are close to unlocking the mystery of Castle View.

I have one final task for you. Take the key in this envelope to Moncrieff's Bank in Edinburgh, with two forms of identification each and my death certificate, which you may obtain from Mr Matthews, my solicitor. He is awaiting your request.

This key opens a safety deposit box at the bank. The box contains the answers to most – if not all – of the questions you may have about me, the house, and our family. I also hope that what you find will help you.

Please forgive an old woman her dramatics, and accept my love.

Isobel

'A safety deposit box!' Bridget exclaimed, taking the letter from Catie and reading it. 'We have to go. We have to see what's in it!'

'Okay, Yes. Definitely.' Catie nodded. 'Oh, my goodness!

This is so exciting! What do you think might be in it?' She sat on the edge of Skye's bed. Skye sat beside her and read the letter for herself.

'Absolutely no idea.' Bridget grinned. 'But it's going to be fun finding out, isn't it?'

'One thousand per cent,' Skye whooped. 'Mum! Can I please make a story for socials about all of this? I promise I won't give any personal information. Not the name of the bank, or anyone's private details. Just, like, showing the wall safe, opening it, the key, that kind of thing. The sketchbooks and stuff.'

'All right. As long as you don't put anything personal in it.' Catie gave her daughter a hug.

'Thanks, Mum!' Skye jumped up and got her phone out immediately. Catie knew that this was important to her – not the making of this reel in particular, but connecting with her friends online. Previously she had scolded her daughter for it, but, now, she understood how important it was for Skye to connect with other kids her age, however she was doing it.

Castle View has changed us all, Catie thought. She thought about how it was when Bridget, Sky and herself had moved in to the mysterious house. How separate they had been from each other; how disconnected. And, over a short time, the house seemed to have worked a strange magic, bringing them together in a way Catie could never have expected. And she was so, so glad.

32

The bank sat on a side street in the city, its stone facades unchanged from when it was built, adorned with carvings of dragons and gargoyles. Now, the stone was sooty and there were places of disrepair, but it still had a grandness about it.

Catie exchanged a glance with her sister as they stood on the threshold of the building; its once-grand stone entrance had been built over with practical and modern glass revolving doors.

'Are we sure we want to do this?' she asked, suddenly unsure.

'Yes. Why not?' Bridget hugged her coat around her as a gust of wind cut down the narrow side street. 'Come on, Kaybear. We came all this way.'

Moncrieff's was an old bank in Aberdeen – ironically, Catie realised that she had probably walked past it several times when she'd lived there. It was strange when that kind of synchronicity happened. She wondered what other hidden secrets she had been close to in her life, and not known: secrets that were fated for her to find, at some point in the future.

'I know. I guess it's just...' She paused for a moment. 'What if we find out something bad? About Isobel?'

'What would we find out that would be bad?' Bridget frowned.

'I don't know. But that fire, on Half Moon Lane... that was bad. What if Isobel was involved with it somehow?'

'Catie. Listen to me.' Bridget rummaged in her handbag, pulled out a boiled sweet and popped it in her mouth. She held out another one for her sister, but Catie shook her head. 'Isobel was family. We have a right to know what's in that box, and when we do know, it will give us clarity. Even if we discover she was a serial killer, at least we'll know. Knowing is always better than not knowing. Right?'

'Right.' Catie nodded. 'You're right. I shouldn't be as cautious. I don't know what I'm expecting, that's all. And I hate not knowing.'

'No one likes mystery. That's why there are all those TV shows dedicated to finding out who murdered the vicar in the small village and what have you,' Bridget sniffed. 'Humans have an innate need to tie up loose ends and know what happened. Goodness knows why; life isn't neat. There aren't as many opportunities for closure and tidiness as you might think.'

Bridget pushed her way through the door to the bank and Catie followed her inside.

'How did you get to be so wise?' she asked her sister, as they entered a modest reception area and approached the front desk.

'I always was.' Bridget gave her a wry smile and turned to talk to the receptionist for a moment. The young man behind the desk listened, looked at the paperwork they'd brought with them, then nodded. 'You just spent a long time not listening to me.'

'Just a minute, ladies. I'll call my colleague to take you to the safety deposit area,' the receptionist said, picking up the phone and speaking quietly to someone at the other end.

In a few more minutes, a middle-aged woman with her hair

in a neat bun, wearing a pencil skirt and smart blouse, appeared in reception and approached them.

'Miss McGovern?' she asked, looking at them both. They both replied *yes* at the same time.

'Very good. I'm Sophie Leavenworth, the assistant manager here. Let me take you down.' She led them to a lift to the left of the reception desk.

Catie followed her sister into the lift, which had an antiquated feel, with a brass handrail and art deco style buttons.

'Lovely, isn't it?' Sophie commented as she pressed a button marked B. 'We've kept as many old features of the bank as we could.'

'It's gorgeous,' Catie agreed. 'I never would have known it was even here, down that little side street.'

'No, I know. But it's a bit of an institution, in its way. It was often used by people who had treasures to keep securely somewhere, because our vault is much more sizeable and secure than many other banks. You'll see when we get down there.' Sophie nodded.

They rode down a few floors until they reached the basement, and stepped out into a very different space than the modest reception area they had walked into, several floors above. Catie was surprised that the bank even had as many other floors as it seemed to, judging from the buttons on the control panel of the lift.

The basement was cool and silent. When she stepped out of the lift, Catie felt a sense of the ground above them pressing down above their heads and shivered involuntarily.

'This way.' Sophie led them down a long corridor that featured many dark wooden doors, all with brass handles. They were numbered, and Sophie led them to room 8. Catie wondered what was in the other rooms; she was intrigued at Sophie's mention of *treasures*. What else was down there?

Priceless paintings? Jewels? Ancient, banned and secret manuscripts?

Sophie flicked on the overhead light, and the room lit up with a soft, gold glow.

'Have a seat.' Sophie indicated a central table made of what looked like a dark oak, and two generous black leather seats that sat against it. 'I'll be back with your box in a moment.' She left, and they heard her walk back into the corridor and open another door.

'I thought the box would be in here,' Catie whispered.

'This just looks like a room they take you where you can look at your stuff, I guess,' Bridget said, looking around at the low walls which featured a couple of framed, nondescript prints of the Scottish countryside and little else. 'They must be very private about the storage areas. I guess that's good.'

'I guess so,' Catie said, looking up as Sophie returned, holding a medium-sized steel-coloured metal box.

'Here we are,' she said pleasantly, placing it on the table. 'Isobel McGovern. The top slides off easily,' she said, demonstrating the movement with her hand. 'I'll leave you with it; there's no rush at all, and when you're ready to go, I'll be in room 7 next door. Just give me a knock and I'll take you back up.'

'Thank you, Miss Leavenworth.' Catie looked up, offering Sophie a smile. 'We appreciate it.'

'Not at all.' Sophie nodded, and left the room.

'Well, here we are, then.' Bridget raised her eyebrows. 'Shall we?'

'Okay.' Catie slid the box open in the way that Sophie had shown her, and they both looked inside.

'Looks like letters. Old paperwork, mostly,' Bridget said. 'And some boxes. Oh my god. It looks like jewellery.'

'Oh, goodness. Open one of them.' Catie leaned forward, intrigued.

Bridget clicked open a red velvet box and took in a deep breath, then turned the box so that Catie could see what was inside.

On a bed of black velvet lay a beautiful triple string pearl necklace with what looked like a large diamond clasp in the middle. Bridget lifted it out carefully and handed it to her sister.

'Wow. That's beautiful. If it's real pearls it would be worth a bit of money now, wouldn't it?' Catie asked, holding it up to the light.

'It must be real. Look at the box,' Bridget said: on the top of the velvet read the name *Cartier*.

'Oh, god. It must be worth thousands.' Hastily, Catie laid it back in the box. 'I don't even want to risk touching something that valuable.'

'There are other Cartier boxes here too. She must have been *loaded*,' Bridget said, picking up four more similar sized boxes. 'I can't believe that great aunt Isobel was this wealthy and we didn't know!'

'It's amazing,' Catie agreed, opening a letter from on top of a small pile that were tied together with a piece of ribbon. 'Oh, my. Wow. Listen to this.'

She read the letter aloud slowly, getting to grips with the old-fashioned style of handwriting.

Dear Frank

I wish you would reply to one of these letters. I write to you ever week, and hear nothing back. The only way that I know you are in the house is from the housekeeper, who tells me that you hardly leave.

There is a lot of ill will towards you in the village. I have asked you repeatedly to try and repair things with the Emerson family, but I know that you will not.

Like it or not, your actions have an effect on me. I don't feel that I can ever come back to Loch Cameron now, but I have tried, where I can, to repair what you have done.

I know that you say it was an accident. No one will ever really know except you and Simon, and Simon has gone.

Castle View is yours to live in for as long as you need it. I will continue paying all the bills, and maintain your weekly appointment with Dr Brown, even though you refuse to attend. If you need anything additional, all you need to do is write to me c/o the solicitor's address above. They will forward all correspondence to me.

Your sister,

Isobel

'Bloody hell.' Bridget looked up from the jewellery boxes, which she had arranged in a line on the table. 'Catie. You know, these necklaces and earrings – look.' She opened another, smaller box, and showed her sister two large round pearl studs edged with diamonds. Each diamond looked about the size of one that you'd find in an average engagement ring. 'They must be worth hundreds of thousands of pounds. I mean, *Cartier*.' Her eyes were wide.

'I know. I don't actually know what we should do with them.' Catie looked up from the letter.

'Skye would love them.' Bridget chuckled.

'I am not giving half a million pounds' worth of jewellery to my teenage daughter to show off on social media.' Catie rolled her eyes.

'No, perhaps you're right.' Bridget nodded. 'Is there a follow up to that letter? I want to know more about this Frank. So, he was Isobel's brother?'

'Hmm. Yes. That makes him our great-uncle. Listen.' Catie read the second letter in the pile aloud.

Dear Frank

I am writing, not because I think you will reply, but because I have contacted the Emerson family and tried to make some reparations with them.

Nothing I can do can bring Simon back, but I have offered to fund a memorial in the village for him, and a fund to support victims of violence in the village. I have donated a large sum to the Laird and he promises me that it will be put to good use.

Simon's family are understandably bereft without their son, and it fills them with terrible grief that you are still in the village. However, I have explained to them that you are my brother and it is therefore my responsibility to provide a home for you.

I think they would appreciate an apology, if you could be decent enough to go to them and at least give them that. I know it was an accident. They suspect otherwise: surely it makes sense to allay their doubts and help them lay their grief to rest as kindly as you can.

Your sister,

Isobel

'Dramatic.' Bridget frowned. 'Are there more?'

Catie flicked through the pile of papers that had been tied with a ribbon.

'Yes. Wait. There's a newspaper clipping.' She read it aloud.

ACCIDENT KILLS LOCAL MAN, INJURES OTHER

The residents of Loch Cameron are shocked this week at the terrible loss of one of their own.

Simon Emerson, of Gowdie Street, was walking with a

friend on the pathway alongside the loch when the ground gave way and he fell into the water. Because of the icy temperature of the water and its depth, his companion – Frank McGovern of Gillington Row, Loch Cameron – was unable to save him, and Emerson died of hypothermia.

The point on the loch path at which Emerson fell was well-known as a perilous spot, raised above the water with a small wooden bridge. While the loch path generally leads around the perimeter of Loch Cameron, and follows the shallow shore line, the bridge and the high mud embankment leading up to it traverses a deep part of the natural lake.

The Laird of Loch Cameron, Donald Cameron, said:

'We are deeply saddened to learn of Simon Emerson's accidental death. Safety has always been of utmost importance on the Loch Cameron estate, and I will be looking into making improvements to the bridge and mud embankment where Simon fell.

'Simon was a much-loved member of the community, and our thoughts and prayers are with his family.'

Emerson's companion, Frank McGovern, suffered frostbite and shock but was otherwise unaffected. He was unavailable for comment.

Emerson was studying art at Glasgow University and was home for the Christmas holidays when the accident happened. He was twenty years old.

Simon is survived by his mother, Patsy, his father, Brian, and his sister, Eleanor. It is the second tragedy for the family, whose cottage had previously burnt down during a fire on Half Moon Lane.

'Oh my goodness.' Catie's eyes widened as she read the article. 'It seems from Isobel's letters... it kind of reads as though Frank pushed this Simon in? Or at the very least, did something on purpose.'

33

'What if there was something suspicious about the fire as well? Something to do with Frank?' Catie's eyes widened, remembering the police report Matt had read aloud to her at the castle. She had told Bridget about it when she'd got home, but, typically, Bridget had thought it was nothing at the time. 'The police report said that Simon went for a walk at the time of the fire, and he was seen with another man. That must have been Frank. Do you think they were in a relationship? I mean, with all the drawings of Simon we found... if they were Frank's, it would sort of look that way.'

'It does.' Bridget frowned. 'It doesn't seem like anyone knew Simon and Frank were an item, though.'

'I guess they didn't feel comfortable being open about being gay here then,' Catie said. 'When was this? Dotty said, thirty, forty years ago.'

'Well, that would be the 80s or 90s. I mean, people were out then. It was a long time since it was illegal.' Bridget shrugged.

'Yeah... but there was still a lot of prejudice. Maybe Frank or Simon had experienced that. Maybe Simon's family were homophobic. Or very religious. Sometimes that means people are afraid to come out to their own families.'

'I guess so. Isobel knew. That much is obvious.'

Bridget rummaged through some other papers in the box. She pulled out a small, burgundy leather-bound diary, no bigger than her palm. On the front, DIARY was embossed in faded gold lettering. 'Oh. Look at this!'

'What is it?' Catie craned her neck to look at what was in her sister's hands.

'I think it was Great-Aunt Isobel's,' Bridget said, flicking to the first few pages. 'Yes. Here, look.' She showed Catie a page where Isobel had written her name in the same copperplate handwriting as the letters were written in.

'What does it say?' Catie asked.

'I don't know, Catie. Generally, you have to read a book to know what it says,' her sister snapped at her, but not unkindly. 'Listen.

> *Frank is out again. He has been impossible since the accident.*
> *Inconsolable. That poor boy was his friend. More than a friend,*
> *I thought.*

She must mean Simon Emerson,' Bridget said.

'It sounds like it.' Catie frowned. 'What else does it say?'

'Oh, you read it. I can hardly make out the tiny lettering.' Bridget handed her the book.

'Okay. Let's see.' Catie frowned at the tiny, neat hand-writing in brown ink.

> *More than a friend, I thought. Though Frank would never have*
> *said it.*
>
> *I asked him what happened, and he told me that they were*
> *walking, they had an argument. Simon pushed him, so Frank*
> *pushed him back. Simon fell into the loch. It was an accident;*

> *Frank panicked. He can't swim. "I wanted to jump in after him," he said to me, on the one moment he would talk to me, "But I didn't. I just stood there."*
>
> *I think he will hold that regret with him for the rest of his life.*
>
> *Frank has always been difficult. I feel pity for him; I always have. But, I also know that he has done wrong in his life and probably will continue to do so.*

'Siblings.' Bridget raised an eyebrow. 'Looks like there were always issues in our family.'

'Show me a family where there isn't.'

'Well, at least we got through it to the other side.' Bridget gave Catie a wry smile.

Catie smiled back, and turned the page. She read aloud again.

> *He never exactly told me what happened when the fire started in Half Moon Lane, but I know that he got home that night stinking of smoke. When I asked him about it, he said "they got what was coming to them" and when I said, "Who, Frank? What have you done?" He turned away with an unpleasant smirk on his face and said "If they don't approve of me, then I don't approve of them.'*

'Bloody hell!' Bridget exclaimed. 'You were right! This is intense.'

'I know. There's more.' Catie returned to the diary.

> January 18th, 1991
>
> *I have left the village. I cannot be there any longer with all the bad feeling towards Frank. He is growing worse by the day: shouts, is violent. The last straw was when he struck me. I*

cannot live at home any longer. It is too small for me to live in with a madman and the walls are paper thin; I hear him pacing at night like a caged wolf.

I fear him. If he started the fire on Half Moon Lane then he has criminal urges. It was luck that nobody was harmed, but Frank's temper is bad. He has never been able to control it.

I can believe that – if he was more than friends with Simon Emerson, which I think was the case – if Simon's family found out about them, then they disapproved. Who knows what may have happened, but Frank... Frank is a man of deep passions who does not always think before he acts.

Now that our parents have both passed away, he refuses to leave the house at all. I have employed a carer to look after him, but goodness knows how long she will put up with his rages. I feel terrible, but I must look after myself too.

I am going away. To America, to make a new life and leave the sorrow of this one behind me.

'Oh, wow. It's so sad.' Catie looked up. 'Poor Isobel. And this would seem to suggest that Frank started the fire on Half Moon Lane. I guess as a revenge? Maybe Simon's parents found out about their relationship and there was some kind of row. Maybe they forbade Simon from seeing Frank. And Frank retaliated.'

'Jeez. That is intense.' Bridget exhaled. 'Do you think that's what happened?'

'I don't know. I guess we'll never really know. But I felt Frank's energy in the house. Didn't you? He was so angry. Sad, too.'

'Yeah. He was.' Bridget nodded, grimly. 'God. Those poor people. If he really did start the fire, he could have killed all of them. Including Simon.'

'Makes you wonder whether Simon's accident was really an accident.' Catie grimaced.

'I know. It's dark, this whole Frank story. Poor Isobel.' Bridget shook her head. 'You know, I want to know how Isobel got Castle View. I don't think she owned it at the point you're reading from. She said the house had thin walls? Castle View has thick walls.'

'You're right,' Catie mused. 'They must have been living at the family home somewhere in the village.' She flicked through a few blank pages, and then the entries began again. 'Oh, wow. Okay. Listen to this. Dated a few years after.'

My life is so different now, I can hardly believe that it is the same me that wakes up in the morning and goes to bed at night.

The fact that I have found a well-paid job here and live such a luxurious lifestyle astounds me every day. Here, I am a well-educated lady and my books are in great demand. Who would have thought that my silly stories about a village not unlike Loch Cameron would sell so well?

New York is a playground, full of novelty. Yet, when I walk in the park here, I compare it to the loch and find it wanting. Still, I have friends here, and a good apartment. I am happy.

Frank worries me. He is no better, and in fact, much worse. I live in constant worry that he will do something awful again, or hurt himself. When I call, sometimes he picks up the phone, but will not talk.

March 3rd, 1994

I have bought a house in Loch Cameron, Castle View.

Though some in the village think that the laird, Donald Cameron, is a hard taskmaster, he has become a correspondent of mine and, over time, I have confessed my concerns about Frank to him.

We began writing when I set up the fund in the village. I was desperate to do something in the wake of Simon's death, and, when I started to do well out here, I contacted the laird and wired him some money. In fact, it was the advance for my third book, Destiny's Secret, which was so large that I hardly knew what to do with it, that I used.

I have also invested in the stock market, and my broker assures me that this is the way I will drastically increase my finances further.

In return, the laird has kindly been keeping an eye on my brother for me, and it was him that suggested the purchase of Castle View. It has long been under the ownership of the Cameron clan, but the laird has some debts he needs to settle; I am not supposed to tell anyone, but he is a gambler and a drinker, and has played a little fast and loose with the family money.

He has offered me Castle View at a decent rate for cash and I am going to take it.

I am not going to live in it, though. The house is for Frank.

Castle View sits away from the village, on its own, on a promontory of rock overlooking the loch and the castle. At Castle View, he will be safe, and safely far away from the village so as not to endanger anyone. Or, at least, as few people as possible.

I will engage a specialist staff to care for him; to keep the house in good condition and to keep him safe and well, so that no one has any cause to complain about my brother ever again.

'Wow. So that was how she came to buy the house,' Bridget said. 'She was protecting Frank.'

'Even though it doesn't sound like he deserved it.' Catie nodded. She turned to the back pages of the diary, which contained lists of names. 'Look at this. Names and dates. Georgia McHale. Charlotte Sweeney. Eliza Beddington. Alan Carstairs. Maybe these were all the names of the staff she hired to look after him. None of them stayed for long.'

'You wouldn't, would you? If Frank was as bad as she says he was.' Bridget shuddered.

'No. It's horrible to think all that happened in our house.' Catie made a face at her sister. 'But it also makes sense. The bad energy. The dreams. Maybe Frank's energy never really moved on from Castle View, after he died. I don't know if what Isobel did was kind or not, in the end.'

'Yeah. But she did what she thought was best, I guess.' Bridget whistled. 'Frank was a wrong 'un, and she knew it. She tried to contain the situation as best she could, but Castle View ended up being Frank's prison.'

'It's a really sad story.' Catie nodded. 'You know, I've been wondering why Isobel stipulated that we had to live at Castle View for a year together to inherit the house. But I think I realise now. She must have known that we were estranged. That we didn't get on. Remember, Mum and Dad said that they used to be in contact with Isobel when we were younger?'

'Yeah. I remember. And then after a certain point they lost contact.'

'Right. Well, I think Isobel must have reflected on the fact that she and Frank had always had this difficult relationship, and if she thought we were heading sort of the same way – without one of us being as troubled as Frank, admittedly – maybe she wanted to bring us back together. So, she made us live together at Castle View. With the hope we'd sort our stuff out.' Catie reached for Bridget's hands and clasped them in hers.

'And we did.' Her sister nodded, squeezing Catie's hands. 'It worked. And I'm glad.'

'Me too.' Catie thought about how far she and Bridget had come. Great-Aunt Isobel had saved them both from a life of sadness and disconnection. 'Is there anything else in that box?' she added, still curious.

Bridget let go of her sister's hands and rummaged in the box again. 'Hmm. Financial stuff. Old statements and chequebooks. Wow. She wasn't kidding. She definitely was loaded. Look at this.' She handed Catie a sheaf of papers detailing large amounts of money going in and out of Isobel's bank account.

'Goodness.' Catie raised an eyebrow. 'That would explain the jewellery. It looks like Castle View wasn't her only asset. Look, she gave a lot of money to charity, too. Look at these letters. Children's charities. Mental health charities. LGBTQI charities.' Catie flicked through a stack of paperwork, all addressed to Isobel. 'She was a real philanthropist.'

'Ah. Look. Frank's death certificate.' Bridget took out a piece of thick, cream-coloured paper. 'Frank McGovern. Died of heart attack caused by prolonged alcoholism. He wasn't that old.' She handed it to Catie, who looked at Frank's birthdate and did some quick maths.

'In his fifties. Not old at all.' Catie sighed. 'The drink killed him.'

'Maybe he could never get over Simon's death,' Bridget said. 'I'm not excusing him. I mean, he was clearly a bad man. But maybe he was also grieving.'

'Maybe. I think what we can take away from this, though, was that Isobel loved him. Despite everything. She tried to care for him as much as she could, in the best way she could think of. And she did all this good, but never wanted anyone to know. Look at these letters from the charities. These huge sums. But the donations were all anonymous. She didn't want thanks and praise. Same with the Loch Cameron fund,' Catie said.

'It's like she was trying to atone for Frank's behaviour.' Bridget nodded. 'Siblings. We're always so deeply connected, even when it hurts. Those years when we weren't friends almost killed me. But I was so hurt.'

'I know. It hurt me too, not to be able to talk to you every day. For us not to be close.' Catie took her sister's hand. 'But, that's over now. Because of Isobel.'

'I'm glad. And, we also own a kickass house. I never thought I'd live somewhere like Castle View.' Bridget grinned.

'It was her last good deed.' Catie wiped a tear from her eye. 'Even beyond death, she was helping people. I can't believe that she kept it all so quiet. All of her good works. She was a legend.'

'She really was.' Bridget hugged her sister. 'She really was.'

34

'Wow. This is *beautiful*,' Catie whispered to Bridget as they joined the queue of people filing patiently onto the private beach at the foot of Loch Cameron Castle.

In front of them, circular rows of chairs had been set up around the focal point of the stone circle that stood on the beach. Every now and again, the sun shone through the clouds and a shaft of light would catch the stones, bathing them in a golden glow.

Around the base of the stones, summer flowers had been arranged in a circle, and the stones themselves had been decorated with pink and white ribbons that made the shapes of hearts and stars. Catie was reminded of the old-fashioned maypoles she'd seen as a child; the stones had the same flower-bedecked, ribbony look that made her think of dancing and merriment. In the space at the centre of the stones, a string quartet were setting up: four young women, all wearing beautiful long, full-skirted tartan dresses with spaghetti straps and scoop necks. They wore flowers in their hair.

Flowers – pink and white roses, the traditional purple thistle of Scotland, and deep pink peonies – garlanded the backs of the chairs. To one side of the seating, a piper in full Highland dress played an upbeat traditional tune.

The whole village was in attendance: clearly, after Hal's open invitation at the Inn weeks ago, people had taken him at his word. And, in the weeks following, formal invitations had also dropped on the mat of every house in the village: Catie had had one at the library, and one at Castle View. It had said:

> *You are cordially invited to the wedding of*
> *Harold Donald St John Cameron, Laird of Loch*
> *Cameron*
> *and*
> *Miss Zelda Hicks*
> *At Loch Cameron Castle, 21ˢᵗ June 2024, 2pm*
> *The ceremony will begin at the stone circle, followed by a*
> *drinks reception, then dinner and dancing in the Great*
> *Hall.*
> *Dress code: Dazzle us!*

Catie wouldn't normally have considered herself dazzling, but she had worn her fanciest dress, which she had, in fact, bought from Fiona's Fashions in the village as Zelda had suggested. It was a full length, one shoulder maxi dress in white with a pattern of blue roses, and Catie felt both comfortable and pretty in it. She didn't usually put "pretty" as a priority in choosing clothes; usually, especially working in the library, she was looking for "warm" since the heating in the building was archaic to say the least. But, today, it had been nice to get dressed up.

Not only that: Catie, Bridget and Skye had each chosen a piece of Isobel's jewellery to wear for the wedding. Catie had felt too self-conscious to wear one of the necklaces, but she'd chosen a large, smoky-coloured diamond ring which fit just right on her middle finger. Even though it wasn't as eye-catching as the necklaces, Catie was all too aware of the weight on her hand and the way it caught the light.

'Are you *sure,* Mum?' Skye had asked, open mouthed, as Catie had spread the Cartier boxes out on the kitchen table in front of them.

'Absolutely. Isobel would have wanted us to wear these. They're too beautiful to be mouldering inside a safety deposit box,' Catie had said. 'And – I've been thinking. Bridge, if it's okay with you, I think we should all take one thing to keep, and the rest, put towards Skye's university fund.'

'That's awesome. And maybe, now that we know about Isobel's investments, we can help Mum and Dad out too.' Bridget had nodded, grinning.

'Yes. I was also thinking that,' Catie had nodded. 'Skye. If you want to study fashion, then we can afford for you to do that now. In London, or wherever you want. But you have to study hard to get there.'

'Yes! Yes, I do!' Skye had whooped and enveloped her mum and aunt in a joint hug that knocked the wind out of them. 'Thank you, Mum!'

Bridget wore a simple pink shift dress, white sandals and a little white cardigan over her arms. She had chosen to wear a diamond teardrop necklace, and it sparkled like a cluster of stars around her neck.

Skye was wearing one of her own creations, which fitted her perfectly: a light blue gingham dress with a fitted bodice, sweetheart neckline and a full skirt. She had chosen the triple-strand pearl necklace and it matched the dress perfectly.

'You look absolutely gorgeous, Skye.' Catie put her arm around her daughter and gave her a squeeze. 'I'm so proud that you made that dress!'

'I know. I want you to make one for me now,' Bridget added as they filed into their seats.

'I'll make you a dress if you want, Auntie Bridget,' Skye replied. 'You too, Mum. If you want.'

'I'd love that, sweetheart. Definitely.' Catie was touched. It had been a long time since Skye had offered to do anything nice with her. 'That would be a really fun project we could do together. We could go and look for a pattern and the fabric at that shop you like in Loch Awe, if you like.'

'I'd love that.' Skye's face lit up, and Catie reached for her daughter's hand.

'So would I,' she whispered.

The crowd hushed, and the piper stopped playing.

'Please be upstanding for the groom!' the piper called out. Everyone stood to watch Hal Cameron walk down the central aisle that split the circle of chairs around the stones. He was certainly handsome, Catie thought, as she watched him make his way to the central point where the local vicar – a friendly, middle-aged woman dressed in a purple robe and a colourful surplice with Celtic style embroidery – stood waiting for him.

The resemblance to Matt was definitely there – Hal and Matt both had the same classic Scots colouring of auburn-reddish hair and blue eyes. Hal was a little taller, but they were both broad in the shoulders and had the same strong jaw and wholesome, ruddy-cheeked good looks. Hal wore full Cameron clan formal regalia: he had chosen a red and white Cameron tartan with a subtle yellow stripe as a kilt, a formal black jacket with tails, white shirt and socks and black leather lace-up shoes. He wore a thistle and floral buttonhole that matched the floral arrangements on the backs of the chairs, and Catie had to admit that he looked very dashing indeed.

However, Catie reflected that there were differences between the brothers. Matt had a more reserved energy. He'd told her he was *a little weird*, and she could see that Hal was the more outgoing brother, as he shook hands with the villagers in the crowd and had a kind word and a smile for everyone. Matt was kind too, but Catie knew he was more introspective and thoughtful. He was the one who had had the vision for a tech business; who had studied coding and left to make a life for himself in America. Perhaps Hal was the more responsible of the two: the more extroverted and community-minded.

Matt was smart, intelligent, a tech wizard. But he was still kind, in a quieter way than Hal: it had been Matt that had sorted out the library systems for her and made them work when the IT consultant they'd been working with for ages couldn't. It was Matt that had made the Reading Rocks portal for her, listened carefully to what she wanted and checked in with her to test that it was the way it should have been. It was Matt that had listened to her talk about her troubles with her family and been supportive.

But Matt was also the one who had mismanaged the Cameron family finances so badly that it had necessitated a rent increase for every tenant in the village – many of whom were on the breadline because of it. That made her furious with him.

Catie had liked him. She'd liked him a lot, but whether she'd liked him a lot or a little didn't matter anymore, because he'd left to go back to America. And he hadn't even stayed for his own brother's wedding, at which he was supposed to be the best man. That said everything that she or anyone else needed to know about his character.

Ben Douglas, the owner of the Loch Cameron Distillery, joined Hal; everyone knew that Hal had had to find someone to stand in for Matt, who was supposed to be standing there. Catie could only imagine how sad and angry Hal must have been when Matt had disappeared. She'd heard, second-hand, from the gossip of the crochet coven how upset Hal and Zelda were, and she could understand why. Despite the fact that she liked Matt – had begun to have feelings for him, even – she thought that if she'd been in Hal's shoes, she would never have forgiven Matt for leaving him in the lurch at the last minute – never mind his putting the estate at risk financially. It was insulting and thoughtless, and showed exactly what he thought of his family, his heritage and of Hal and Zelda's relationship: nothing at all.

The string quartet began to play, and Catie looked around again, watching Zelda make her way down the aisle.

Touchingly, Zelda was accompanied by the owner of the Loch Cameron Inn, Eric Ballantyne – Dotty's husband. Catie assumed that Zelda must have a good friendship with the elderly couple.

Zelda wore a stunning wedding dress: white, full skirted and with an asymmetric neckline and corset which had the kind of punky style of one of Skye's favourite designers, who, Skye had once informed her, had begun her career with bondage-inspired pieces before moving into tailoring, couture and streetwear. Catie didn't know much about the bondage side of things, but she knew that Zelda's dress looked like it was made by a designer. It also featured a tartan sash to match Hal's, and she wore a pearl choker and flowers in her hair.

'Wow.' Skye was open-mouthed as Zelda glided past them, her arm in Eric's. 'That looks like a vintage Vivienne Westwood. I'm sure it is,' she whispered to Catie, who nodded, relieved that she had enough fashion sense to have thought the same. 'She looks so beautiful. And so *cool*.'

Catie smiled fondly at her daughter and the sense of reverence in her voice. It was hard to impress a teenager, especially when it came to fashion, Catie had found, and she resolved to try and introduce her daughter to Zelda Hicks at some point during the day. She had said hello to Zelda a couple of times around the village, but she didn't really know her. However, she knew that Zelda worked on a fancy home interiors magazine in the US, and that she probably had some friends in the fashion industry. It would be inspiring for Skye to talk to her.

Zelda and Eric reached the stones, where Hal stood, gazing

raptly at Zelda. Everyone could see that they only had eyes for each other; Catie was sitting at just the right place to see Hal say *you're beautiful* to Zelda, before kissing her.

It was a touching moment; deep in Catie's heart, a feeling stirred. It was longing.

It was an unfamiliar feeling. Catie had spent so long focusing on being a good mother and on her career after she and Greg had split up that she had hardly thought about love at all. Love was something for novels or TV shows. It wasn't real life, as far as she was concerned.

And, then, Matt Cameron had walked into her life and woken her from a long sleep. *Just like the fairy tale,* she thought. Only, in her case, Prince Charming had caught her attention and then, just when she had got interested, relocated to California, never to be seen again.

That wasn't quite the fairytale *anyone* had read.

But, despite the way it had ended – or, never really begun – watching Hal and Zelda together awoke a longing in Catie's heart. The way that they looked at each other. The energy between them. The wonderful celebration of their love that was this beautiful wedding. The sudden yearning spread from a pinprick in Catie's heart, into a rose of warmth across her chest and through her whole body. *Love.* What it would be to be so loved, and to love someone else so completely?

'Welcome, everyone.' The vicar held up her hands for quiet. 'Please, take a seat. We're here to celebrate the wedding of Hal and Zelda, on this beautiful day in Loch Cameron,' she began, but, suddenly, there was a raised voice from beyond the seating.

'Not without me.'

Catie looked around to see Matt Cameron striding purposefully down the aisle, and the rose of longing that had bloomed in her heart thrummed with a sudden, vivid resonance.

35

When Matt reached Hal and Zelda, he stood uncertainly before them, as if awaiting their judgement. Zelda looked shocked, but Hal stared at his brother for a long moment without saying anything.

'Hal. I'm sorry. I should have been here. I shouldn't have left,' Matt said in a low voice. Everyone could hear, despite his low tone. Catie realised she was holding her breath; she let it go, slowly. But, she could sense the tension in the crowd; everyone was on tenterhooks, waiting to see what Hal would do.

Hal regarded his brother for another long moment, not saying anything, but then Zelda took Hal's hand and turned to Matt.

'Thank you, Matt. We're so glad you could make it,' she said, and leaned forward to kiss her brother-in-law-to-be on the cheek.

Hal gazed lovingly at Zelda, and closed his eyes for a minute with a wry smile. Then, he enveloped his brother in a bear hug.

'Thanks, man. I'm glad you're here,' Hal said. There was an audible sigh of relief from the crowd; there had been a moment,

Catie thought, when it wasn't clear if Hal was going to punch Matt in the nose or tell him to leave. But, sense – and brotherly love – had prevailed.

No one would have blamed Hal for spurning his brother. And there were a fair few sour looks being aimed at Matt from the crowd, as Ben Douglas handed the ring boxes to Matt and stood to one side and the vicar resumed the service.

Despite everything – and despite the whisperings of the people around her, who she knew definitely weren't fans of Matt – Catie couldn't take her eyes off him. He wore the same formal jacket, kilt and shirt as Hal, and he looked incredibly handsome. Catie had only ever seen him in casual clothes, and the effect of his traditional Scottish dress was remarkably sexy.

Her feelings were all over the place, seeing him so unex-pectedly. As far as she had known, she was never going to see Matt Cameron again; he had left to restart his life in California. Did this mean he was back now, or had he simply felt bad about missing his brother's wedding, and flown back for a couple of days? What would she say to him if he came and talked to her? Would he even bother talking to her? There was no reason why he should.

As she watched Hal and Zelda take their vows, her eyes met Matt's across the crowd. He stared at her without breaking his gaze. He didn't smile, but something seemed to pass between them. An intensity of feeling; something that Catie couldn't explain.

'The cheek of it!' Kathy, one of the crochet coven – a girl with two-tone black and white hair wearing a bright red summer dress – muttered, in Catie's earshot. 'He just turns up in front of everyone, after what he did!' she shook her head. 'Not okay.'

It wasn't okay. Kathy – and everyone else in the crowd – knew it. Catie knew what Matt had done. But she couldn't deny

KENNEDY KERR

the chemistry that had flared between them, the second he had walked through the crowd.

'Harold Donald St John Cameron, Laird of Loch Cameron, do you take this woman, Zelda Hicks, as your lawfully married wife? To have and to hold, in sickness and in health, until death parts you?' the vicar asked; Catie tore her eyes away from Matt and focused back on the couple as they held each other's hands and repeated the vows. *Such promises,* Catie thought. *Such love.*

'I do,' Hal said. Zelda repeated the vows, and said *I do.* There were tears in her eyes.

But, Catie could feel Matt's eyes on her, still, and when she looked back to him, he was staring straight at her.

36

'Lovely ceremony. Didn't she look gorgeous?' Fiona, the owner of the local fashion boutique, where Catie had bought her dress for the wedding, held out her champagne glass for a refill as one of the waiting staff walked by. 'I won't say no. Thank you.' She grinned as the waiter filled her glass.

'Miss?' He held the half-full bottle towards Catie and Bridget, who was standing next to her.

'Why not? Thank you.' She accepted, and chuckled as Skye looked pleadingly at both of them. 'Just one, then.'

Skye was technically underage, but she was the same height and weight as Catie now, and it was a wedding. Catie thought that her daughter was allowed one glass of bubbles.

'Thanks, Mum! You're the best!' Skye grinned. Catie thought briefly about how things used to be between her, Bridget and Skye: about how she had always got cross when Bridget and Skye had sided against her.

It was good not to be the one left out, now, and to feel able to be a little more bonded with her daughter. It was nice to feel like the "cool mum" for once, and not the eternal disciplinarian.

'Don't drink it all in one go.' Catie held up one finger in

warning; there was still a sensible level of disciplinarian in her, after all. 'Oh, Zelda looked fantastic. I mean, I expected she would. She's in that world, isn't she? So glamorous.'

'Aye. From New York originally.' Fiona nodded. 'But, you know what? She helped me out so much wi' the shop an' getting' it out there on the socials. It's just gone from strength tae strength in the past few years, an' a lot o' that is because Zelda helped me become more confident in running a fashion business.'

'That's awesome.' Catie nodded. 'Skye makes her own clothes, you know. She made what she's wearing. She'd love to work in fashion one day, wouldn't you, love?'

'No. You made this?' Fiona looked genuinely surprised. 'It's gorgeous!'

'Thanks,' Skye said, shyly. 'I love clothes. This is from a vintage pattern.' She held out the full skirt with one hand, the champagne glass in the other.

'Well, I'm impressed,' Fiona cooed. 'Good for you! Are you going to go to fashion college? You should.'

'I don't know. Maybe. I'd like to.' Skye shrugged.

'You should. And if you're interested in a part time job, I might be able to help you out. I've been thinking that I could do with some help, recently.' Fiona looked thoughtful.

'Really? Wow. That would be so cool! I've been in your shop. You have really cool taste,' Skye chattered, more excited than Catie had seen her in a long time. She watched her daughter with a sense of joy in her heart: it was so good to see her so alive, so enthusiastic. Skye had been in a dark place for too long, and Catie hadn't known how to pull her daughter out of it. She exchanged a warm smile with Bridget; she could tell that her sister was thinking the same thing.

'Bit of a scandal, the young laird turning up, last minute!' Fiona said, her eyes bright with the gossip.

'I know. The cheek of it!' Bridget agreed. 'Catie dated him, you know.' Fiona looked expectantly at Catie, who blushed.

'Well, *hardly*,' she said. 'He was helping me out at the library. I didn't know anything about what he did, until much later. With the rent increases and everything.'

'Ladies, some fantastic looks going on over here.' Zelda, who had been chatting with some of the crochet coven nearby, wandered towards them. 'Thank you all so much for coming. Catie, I heard that your dad wasn't too well. We did invite your mum and dad, but I guess he didn't feel up to it?' she asked, kindly. 'Please do give them our love. The people that couldn't come today, we're sending them all a little gift. Just a bottle of champagne and some wedding cake, so people can celebrate with us in their own time,' she added.

'That's very kind of you, Zelda,' Bridget said. 'Thank you. Our dad is improving slowly. He's got a really great physiotherapist and he's doing speech therapy.'

'I'm glad. Hal said it was a stroke?' Zelda enquired. Catie reflected what kindness Zelda had, to be asking after someone she didn't even know, on the day of her wedding. But, then, that was part of being the Laird's Lady, she supposed.

'Yes. It's been a stressful time, but we're getting past it now, we hope,' Catie interjected. 'Anyway, it's your wedding day! We were all just admiring your dress. It's absolutely beautiful.'

'Oh, you're too sweet! Thank you.' Zelda held out her skirts and did a curtsey. 'This is actually a dress that belonged to Hal's mom. She had quite the couture collection, let me tell you.' Zelda lowered her voice and leaned in towards them, confidentially. 'The late Lady Cameron was a glamourpuss. A hundred per cent. This is a Vivienne Westwood, and I had it altered to fit me, and added the sash. I absolutely love it, though.'

'That's what I thought it was!' Skye exclaimed. 'You can tell by the neckline and the tailoring. It's stunning.'

'Oh, thank you! Something borrowed, something blue,

right? This is something borrowed.' Zelda smiled warmly at Skye. 'You're into fashion, then? And hello, I'm Zelda, I don't think we've met.' She held out her hand and Skye shook it.

'Skye. Hi. Happy wedding day.'

'She made the dress she's wearing!' Fiona chipped in, excitedly. 'Isn't that brilliant?'

'Oh, wow! That's so cool!' Zelda enthused. 'Are you on social media? Do you post about what you make? I love that kinda thing. Like, watching a garment be made from scratch.'

'No, but that's a really cool idea,' Skye replied; Catie could see her thinking about it, and the joy she was already feeling for her daughter intensified. She could see Skye growing more and more inspired around these women, and she was so very glad of it. Catie had thought that sending Skye to the best school in the area was the best she could do for her; that it would be school that would provide her with opportunities and inspiration. But, actually, it was the community of Loch Cameron that had made Skye's face light up.

Who knew? Catie thought. *Who knew that when we moved here to be closer to mum and dad, that this little village would give us so much?*

'Catie?' A man's voice behind her made her heart flutter; there was no mistaking his deep tone, and the way that he said her name which lit a warm glow in her abdomen and her heart. *Matt.*

'Hello.' She turned to find him standing behind her. He looked even better close up, and he smelt good too. He always did. It wasn't anything in particular, just the overall sense of him that made her feel calm and grounded – as well as desperately aroused.

'Hi.' They stood, staring at each other *like a couple of idiots,* Catie thought, but she couldn't stop looking at him, just like she couldn't during the ceremony.

'Do you have a minute?' he asked; Catie blushed, knowing

that Bridget, Zelda, Fiona and Skye were all watching them. But she nodded.

'Sure.' She nodded, trying to seem natural.

'Shall we get a drink?' he asked, though they both held half-full champagne glasses. He smiled his sudden, warm smile at the group of women. 'Ladies. Will you excuse us for a minute?' He held out his hand to Catie, and, baffled, Catie took it.

What is happening? she thought, as Matt led her through the crowd on the castle lawn to a quiet spot next to some topiary trees, overlooking the loch.

'Catie. It's so good to see you,' he began. 'There's something I have to tell you. And it absolutely cannot wait a moment longer.'

37

'What is it?' she asked, wondering what all this cloak and dagger stuff was about. 'I thought you were in California.'

'I was. I came back,' he said.

'I can see that. I think what I was asking was, why are you back and what happened with the new business deal.' *And the ex-girlfriend*, she added, in her mind. *Who, now, presumably, isn't so much of an ex.*

'Straight to it, huh.' A grin tugged at the edge of his lips. 'Direct as ever.'

'Well, yes. Because I'm here at a very lovely wedding with my sister and my daughter, and I don't really have the inclination to be pulled aside for meaningless chats with men who ask me out on dates and then disappear to other countries. After defrauding their families, and forcing their local community into penury.' Catie found herself annoyed by Matt's attitude – never mind the fact that he'd left in such a dramatic fashion, only to reappear unexpectedly.

'Wow. Okay.' Matt took a drink from his champagne and let out a long breath. 'Well... let me address those things one by one. First, I realised that I should be at my brother's wedding.

It's a big deal, I was supposed to be the best man, I said I would be the best man, so I came back.'

'Right.' Catie frowned. 'So, just here for the wedding, then?'

'Maybe.' He looked evasive.

For goodness' sake, Catie thought, exasperated. This was worse than talking to Skye when she was in a mood.

'What do you mean, *maybe*? Matt, you don't owe me anything here,' she snapped. 'Nothing ever really happened between us. You don't have to apologise to me for coming to your own brother's wedding. I mean, well done?! It's what you should have done, so... Great. Excellent. Congratulations on doing what anyone with a shred of decency would have done, without expecting a medal for. I'll be going back to the reception now, if that's all right with you.'

She turned to go, incensed at his overly dramatic behaviour. What was he intending on doing, exactly? Having a fumble with her in the bushes, just because he felt like it? Did he think that just because he looked especially handsome today, and because he'd appeared out of the blue, she was going to drop her knickers for him, no questions asked?

I bloody think not, she thought, fuming at the idea.

'Catie. Wait, please.' He barred her way and held out a gentle hand to stop her leaving the enclosure of trees they stood in.

'What?' she snapped. 'I don't understand what's so important that you had to drag me away from a perfectly lovely wedding reception. And, by the way, I don't know how you have the gall to turn up, considering that everyone here thinks you're a total bastard for making Hal put the rents up for everyone. I cannot believe that happened because of your ineptitude. You know that people are suffering because of you? Quite how Hal decided that was the only option also beggars belief.' She was furious now, and she didn't care if she hurt Matt's feelings.

'Fine. Well, first, yes, I messed up. But when I was back in

California I also called in some debts and released some assets, so I've repaid the money I owe to the estate. Hal won't have to adjust the rents anymore. He can keep them at the low rate they were before. Which, by the way, is quite far below market value.'

'What assets?' she frowned. 'And, yes, that may be true about the rents, and that's something that everyone has always appreciated. Living in Loch Cameron is a lot more possible than it is elsewhere, nowadays.'

'My house. Shares in another business that I'd kept. My cars.'

'How many cars did you *have*?' She assumed that they weren't the basic models that most people in the village drove.

'Well, I'm a motoring enthusiast. I had a Ferrari, a Bentley, a McLaren.' He looked almost embarrassed. 'But, if I'm going to be staying in Loch Cameron, I don't need to keep them in a garage in LA. Nor do I need to keep my house out there.'

'Right.' Catie blinked, taking in what he'd just said. 'I mean, that's great, for the village. I guess I'm wondering why you didn't do that in the first place.' She raised an eyebrow.

'Because, I didn't know Hal was going to do that. I didn't realise it was such a big deal, I guess? And I didn't think I was going to stay here. I thought I was going back to live my life in LA. Because I was a selfish idiot. Okay? I admit that.'

'Well, at least you're self-aware.' She shook her head.

The thing was that, despite everything, she still felt an attraction and a bond with Matt that was undeniable. Yes, she was giving him a hard time. But it was because she felt betrayed: to some extent she had "invested" in Matt. She had invested her liking and attention, and then found out that he wasn't someone that deserved either. That hurt.

'Listen. I haven't said what I need to say, yet,' he said, gently. 'Can you just listen for one minute? Please?'

'Fine. One minute.' She crossed her arms over her chest and raised both eyebrows.

'Catie. I like you,' he began, nervously.

'Fifty-eight seconds. I like you too. So what?' She looked at her watch.

'Oh, for...' he swore under his breath. 'Can you not time me? It's really off-putting.'

'You asked for a minute,' she said, pointedly.

'Great. Okay.' He sighed. 'Catie. When I got to California, I missed you. And I regretted not spending more time with you.'

'Right. But, the way you explained it, it was unavoidable. The new business. The girlfriend. I got the impression you were walking into a whole new life. Or, back into your old life, perhaps. We were never a thing.'

'I know. But I did want us to be a thing.' He ran a hand through his hair. 'Listen. I've been away from Loch Cameron for a long time. I never felt that it was really home for me, you know? I spent most of my childhood away at school, then university. Then we lost our parents, and I was never that close with dad, but losing mum really hurt. I didn't want to be here at all, really.' He took a deep breath.

'I'm sorry. I know you really loved your mum,' Catie said, kindly. Regardless of the situation, she would always feel compassion for someone who had lost someone dear to them.

'Thank you. I know you understand.' He smiled, catching her eye. 'You're a deeply kind person, which is one of the things I... really fell for.'

'Fell for?' She frowned. *What?* She had never allowed herself to imagine that Matt might have real feelings for her. He had flirted with her and asked her out, but surely, he was just amusing himself.

'Yes. Catie, that's what I'm – very inarticulately – trying to tell you.' He took her hand in his. 'The business opportunity turned out to be a fantasy on the part of my ex. She wanted us to get back together, and she manufactured this plan... which I realised was complete rubbish as soon as I got there.'

'Rubbish? How?'

'Umm... basically, she lied about having got investors interested in an old business concept of mine. She knew that it was something really close to my heart, but I could never get it off the ground. I guess she knew how to manipulate me.' A dark expression crossed his face.

'Oh. Wow.' Catie raised an eyebrow. 'That's *really* manipulative.'

'Tell me about it. When I was here, back in Loch Cameron after my previous business failed, I was feeling like I'd lost myself. I'd lost a good chunk of the family money, and Hal was furious with me. I'd left Angelica because the relationship was over; she wanted us to get married and have a baby, but I never wanted a baby. I was okay with her having kids – they were hers, and they were nice humans in their own right, already. I never really wanted to go through the baby stage with anyone, and the urge for my own kids was never really there. And, anyway, she had started being really underhand about stuff, like not taking her birth control and saying it wouldn't be the worst thing in the world if she got pregnant accidentally.'

'Oh. That's not great either.' Catie frowned. 'I mean, I'm not with Skye's dad anymore, but when she was born, she was planned, and we were both happy about it.'

'I know. I know. I should have guessed that all this talk of the business and huge investment was rubbish, but...' he shrugged. 'I really wanted it to happen, you know? I wanted to be a success again. I wanted... I wanted to feel like a man again.' He ended his sentence quietly.

'You were always a man, Matt,' Catie said, softly. She felt for him; clearly, what he was telling her was difficult.

'On the outside. We're all sad little boys underneath, I guess.' He shrugged. 'Look, I have a therapist. I know all this stuff. I've worked through most of it. But Angelica really pushed my buttons, I guess. I guess I didn't realise how much the business failing really hurt me. It really hurt, having to come back home and do as I was told by Hal. And I knew I'd done wrong, you know? But I didn't want to admit it. And then...' he trailed off.

'Then what?'

'And then I met you.' He held her eyes with a deep, meaningful gaze.

'And?' She was being a bitch, maybe, but she felt like it was justified. More than that, though, Catie was protecting herself. Because what Matt was saying cut to the quick.

'And you were so different to any woman I'd met in such a long time,' he continued gazing into her eyes, and now there was nothing but an honest openness there. It made Catie's heart glow with a fierce softness she had only felt a tiny part of, before. Now, it felt like her chest was melting.

'You were – are – kind. And *real*,' he continued. 'You just have this aura about you. Calm. Centred. And you're funny and weird and... really, really hot.' He gazed helplessly at her.

'*What?*' Catie couldn't help herself; she laughed, completely dispelling her previous anger. The notion that she was a hot librarian tickled her. 'Matt. I am a middle-aged librarian that wears cardigans, and the mother of a stroppy teenager.'

'I know.' He was still holding her hand. 'But I love all of that about you.'

'Why?' Catie was genuinely flabbergasted. 'I just don't get it. You had... I don't know. What seemed like a very glamorous life. I mean, I understand what you're saying about your ex, but... I'm not some Californian model. You do know that.'

'Of course I know that. But... you're you, Catie, and that means so much more. I like you. And I've decided to stay in Loch Cameron for a while. I also realised when I was here that I liked it here. I liked being able to make a real difference, even though it was nothing like the work I was used to. I liked being able to help you at the library. And Hal, with the estate. I should have been helping for a long time before now.'

'So, you're staying?' Catie smiled over at Bridget, who was hovering nearby. Her sister gestured to her with a quizzical expression; Catie knew that Bridget was checking up on her to see if she needed rescuing. Subtly, she shook her head.

'Yes. I'll be living at the castle. And I've promised Hal that I'll focus my expertise on helping the village. We've already got some great ideas for things like improving connectivity in Loch Cameron.'

'That sounds really positive.' Catie smiled.

'And... if possible, I'd like to take you on that second date. If you didn't have any objection.' He let go of her hand, and jammed his hands in the pockets of his dress jacket.

'A second date, huh.' She smiled, looking up at him under her eyelashes. 'I expect that's possible.'

'I'd like that.' He grinned back. 'I'd also really like to kiss you now. If that was also possible.'

Catie was taken aback, but Matt had impressed her with his maturity and thoughtfulness. He'd admitted that he'd been wrong, and taken steps to solve the problem. That was what a good man did.

'It is,' Catie said, a wave of anticipation filling her; it felt as though she was suddenly full of bubbles.

She had wanted this. She had tried to forget about Matt, and she had convinced herself that she didn't want him. That he was unsuitable, a bastard, a liar.

But she had wanted him, nonetheless, and, suddenly, here he was, having made everything right, and leaving another continent to find her.

She had to admit that was kind of hot.

She leaned in, a little, and Matt put his hand in the small of her back.

When his lips met hers, she gasped a little at the sudden spark of electricity that fizzed between them. His kiss was warm and tender, but Catie sensed a reservoir of passion behind it.

Her mouth opened slightly, and she sighed involuntarily: a sound of desire that escaped her before she had a chance to control it. It was the sound of her emotional surrender to the kiss: she felt that she was going under, pleasurably, to a place of softness. A place where time stopped, and all that was left was the kiss.

His lips were so soft on hers, and the edge of his tongue caressed them so very slightly, sending shivers down her spine. It felt as though they had all the time in the world to connect with each other, to touch and be touched, to meet with their lips in a new world of sensuality and the promise of so much more.

Matt pulled her closer to him, and she felt as though she was melting into his chest and his strong arms that held her. The kiss deepened. He was still tender, but she felt his unmistakeable masculinity envelop her. She had forgotten everything of where they were, just for those few moments.

Slowly, they stopped kissing, and Catie pulled away, blinking in the light.

'Well. That was... um. Something.' Matt looked slightly shellshocked.

'Mmm. It... errr... certainly was,' she said, also lost for words. The chemistry between them had always been good, but that kiss... she'd never had a kiss like that before. It felt as though it was re-engineering her body chemistry in some kind of subtle but essential way. On a primal level, the moment that she had stepped away from his body, she instantly wanted to be back there, nuzzling against his neck.

'Well, I should be getting back to the wedding.' Catie

looked round, collecting herself and hoping that no one had noticed their moment of passion.

'Sure. So, can I call you? Can I take you out soon?' Matt followed her as she walked back to the reception. *Like a little puppy*, she thought, as she looked at his wide, adoring eyes. She didn't think she'd ever been looked at like that before, and she liked it.

'You have my number.' Catie smiled graciously.

As she walked away from him, she realised that she felt different. What had changed?

Part of it was understanding the truth about what had happened between her and Matt – she felt that she had clarity now, about why he'd disappeared, who he was and what he wanted. But, most of it was the sudden realisation that she hadn't had to do anything different. All she had done was be herself and let Matt do what he needed to do, and he had come to her and confessed all of his deepest feelings for her.

She hadn't made that happen by any effort of her own. All she had done was accept that he left; she'd moved on and concentrated on her life, and then, when he'd realised the error of his ways, she'd been there.

For the first time in what felt like forever, Catie felt that a weight had been lifted from her shoulders. And the weight was an ongoing sense of gloom and self-doubt that she had had for so long that she'd almost forgotten how to be without it.

The kiss had been lovely. Matt was lovely. But it wasn't the kiss or Matt that had changed her. It was the knowledge that she had just had to be herself and go about what was important to her – being with her daughter, rebuilding her relationship with her family, working on Reading Rocks – and life sorted the rest out.

Since her childhood illness, Catie had never really believed that life could sort anything out for the good. All she'd known at that time was illness, pain and solitude. And that had set the programme for her life: expect the worst.

Idly, she wondered if the house clearance had done something for her – and for Bridget and Skye. After all, she and Bridget had mended their relationship since Kevin had blessed the house; Skye had definitely turned a corner when it came to confidence and happiness since he'd come and said his prayers in the house, and Catie herself – well, this felt like a new energy entering her life. She felt positive, happy, open to new things for the first time in such a long time.

There was a little girl inside her who had wanted to be free for all these years. The little girl who hadn't expected the worst; who had run and played freely, before she was sick. And that little girl had returned.

EPILOGUE

Loch Cameron Open Season: Castle View

Closed to the public for many years, the mysterious Castle View is now open to visitors for the month of June as part of Loch Cameron Open Season.

Purchased by the philanthropist and writer Isobel McGovern, Castle View remains a wonderful example of Victorian Gothic architecture. Its gardens show influences of design by Capability Brown and its main staircase is reminiscent of the Entrance Hall at Loch Cameron Castle, being designed by the popular interior builder and designer of the time, Lothiel Whistance.

Rumours of the house being haunted were popular in the village for many years, mainly due to the house being left empty after its last tenant, Frank McGovern, died. These rumours have proved unsubstantiated, and the current owners have assigned rumours about supernatural happenings at the house to its dramatic architecture.

Originally from Loch Cameron, Isobel McGovern wrote many bestselling novels under a variety of pen names, living mostly in America until her death in 2024. She was a multi-millionaire and an active philanthropist, contributing in secret to various projects in Loch Cameron as well as to charities across the world. Her estate continues to support a number of those charities.

Castle View was bequeathed to Catriona and Bridget McGovern and remains their family home.

A LETTER FROM KENNEDY

Dear reader,

I want to say a huge thank you for choosing to read *Inheriting the Cottage by the Loch*. If you did enjoy it, and want to keep up to date with all my latest releases, just sign up at the following link. Your email address will never be shared and you can unsubscribe at any time.

www.bookouture.com/kennedy-kerr

I hope you loved *Inheriting the Cottage by the Loch* and if you did I would be very grateful if you could write a review. I'd love to hear what you think, and it makes such a difference helping new readers to discover one of my books for the first time.

I love hearing from my readers – you can get in touch through social media.

Thanks,

Kennedy

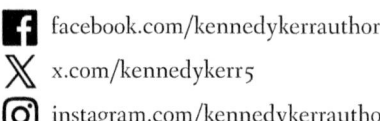

facebook.com/kennedykerrauthor
x.com/kennedykerr5
instagram.com/kennedykerrauthor

AUTHOR'S NOTE

Regular readers will know that I based Loch Cameron Castle on Inverary Castle, the home of the present Duke of Argyll, who is also the head of the Campbell clan. I have taken the castle's basic history as being constructed in its current form as a grey stone castle with turrets in the 1700s from Inverary's history. However, my other inspiration for the village of Loch Cameron is the village of Dornie, close to Eilean Donan castle on Loch Duich, approaching Kyle of Lochalsh on the road to the Isle of Skye. The castle of Eilean Donan also has a fascinating history, and its interiors inspired some of the castle-set scenes in this series.

The Camerons are a real Scottish clan. My depictions of Hal Cameron, his castle and his family are in no way connected to the real Cameron family or the Campbell clan.

www.shortlist.com/news/what-is-exorcism-how-to-become-an-exorcist is an interesting article regarding the training of ministers of the Church in exorcism and house cleansing or healing methods. When I was a child, we had some unsettling activity in our house and it was blessed by our local vicar. He told my mother, as Kevin tells Catie and Bridget, "it's much more common than you think". My feeling with the haunted house theme in this novel was that it was Frank's sadness that had somehow seeped into the house and created an atmosphere that the sisters would find difficult to live alongside – and seek to set right, which they do. This article would suggest that exorcisms are on the rise, but also that the majority of activity that exorcism teams are called out to tends to relate to mental health issues rather than the supernatural demonic possessions we might see in films and TV, which (like the 80s classic *Poltergeist* I referenced in this novel) tend towards the sensational.

Some of my inspiration for Isobel's jewellery collection was taken from the marvellous online catalogue from Elizabeth Taylor's jewellery collection which was auctioned by Christie's in New York on 13 December 2011. The joy of finding a secret safety deposit box containing treasures like these has to be one of my favourite fantasies, being a fan of all things beautiful.

You can view Elizabeth Taylor's beautiful items here: www. christies.com/auction/auction-2623-nyr

Finally, I did have to research what would happen if you found a random key for a safety deposit box, as they usually do not have the name of the bank or secure facility marked on them. This means that, fascinatingly, if you come into possession of a safety deposit key but don't know where it belongs, you can spend years researching what different keys look like and the banks they belong to – and then, contacting the different branches of those banks – to see if there is a deposit box there in the name you're looking for. (A cautionary tale if you plan to stash your treasures somewhere: make sure that your descendants know where it is.) In the interests of the story, I had to change the facts a little and make it so that Catie and Bridget would find a key with the bank's name on it.

PUBLISHING TEAM

Turning a manuscript into a book requires the efforts of many people. The publishing team at Bookouture would like to acknowledge everyone who contributed to this publication.

Commercial
Lauren Morrissette
Hannah Richmond
Imogen Allport

Cover design
Emma Graves

Data and analysis
Mark Alder
Mohamed Bussuri

Editorial
Kelsie Marsden
Sinead O'Connor

Copyeditor
Claire Rushbrook

Proofreader
Tom Feltham

RAISING READERS
Books Build Bright Futures

Dear Reader,

We'd love your attention for one more page to tell you about the crisis in children's reading, and what we can all do.

Studies have shown that reading for fun is the **single biggest predictor of a child's future success** – more than family circumstance, parents' educational background or income. It improves academic results, mental health, wealth, communication skills, and ambition.

The number of children reading for fun is in rapid decline. Young people have a lot of competition for their time, and a worryingly high number do not have a single book at home.

Our business works extensively with schools, libraries and literacy charities, but here are some ways we can all raise more readers:

- Reading to children for just 10 minutes a day makes a difference
- Don't give up if children aren't regular readers – there will be books for them!

- Visit bookshops and libraries to get recommendations
- Encourage them to listen to audiobooks
- Support school libraries
- Give books as gifts

Thank you for reading: there's a lot more information about how to encourage children to read on our website.

www.JoinRaisingReaders.com

Printed in Dunstable, United Kingdom